On my short list of must-read authors of biblical fiction

When I read Lana Christian's debut novel, *New Star,* she joined my short list of must-read authors of biblical fiction. Her novels read like political thrillers and keep me reading way past bedtime. Her first story of political intrigue, spiritual challenges, difficult relationships, and physical dangers kept me reading and losing sleep for "just one more chapter" (when I should have been working on my own writing). *Survival Secrets,* the second novel in *The Magi's Encounters* series, is a fitting successor to the first one. As the journey continues, the grave dangers and many problems the characters face kept me reading eagerly, just like *New Star* did. With a cast of characters you're sure to care about and exotic settings based on careful research, I can heartily recommend both books to anyone who loves biblical fiction or historical fiction set in ancient times.

—Carol Ashby, author of the 14-book standalone
biblical fiction series, *Light in the Empire*

Deeply satisfying; the best kind of sequel

When we read a story, especially a good one with intrigue, danger, and noble main characters, we want it to go on. We want to know what happens next. In the Gospel of Matthew, the Magi's journey to Bethlehem abruptly ends with them being told in a dream to go home by a different route. But we know that could not have been the end. Not with power-hungry Herod being threatened by the Magi's announcement of a new king.

Fortunately, Lana Christian, who retold their story in her excellent first book, *New Star*, has returned to continue the Magi's journey as they head off on this "different route." Inspired by her thorough research into the history of the area at the time of Jesus' birth, she presents a likely scenario of the spiritual and physical testing they must endure in order to make it back home. *Survival Secrets* is the best kind of sequel. It helps us to imagine "what happens next" in the lives of these brave Magi, people we care about, when an abrupt ending just doesn't satisfy.

—Tony Perona, author of the *Nick Bertetto* mystery series; coauthor with Liz Dombrosky, writing as Elizabeth Perona, of the *Bucket List* mystery series

A powerful story of faith in the face of an uncertain future

Lana Christian continues the intrigue of the Wise Men as they flee the perils of King Herod after finding a child who alters their lives and changes their hearts. Akilah returns with his fellow Magi as unexpected travels teach them to deepen their faith and wrestle with an uncertain future. Another encounter with the Christ child has Akilah learning the true meaning of the Scriptures he has studied. Akilah's cousin is on her own trajectory of faith as she encounters her late husband's Levite friend and ponders his teachings. Will the star, the child-king, and their meaning upend Magi society forever? Creativity and history collide for a powerful sophomore novel by Christian.

—Barbara M. Britton, author of the *Tribes of Israel* series and *Daughters of Zelophehad* series

A meticulously researched, intricate story

We really don't know much about the Magi who visited the Christ child. Scripture tells us they were supposed to report to Herod when they found the child, but "they left for their own country by another way." In this second installment of *The Magi's Encounters* series, Lana Christian has crafted a compelling fictional account of the Magi's journey home. Meticulously researched, Christian weaves an intricate tapestry that blends characters, challenges, dangers, and surprises, with godly provision. And, as the title suggests, everyone has a secret. Any fan of believable fiction will love this book.

—Stan Priebe, author of
Walk With Me Through Genesis

Another dynamic story from Lana Christian!

Survival Secrets picks up right where *New Star* leaves off, as Akilah and the rest of the Wise Men "go home a different way" after meeting Jesus. The tension builds through the entire book in a fast-paced, dangerous adventure. The Wise Men's learning and knowledge may be no match for navigating political intrigue in Parthia, dissension within the caravan, a perilous journey across uncharted wilderness, and other hardships. Can their secrets help them survive? Or will the truth of Jesus strengthen them through their trials and reconcile them with a greater goal? Readers of biblical fiction will not want to miss *The Magi's Encounters* series!

—Naomi Craig, author of the *Acts of Faith* series (part of the Early Church anthology *And Their Numbers Grew*)

BOOK TWO OF THE MAGI'S ENCOUNTERS

SURVIVAL SECRETS

LANA CHRISTIAN

Scrivenings
PRESS
Quench your thirst for story.
www.ScriveningsPress.com

Copyright © 2025 by Lana Christian

Published by Scrivenings Press LLC

15 Lucky Lane
Morrilton, Arkansas 72110
https://ScriveningsPress.com

Printed in the United States of America

All rights reserved. No part of this publication may be reproduced, stored in a retrieval system, or transmitted in any form or by any means—for example, electronic, photocopy, or recording—without the prior written permission of the publisher. The only exception is brief quotations in printed reviews.

Paperback ISBN 978-1-64917-502-1
eBook ISBN 978-1-64917-503-8

Editor: Suzie Waltner

Cover by Linda Fulkerson, www.bookmarketinggraphics.com

Original artwork (maps and scene break image) by Bree Cook, Illustrator and Graphic Designer

All characters are fictional, and any resemblance to real people, either factual or historical, is purely coincidental.

Scripture quotations marked ESV are taken from the ESV® Bible (The Holy Bible, English Standard Version®), copyright © 2001 by Crossway, a publishing ministry of Good News Publishers. Used by permission. All rights reserved.

Scripture quotations marked NIV are taken from The Holy Bible, New International Version® NIV® Copyright © 1973, 1978, 1984, 2011 by Biblica, Inc. Used with permission. All rights reserved worldwide.

Scripture quotations marked BSB are from The Holy Bible, Berean Study Bible, BSB. Copyright ©2016, 2018 by Bible Hub. Used by Permission. All Rights Reserved Worldwide.

NO AI TRAINING: Without in any way limiting the author's [and publisher's] exclusive rights under copyright, any use of this publication to "train" generative artificial intelligence (AI) technologies to generate text is expressly prohibited. The author reserves all rights to license uses of this work for generative AI training and development of machine learning language models.

This book is dedicated to everyone who has ever said,
"My problem is too big. The task is too hard.
I can't see a way through this."

"Blessed be the name of God forever and ever,
for wisdom and power belong to Him.
He changes the times and seasons; He removes kings and establishes them.
He gives wisdom to the wise and knowledge to the discerning.
He reveals the deep and hidden things;
He knows what lies in darkness,
and light dwells with Him.
Daniel 2:20-22 (BSB)

What's Happened So Far

(Recap of *New Star*, Book 1 of *The Magi's Encounters*)

As the Parthian Empire stands on the brink of an unpopular king being replaced by a worse option, Akilah, a highly respected astronomer and priest-scholar in Magi society, has a once-in-a-lifetime chance to influence that change of power. He is offered a position in the Upper Council as a Megistane—the elite group of Magi that decide who will become king. Instead, Akilah pours his energies into studying an elusive star prophesied to herald a new king. But not just any king—a Hebrew child-king who is supposed to rule eternally. As Akilah pursues slim leads that link Hebrew prophesies with the remarkable star he's seen only once, resistance to his study builds. Although the Parthian Empire tolerates many religions, it maintains a national religion that all Magi are sworn to uphold.

People in high places are threatened by the implications of Akilah's "star study"—and take increasingly drastic measures to prevent him from finding the prophesied child-king. Eventually Akilah must rely on help from the people he wants to avoid the most—his estranged father (the Chief Megistane) and his cousin, Farzaneh, who bears deep wounds from a fateful decision Akilah had made three decades prior.

The Wise Men embark on a perilous physical journey as well as a faith journey—making new enemies as they search for the child-king Yeshua. Although they find Him, it comes at a great price, forcing them to abandon their route to return home. Their first alternate route places them in even graver danger than before. Desperate to flee beyond Herod's control, they head into the Wilderness of Paran. Will they survive?

Familiar Faces and a Few New Ones

Survival Secrets reprises most of the characters from *New Star*, but you'll also meet a few new characters (and one special camel) in this book. New characters appear at the end of this list, shaded in gray. Names are listed in alphabetical order, not order of appearance. Can you find similarities in the characters' names and their behaviors?

Character	Pronunciation	Meaning	Origin	Notes
Akilah	a-KEE-lah OR AK-i-lah	Wise	Arabic	Lead Wise Man His head servant: Hakeem His camel: Dain
Antipas	AN-ti-pus	Against the father; instead of the father	Greek	A son of Herod the Great
Azazel	a-ZAZ-el	Scapegoat	Hebrew	Sassanak's closest colleague In Jewish culture, Azazel was an evil spirit or fallen angel
Babayi	ba-ba-EE	Grandfather	Arabic	How children commonly address their grandfather
Burhan	BUR-han	Religion	Arabic	An Orderal; he catalogs Magi research and writings His full name, Burhan Al-din, means "proof of religion"
Fakhri	FAHK-ree	Honorary	Arabic	Alludes to his status as a Magus Honorific (like a professor emeritus)
Farzaneh	FAHR-za-NEH	Wise and intelligent	Persian	Akilah's orphaned cousin
Gadiel	GAD-ee-ul	God is my wealth	Arabic	Chief Megistane of the Upper Council and Akilah's estranged father
Hadi	HAH-dee	Leader; guider	Persian	Farzaneh's Persian mastiff, her guard dog
Hakeem	Hah-KEEM	Wise	Arabic	Akilah's head servant
Haruz	HARE-us	Earnest; zealous	Hebrew	Hesed's father, a devoted Jew
Hesed	HAH-sed	Kindness	Hebrew	Caravansary owner in Ayla
Ihsan	ih-SAHN	Perfection or excellence; benevolence; compassion	Persian	Farzaneh's second husband; embraced Judaism late in life

Character	Pronunciation	Meaning	Origin	Notes
Javad	jah-VUD	Righteous	Arabic	Farzaneh's head servant
Kassim	KAS-im	Divided	Arabic	Rashidi's head servant Kassim's name reflects his divided desires in this book.
Keket	kee-KET	Goddess of darkness	Egyptian	Alludes to doing dark deeds (with or without Nakal's help)
Malachi	MAL-a-kiy	My messenger	Hebrew	Tallis's head servant
Mamani	ma-man-EE	Grandmother	Arabic	How children commonly address their grandmother
Mekonnen	may-KAHN-uhn	Honorable	Ethiopian	Javad's name in the language of his homeland (Cush)
Nakal	na-KAHL	Swindler	Hebrew	A Susita merchant who takes bribes for dishonorable tasks
Omid	OH-MEED	Hope	Persian	One of Farzaneh's servants; he attempted to ford the Jordan
Rashidi	rah-SHEE-dee	Wise Rightly guide	Egyptian Arabic	Wise Man His head servant: Kassim His camel: Moody
Sadiq	suh-DEEK	Loyal; true	Arabic	Akilah's chief healer on the trip to Jerusalem
Sarbaz	SAR-bahz	Caravan leader	Arabic	A vendor and a mercenary, doing dirty work for others
Sassanak	SASS-a-NAK	(A sibilant name to reflect his character)		Head Magus of the Lower Council
Tahrea	TAR-re-uh	Anger; contention	Hebrew	One of Farzaneh's servants who causes a lot of trouble
Tallis	TA-lis	Wise	Persian	Wise Man His head servant: Malachi His camel: Tashi
Varinius	vahr-IN-ee-us	Versatile	Roman	An informant to Antipas

Character	Pronunciation	Meaning	Origin	Notes
Archaclus	ar-keh-LAY-us	Leading the people	Greek	One of Herod the Great's sons, he inherited Samaria, Judaea, and Idumea; cruel ruler; persecuted the Jews
Aretes IV	ah-REE-tuz	Virtue; excellence; moral goodness	Greek/ Nabataean	Ruler ofNabataea in its "golden age;" his daughter, Phasaelis, married Antipas
Basa	BAA-sah	A great many; too much	Urdu	Oversized, overly nosy landlord in Heliopolis
Eliana	el-cc-AHN-ah	God has answered	Hebrew	Elyakim's wife; also, one of the first displaced people he helped
Elyakim	EI-AY-ah-KIM	God raises/ establishes	Hebrew	A Levite in Arbela (capital of Adiabene)
Gushtasp	GOOSH-tahsp	Related to horses; having an alert stallion	Persian	Farzaneh's most trusted protector
Hazrat	HASS-rat	Presence	Arabic	The youngest servant in the caravan
Helena	HEH-len-ah	Shining light	Greek	Queen of Adiabene; sister and wife of King Monobaz
Ibn	EE-bun	Son of (This is a prefix, not a whole name)	Arabic	A doctor with ties to Elyakim; finds and helps people displaced, captured, or persecuted for their faith
Musa	MOO-sah	Drawn out	Possibly a variant on the Hebrew name Moshe	Italian slave girl given to Phraates IV as a gift; bore a son Phraates V, whom she manipulated to become king of Parthia; she co-reigned with him
Phasaelis	fas-AY-eh-lis	Rescue/deliver; become free	Nabataean	Daughter of King Aretas TV; promised wife of Antipas
Phillip	FILL-ip	Lover of horses	Greek	One of Herod the Great's sons; he inherited the NE lands of Herod's kingdom
Raphael	Ru-FAY-EL	God has restored	Hebrew	Eliana 's son
Suhail	SOO-hayl	Star	Arabic	An older camel that Farzaneh loaned to Akilah
Waqilu	Wah-KEEL-u	Steward, manager, or deputy	Nabataean	Leader of a nomadic Nabataean tribe that Akilah encounters near Egypt
Zabin	zah-BEAN	Gazelle	Nabataean	One of Waqilu's servants

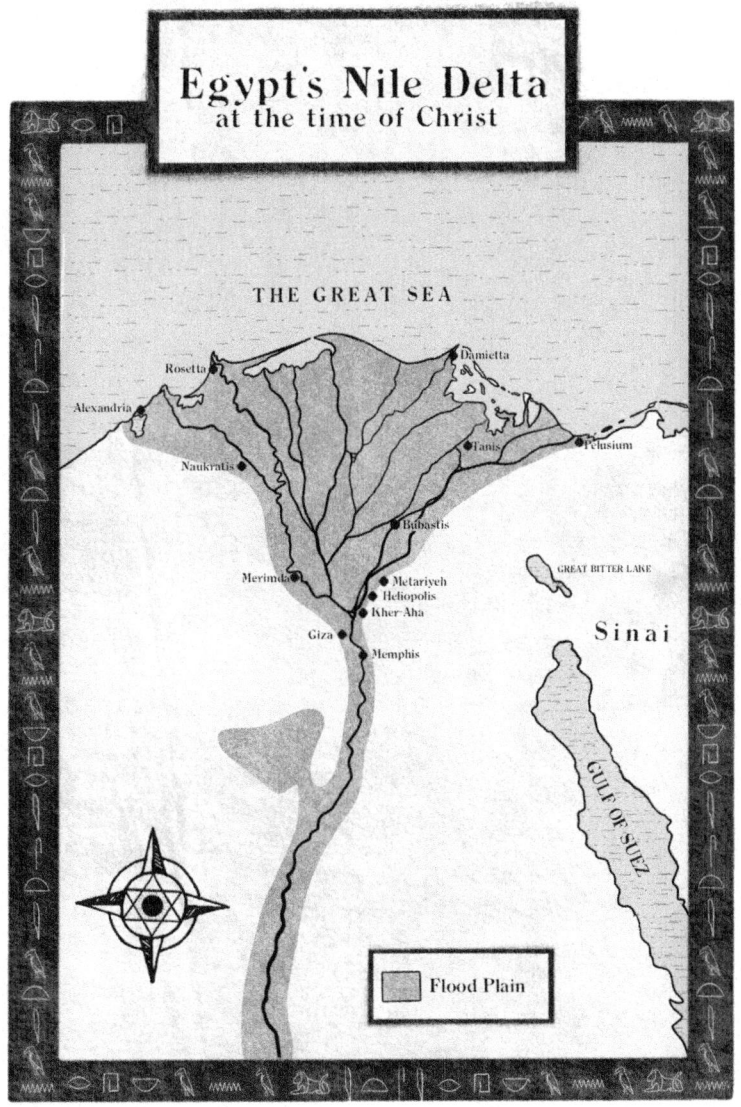

Egypt's Nile Delta
at the time of Christ

THE GREAT SEA

Rosetta
Damietta
Alexandria
Tanis
Naukratis
Pelusium

Bubastis

GREAT BITTER LAKE

Merimda
Metariyeh
Heliopolis
Kher-Aha
Sinai
Giza
Memphis

GULF OF SUEZ

Flood Plain

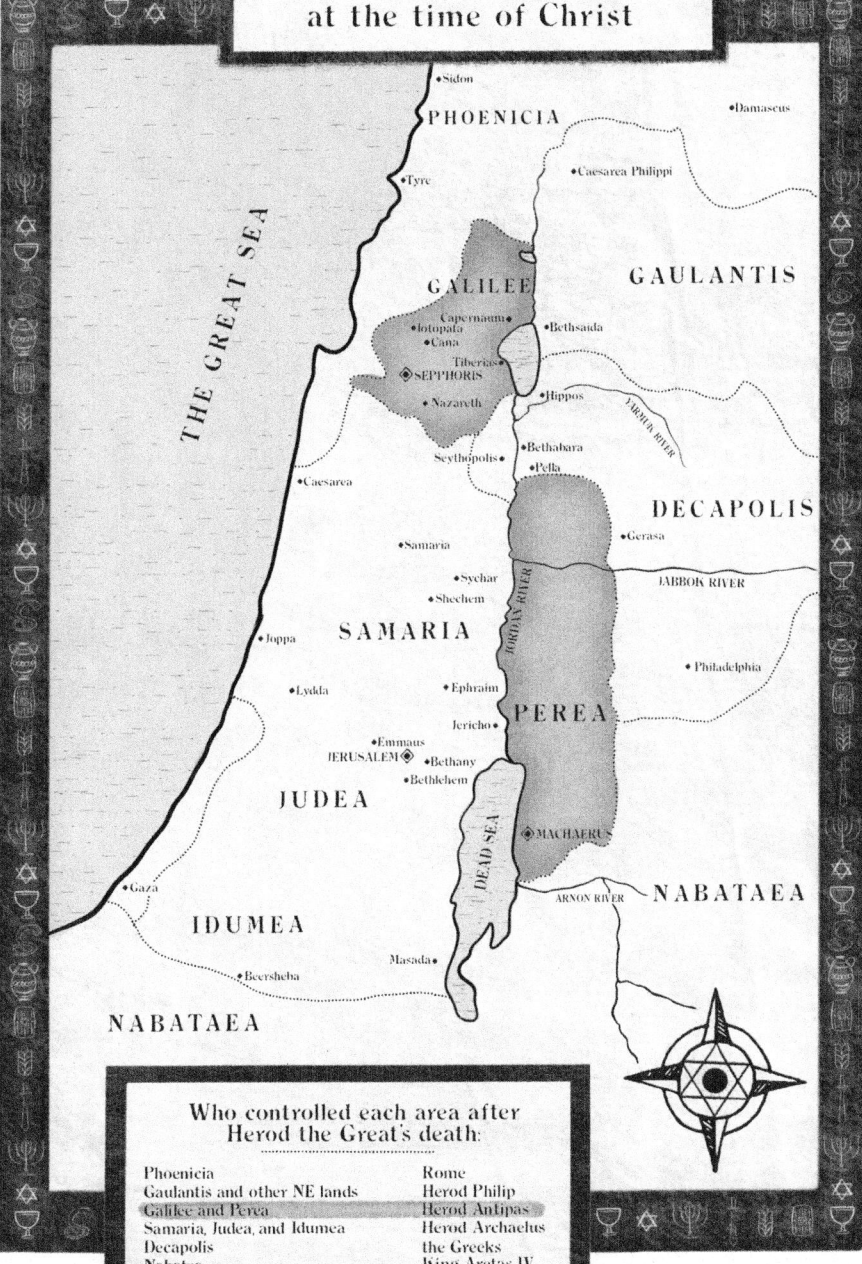

Herod the Great's Divided Kingdom
at the time of Christ

PHOENICIA

•Sidon

•Damascus

•Tyre

•Caesarea Philippi

THE GREAT SEA

GALILEE

GAULANTIS

Capernaum•
•Iotopata
•Cana
Tiberias•
◉SEPPHORIS

•Bethsaida

•Nazareth

•Hippos

YARMUK RIVER

Scythopolis•

•Bethabara
•Pella

•Caesarea

DECAPOLIS

•Samaria

•Gerasa

JABBOK RIVER

•Sychar
•Shechem

•Joppa

SAMARIA

JORDAN RIVER

•Philadelphia

•Lydda

•Ephraim

PEREA

Jericho•

•Emmaus
JERUSALEM◉ •Bethany
•Bethlehem

JUDEA

DEAD SEA

◉MACHAERUS

•Gaza

IDUMEA

ARNON RIVER

NABATAEA

•Beersheba

Masada•

NABATAEA

Who controlled each area after Herod the Great's death:

Phoenicia	Rome
Gaulantis and other NE lands	Herod Philip
Galilee and Perea	Herod Antipas
Samaria, Judea, and Idumea	Herod Archaelus
Decapolis	the Greeks
Nabatea	King Aretas IV

Introduction

In Hebrew culture, the concept of secrets, or hiding something, is significant in daily life and in spiritual contexts. The act can be for protection or survival, as in hiding from enemies. Something deep or hidden often connotes special knowledge that few people possess.

In the Roman and Parthian Empires, knowledge is highly valued but cloaked in superstition and secret. Most cultures believe secret knowledge comes from the gods, so extraordinary efforts are made to curry their favor to attain those secrets.

In Parthia, divine favor, or *farr*, imparts knowledge, wisdom, understanding, and even power. This is crucial for the king to have—because if he does something dreadful to lose farr, the entire kingdom will suffer. Mixing royal Persian with Roman blood tops that list.

As Parthia's power shifts to its young half-blood (Persian-Roman) king and his ambitious Roman mother, power in Herod's kingdom shifts to three of his sons. Archelaus's mistreatment of the Jews is so cruel that Mary and Joseph flee to Egypt. Another of Herod's sons, Antipas, plans to make his corner of the world great in a new way.

Against that backdrop, those who believe in Messiah as the prophecies foretold are in increasing danger.

The risk and cost of knowing about Yeshua have already exacted a toll on the Wise Men. Enemies, the environment, and secrets the Wise Men harbor test their newfound faith in ways they never could have imagined. Some secrets need to be kept in order to survive. Other secrets must be revealed in order to truly live. Their tenuous chance of survival rests with the God they cannot see and know little of.

Chapter 1

The Good Lie

Somewhere in the wilderness of Paran, 3 BC

Was heading to Egypt the right choice? Akilah rimmed his soup bowl with his thumb. The Kings Highway would have taken his caravan from Jerusalem all the way back to the Euphrates River, but traveling home on any Roman road was out of the question. With mathematical precision, Roman watchtowers measured those roads. *Stationarii*, special Roman imperial troops, manned those posts, scouting for runaway slaves and other "undesirables." Akilah and his colleagues had become undesirables the moment they decided to not return to Herod with news of the eternal child-king they had found. Herod undoubtedly had wasted no time dispatching Roman relays with orders for stationarii to intercept the Magi and drag them to Jerusalem in chains.

The caravan might have hazarded sea travel from Ayla if they hadn't crossed paths with one of Herod's scouts and some

Nabataeans there. No, heading northwest toward Egypt was their only option. Akilah had to keep his caravan safe.

Safety. What a precious commodity. Akilah shivered to think of the consequences if he failed at his task.

He sipped his bowl of watery soup. Barren ground had already replaced Ayla's lush beauty. Thankfully, today's unusually cool temperature had allowed the caravan to press on longer than usual—until grumbling stomachs forced them to stop for the day's second meal, a diluted version of the morning meal.

They wouldn't be able to cover this much ground every day. Who knew what challenges this wilderness held for them? Quelling the caravan's fear of the unknown would be an ongoing effort. Akilah had to maintain everyone's focus on covering more ground—even though he had not yet revealed to them where they were going. Heliopolis. It was a wish, a hope, a prayer—at least a month away if all went well. From Heliopolis, they could continue to Alexandria.

Egypt. True safety. Akilah couldn't muster any thought beyond that. Egypt was in the opposite direction of home but was truly out of Herod's reach. They just had to get there.

Akilah watched his head servant, Hakeem, circle the campfire. He had shouldered more responsibility than a servant should ever need to, yet he did so without complaint. Akilah repeatedly struggled to find the right words to express his appreciation. Instead, he said nothing. Silence was more comfortable.

Hakeem bowed before his master. In this rocky wasteland, that simple sign of subservience and respect was a comforting vestige of what had been ... a life of prestige and honor in Magi society. A life Akilah might never return to.

"Master, now would be a good time to address everyone."

Akilah nodded and rose. Stepping close to the fire, he

clapped his hands three times, his signal for the whole caravan to meet.

"We regret that urgent business took us away from lovely Ayla," he started.

"What 'business' would take us into the wilderness?" one servant said, his voice dripping with sarcasm.

Akilah grimaced inwardly. Tahrea. A force to reckon with. Privately. "Business that must be kept secret from certain people."

"Why wouldn't you tell us that 'business' until we were too far from Ayla to turn back on foot?" Tahrea said, his voice rising. "Now we're your captives."

"That's not true."

The servants' unruliness rose like swells in a storm. Logic wouldn't win them over. Something more visceral had to move them. Motioning for silence, Akilah glanced at his fellow Magi leaning against a rock beyond the caravan's campfire circle. He was reasonably sure of Rashidi's thoughts. Less is more. Keep the servants in their place. They're under contract; they must fulfill their obligation, regardless. Tallis's face was an expressionless mask.

"You have a right to know why we aren't going home yet," Akilah said. "It relates to why we went to Jerusalem and what happened there."

Everyone's eyes bored into him.

"It's a good story," he added. The servants liked stories. Maybe that would pique their interest. "In Persia, my colleagues and I studied a star that foretold the birth of a child who would be an eternal ruler and the Savior of the world."

Sniggers and guffaws erupted.

"Inconceivable, yes? But Jewish prophecies over hundreds of years pointed to the birth of a unique person. Not a king born into royalty, but someone we all could relate to."

Silence descended on the camp.

"We traveled from Persia to Jerusalem to find that child. And we did." Akilah's throat tightened. "But some people wanted to harm him. Especially King Herod. He has a habit of killing people when he considers them a threat to his throne. Herod commanded us to report to him when we found the child. We did not."

Akilah shifted in place. "We could not betray the child and His family. Our disobedience to Herod made us targets of his wrath. We couldn't go home the way we came because that's the first place his soldiers would have looked for us." Akilah paused to gauge the servants' reactions. Their silence thickened like gathering fog.

"You defied a king?" One servant finally spoke—slowly, as if testing his words.

"Yes."

"Is the child safe?"

Akilah exhaled a shaky breath. "I hope so."

His answers seemed to fuel other servants' courage to ask questions.

"Do you know where the child is now?"

"No."

"Is Herod still hunting you?"

"I have every reason to believe so."

"Why did we leave Petra? Then Ayla?"

Normally Akilah would not have entertained servants questioning him, but nothing about this trip resembled any other in his career. "Herod has family ties to Petra. We thought we were safe in Ayla, but one of Herod's scouts found us." Akilah swallowed hard. "With help, we escaped that trouble."

The servants' murmurs rose again, this time rippling with notes of awe and respect.

He gestured for quiet. "Herod's men are one threat. Nabataeans are another. In Ayla, we learned a group of them were searching for us—perhaps to turn us over to Herod, punish us for using some of their secret water sources, or both. We didn't know they occupied part of Ayla, plus territory hundreds of miles east of it. That's why we're heading *west*." He paused again. "You could say that makes us renegades on two accounts."

Akilah glanced at Rashidi, expecting a reaction. "Renegades" had become Rashidi's favorite descriptor for their situation.

"So ... you lied and stole but for good reasons?" Some servants seem to like that idea.

"I am committed to getting this caravan to safety."

"Where are we headed?"

"To Egypt."

"Egypt?" Frenzied chatter erupted. The servants' terrified, wide-eyed stares confirmed the limits of their previous travels.

Akilah called for silence. "Egypt will provide true safety for us. It's far from Herod's reach. The Nabataeans can't touch us there either. And Egypt welcomes people who believe in the prophecies we studied."

"How long?" Tahrea shouted.

Irascible voice. If Akilah could channel that servant's skill at sewing discord into a positive direction, he could be a leader someday.

"As long as needed," Akilah said.

"Then we don't know if we'll ever get home." Tahrea pounded the ground.

Akilah clenched his jaw. "We *will* go home. You have my word. This isn't the journey we planned, but its purpose is still unfolding." Hoping to divert the servants' attention, he added, "In Egypt, I promise you will see more glorious things than you could ever imagine."

The servants exploded again with chatter.

Akilah silenced them with difficulty. "Listen well. Our lives —and the lives of that child and his family—depend on your silence. *At all costs.* One person's loose tongue could endanger our caravan, the child, his family, and worse. On the other hand, your silence and faithful service in getting us to Egypt will determine the success of our journey. You could say we have sacred secrets to protect. Will you keep that charge?"

Akilah interpreted their murmurs as an affirmative.

Some servants seemed to revel in the intrigue. Others looked unconvinced.

As everyone retired for the night, Hakeem approached Akilah. "A few servants want to know more about the star and the child," he said. "What the prophecies say and what you believe. Will you tell them?"

Chapter 2

Beyond Value

"Another time." Akilah hurried toward his tent. "I need to check our bearings."

His response was half true. The stark terrain and lack of roads demanded Akilah's daily diligence to ensure they headed west by northwest. But guilt seared his conscience. He was getting better at telling half-truths.

Hakeem hadn't pressed him for when to talk with the servants about Yeshua. But if he said anything, they'd surely ask what he believed about the prophecies. He didn't know how to reconcile what they said with what he'd seen. He might never fully sort his Bethlehem experience, so how could he respond?

He retrieved his case of navigation instruments and retreated to his fellow Magi. They seemed to sense his inner turmoil and respectfully walked in silence with him.

At the nearest hill, Akilah whirled to face them. "Why did we get to see the prophesied child? We're not Jewish."

"Maybe because we paid attention to what others missed," Tallis said.

Rashidi snickered. "What does that say about the priests we'd planned to talk with in Jerusalem?"

Akilah shook his head. "We can't judge them. We never met them."

"Knowing about the child isn't as important as what we do with what we know," Tallis said.

Akilah gripped his instrument case tighter. If he talked to the servants about Yeshua, he wouldn't be able to control what they said. They might forget or twist the facts. Hunger and duress could loosen tongues of the most stalwart men.

If they lived long enough to reach civilization.

Rein in your thoughts, Akilah.

At the hill's crest, he bent to open the case, but the lid wouldn't budge. "Oh, no. Damaged? The lid warped?" He ran his hands across its edges. He jiggled the latch open and pried the lid off with difficulty. Moonlight falling on the interior revealed the culprit—a bag crammed into one corner. He poked it with caution. A familiar rustle replied. His hands trembling, he opened the drawstring.

Pistachios.

"Tallis, did you hide this in my instrument case?"

"Of course not."

Rashidi glanced over Akilah's shoulder. "We know how much you love pistachios, Tallis. But really ... a private reserve? You know that's forbidden."

"I didn't put it there," Tallis protested.

With care, Akilah lifted his astrolabe from its case. When he reached for the tripod, his fingers brushed against a folded cloth underneath it. "What ..."

He sniffed the cloth before spreading its folds. Short stacks of flatbread.

"Haruz." He exhaled sharply. Haruz, the father of the caravansary owner where they stayed in Ayla, must have stowed some extra food in their gear.

What a thoughtful gesture—likely his last act before Herod's scout overtook him. Haruz had suffered greatly to keep the Magi safe in Ayla. Who would sacrifice himself for people he barely knew? Akilah could only hope and pray Haruz would heal from his wounds.

Akilah made a mental note to have Hakeem check every trunk and the rest of the gear tonight for more of Haruz's handiwork—and secure the food before the servants could raid it.

Get your bearings.

Oh, how Akilah wished that incredible star would appear again. He needed its guidance in this vast, uncharted wilderness. Moreover, he needed wisdom and discernment. And, for all the future decisions he couldn't anticipate, he needed help from his colleagues. Akilah knew how to read the sky. Tallis knew how to read the land. Rashidi's engineering expertise would be critical for rigging makeshift repairs. Akilah derived some comfort in telling himself he had chosen well—as if an invisible hand had guided him to people with skills he hadn't anticipated he'd need to depend on.

"Don't move." A voice issued from the darkness.

Like ghosts, four silhouetted figures seemed to appear out of nowhere.

Akilah's blood ran cold. "What do you want?" he rasped.

"Information." A deep, authoritative voice answered. "The most useful one of you will come with us."

Even though the shadowed man spoke Aramaic, he placed one word out of order and twisted others with an odd accent.

Akilah caught his breath. The interloper was Nabataean.

"If you don't get us what we need, Herod's guards will conveniently learn that you are spying on him. Many people are eager to return you to Jerusalem … by whatever means necessary."

Akilah's hands grew clammy. How much did this Nabataean really know of the Magi's recent movements? The night before their caravan left Ayla, the Magi had entrusted Haruz and his son to dispose of Herod's scout. Had they not succeeded? It was impossible to tell from the Nabataean's selectively vague words. "What could we do for you in Jerusalem?"

"Not Jerusalem," the Nabataean snarled.

A clue. But what could they want? Maybe an interpreter. "I speak eight languages—"

"I'm an engineer—"

In one liquid movement, the Nabataean whirled and swung his sword in an arc in front of the Magi, silencing Akilah and Rashidi. Both reflexively drew back, but Tallis held his ground. The sword missed him by less than an inch.

The Nabataean's eyes gleamed as he aimed his sword point at Tallis's throat. "You aren't afraid to die. You must have military training." With his free hand, the Nabataean gestured to the shadows. "Take this one." He jerked his head toward Tallis as two men emerged. "Order the rest to the Magi's camp. Quickly. No killing unless someone resists."

Akilah's face stung with heat. "*No* killing. Take what you need. But no one dies."

"We will take what we want. If you run fast, you might make it back to your camp in time to warn your caravan to not resist."

Akilah's mind raced. "*Wait.*"

At his outburst, either curiosity or cunning spread across the Nabataean's face. He raised his hand to stay his men. "Give me what's most precious to you, and we will kill no one."

"You already took our colleague. Human life is precious beyond price."

Akilah's argument died at the Nabataean's feet.

Think fast. "I have a powerful new navigation device. A mathematical jewel, really."

"We know how to journey through wastelands better than anyone. Your toy is of no use to us."

A holy boldness gripped Akilah. "You didn't ask for what was useful to you. You asked what was most precious to *me.*

Without this device, we will wander in the wilderness. That could cost us our lives." He grabbed his astrolabe from its case and clutched it to his chest with startling ferocity. "This is yours —if you don't harm Tallis *and* he returns to us with this as a sign of your honor. Then leave us in peace. We have no love of Herod but even less desire for entanglements—with anyone. Agreed?"

He glared at the Nabataean. A cloud cleared the moon, shining its wan light on the man's wide gold armband. Red and purple silks wound through gold loops encircled the adornment that covered half of his sinewy upper arm. This Nabataean was no mercenary. He was a leader.

"You understand honor," Akilah said through clenched teeth. "Promise on your honor you will return our colleague to us with my astrolabe. Both intact and unharmed."

The Nabataean lunged for the device.

Akilah spun beyond the Nabataean's reach. Surprisingly, the other man with him didn't intervene.

The leader chuckled. "Don't think yourself brave. I could have killed you twice already if I'd wanted to."

"Then finish your business with us," Akilah hissed. "Agree to the terms. My colleague assists you; you provide his safe return with the astrolabe."

The Nabataean tipped his chin upward. "You took from our secret water sources."

"We won't divulge their location," Akilah said. "You have my word."

The Nabataean spat on the ground. "Persians. Your word means nothing to me."

"Then our map might."

The Nabataean grabbed Akilah's throat. "Speak while you still have breath."

Terror raked furrows across Rashidi's forehead.

"Drew … map …" Akilah choked out between gasps. "Water

... beyond Petra." Blood pounded in his temples. "Take the map ... keep your secrets."

With his hand still on Akilah's throat, the Nabataean summoned another man from the shadows and nodded toward Rashidi. "Take that one's clothes and put them on. Go with this one to retrieve his map. Shield yourself so no one in the camp sees who you are."

His grip tightened around Akilah's neck. "Return with your map in six minutes, and you'll get your Egyptian friend back," the Nabataean said, his voice low and throaty. "If you fail, both your friends' lives will be forfeit—and you'll beg for the same." He shoved Akilah away.

Akilah stifled his coughing as he and the guard slipped down the ridge. From a distance, a protector hailed them at the edge of the camp. "It's just Rashidi and me," Akilah called, turning to block the protector's view of the guard.

Inside his tent, he had barely dug the cat statue from the bottom of his clothing trunk when the guard snatched it from him.

Soon Akilah and the guard were once again on the back side of the ridge where the caravan couldn't see them. Under the light of a small torch, the Nabataean in charge examined the cat statue. With alarming speed, he found its hidden hinge and pulled the map from its hiding place.

He rooted farther, swirling his finger deep inside the cavity. His face hardened.

Don't.

Using a small knife, the Nabataean pried the *stūrīh* from its cramped place in the interior of the statue's head.

"A contract hidden in a statue." He scanned the document. "Most people hide inheritances. But hiding a contract of protection through marriage ... Is this arrangement from honor or necessity?"

Akilah lifted a shoulder. "It depends on which party you ask."

"Is she young? Pretty?" The Nabataean's mouth shifted between a smile and a sneer.

Akilah reached for the crushed document.

The Nabataean snatched it from his reach. "By Persian law, a copy of this should reside in your House of Comparisons. Otherwise, why carry it into the wilderness?" His mocking tone sharpened. "Unless you don't want others to know." His shoulders shook with silent laughter. "You Persians. So truthful, even when secrecy would serve you better." He tossed the *stūrīh* at Akilah's feet but waved the statue in his face. "My souvenir."

"Agree you will return our friend with the astrolabe to us. Both intact and unharmed."

The Nabataean cocked his head, then tucked his chin ever so slightly.

"Your nod is my surety." With his eyes on the interloper, Akilah knelt to grab the *stūrīh*.

The Nabataean signaled to the darkness with his torch. At least a dozen men appeared and streamed down the ridge on a diagonal. Another signal. Another man emerged from the darkness and shoved Rashidi toward Akilah.

The Nabataean bounced the flat of his dagger on Akilah's chest. "You are wise but talk too much. Now *run*."

Akilah and Rashidi fled straight down the hill, leaving the astrolabe and its tripod where they lay.

Akilah had barely enough time to alert Hakeem and the protectors before the plunder began. Thankfully, the servants heeded their warnings to stay in their tents and not interfere during the raid.

With military precision, the Nabataeans took what they wanted of the caravan's supplies. In three minutes, the raiders vanished into the night. All Akilah could do was stand by, helpless.

Rashidi plucked Akilah's sleeve. "About Tallis. We can send—"

"No. The time the Nabataean spent talking to us was planned. It gave his men a longer head start to spirit Tallis away. We can't assume in what direction. If they were on horseback, they could be seven parasangs away by now. We must think of the caravan. Tell our head servants to collect everyone. I'll talk to them while Hakeem inventories what's left."

"What will they make Tallis do?"

"Focus, Rashidi. Go."

"What if they follow us?"

A sinkhole opened in Akilah's heart. "They won't. They got what they wanted."

Chapter 3

Secret Names

After reassuring the terrified servants, Akilah rushed into the Magi's shared tent. The Nabataeans had coldly calculated what likely held the greatest value. Only the locks on their three sturdiest trunks had been broken.

Rashidi barely glanced at the damaged trunks. "Tallis just sacrificed himself for us. You don't seem worried about that."

Akilah turned away, pretending to fuss over how to fix the locks. "There was nothing we could do for him."

"That is cold."

"I know Tallis well enough to know he can take care of himself." He threw the comment over his shoulder.

"Tallis against who-knows-how-many Nabataeans?" Rashidi's voice rose. "What aren't you telling me?"

Akilah repressed a sigh.

Rashidi grabbed Akilah's arm. "Is this about his past? Why keep it a secret?"

"He doesn't want anyone to know of it."

"The Council had to know before his Magi induction."

"Only his sponsor on the Council did."

"But no one else—except you? Why?"

"Rashidi, we have more important things—"

"No, we don't." Rashidi bristled. "Am I an equal on your team or not?"

A stone dropped in Akilah's stomach. He couldn't break his oath to Tallis.

"What other secrets are you keeping?" Rashidi razored his words. "Next thing you know"—he snorted—"you'll tell me you're married."

Akilah's stomach knotted, thrusting that stone up to his throat. What could he say?

Rashidi drew back. "You're not married, are you?"

"I ..."

"You *are?*" Rashidi stepped back, as if distance would dilute his anger.

"Contractually." Akilah forced the word through his lips.

Rashidi snapped his slack jaw shut. "Why should that be a secret?"

"It's complicated."

Rashidi swept his arm in an arc that ended in the direction of the sliver of barren land visible beyond their tent flap. "I don't think life can get more complicated than this." He shook his head. "If we're going to survive this wilderness, we can't keep secrets from each other. Even if you have to settle for me instead of Tallis."

"What?"

"Tallis is trained in survival skills. Without him, you have ... me. Your regret shows."

Akilah stood in stunned silence. He hadn't intended to show favoritism to any colleague. But he and Tallis had shared ten years of travels and dangers in service to Magi society. They had become closer than colleagues. They were friends.

Now Akilah had to live with what he was dealt. Maybe he had assumed Tallis was indispensable. He faced his young colleague. "Rashidi, you are no less skilled than any other

Magus. I need your engineering mind, your innovative thinking, and your knowledge of Egypt to help us get to Alexandria."

"You have my skills but not my trust. Secrets destroy trust."

"For now, secrets and silence are our allies. We should also stay silent about what we saw in Bethlehem. At least for a while."

Rashidi scoffed and swiveled in every direction. "Who is there to tell?"

"Exhaustion, hunger, or capture can coax what's in the heart to come out through the mouth."

"Do you mean—"

"Who knows what enemies we have yet to face?" Akilah turned away. "I've said too much."

"No, you haven't said nearly enough. Explain yourself."

Akilah whirled, his eyes flashing. "Then swear an oath of silence."

Rashidi recoiled with an incredulous look. "The miles have tarnished your perspective. Persians don't make oaths. Neither do I."

"I will not move this caravan another parasang until you do." Akilah ground the words through clenched teeth.

"We could die here." Rashidi scorched the air with each elongated word.

"Yes." Akilah's glare met Rashidi's truculent stare. "With or without you knowing about Tallis. Are you willing to die for what I would tell you about him? Because that could be its price."

"First you say we must keep quiet about what we know of Yeshua. Then I learn you're married. Now you say we can't talk about Tallis. This pattern—"

Akilah grabbed Rashidi's arm. "I am deadly certain about Yeshua *and* Tallis. Ignorance is a safe choice. Knowledge is a dangerous choice. Choose wisely."

"I'll never be an equal in your eyes until I'm equal in

knowledge about the people you picked to work with you." Rashidi shook off Akilah's grip. "Tell me."

Akilah paused. How could he convey the situation's gravity so Rashidi would *want* to keep Tallis's secret, regardless of future duress? Rashidi had conducted himself admirably when raiders near Susita attacked their caravan and tried to capture him. Yet one day later, he had made a snap decision to the detriment of the whole caravan. If the heat of a moment broke his resolve, a careless word about Tallis could have disastrous results. Akilah had to make sure Rashidi would keep Tallis's secrets forever, no matter what.

"I will tell you about Tallis if you tell me your true name."

Rashidi clutched his throat as if poison from a viper bite was slowly stealing his breath.

"Every Egyptian has two names, yes?" Akilah continued. "Your 'good' name—the name by which everyone knows you— and your 'true' name? A name never spoken? A name said to hold the essence of your life?"

Rashidi stiffened. "I haven't believed that for years."

"Then you won't mind telling me your true name."

"I keep it secret to honor my parents and my heritage." Rashidi bristled. "Don't try to compare that to whatever you won't tell me about Tallis."

"You don't believe in the power of your true name, yet you see a threat in sharing it with me."

Rashidi's jaw, set in stone, warned Akilah he was treading on dangerous ground. "As I recall, Egyptians believe that speaking one's true name can make that person vulnerable to bad influences … harm … even jeopardize their ability to enter the afterlife. Did I get that right?"

Rashidi nodded but shot eye daggers at Akilah.

"We're already in harm's way, so why tempt fate for worse, yes? I understand." Akilah's voice softened. "Whether voicing your true name poses a threat to you or not, there's a very real threat in your learning Tallis's past and his true name. I don't exaggerate when I say such knowledge, in the wrong hands, would cost the lives of many people, including possibly everyone in our caravan."

Rashidi tore his tunic from neck to waist. "Don't you trust me?" He palmed his hand toward the east. "I swear on all I value and call holy that I will never divulge to anyone what you tell me about Tallis—even if under threat of death."

Akilah sighed. Was this how parents felt when teaching their children difficult life lessons? He had to make sure Rashidi would never forget this moment. "Very well. Sit."

When Rashidi had settled onto a cushion, Akilah spoke in low tones. "First ... Your true name."

Rashidi gulped.

"Your secret is safe with me." A smile played about the corners of Akilah's mouth. "Although it *is* intriguing to think that saying your true name could subject you to ..." At Rashidi's stricken look, he laughed heartily. "That's a joke, not a promise."

Akilah tapped his ear and leaned in close to Rashidi. "Now ... your true name."

"Zuberi-Bassel," he whispered.

Akilah smiled kindly at his younger colleague. "A noble-sounding name. What does it mean?"

"Strong and courageous."

"Well placed." Akilah clasped Rashidi's shoulders. "You've already proven to be both. If your parents could see—"

"Now you." Rashidi shrugged out of Akilah's grip. "Make it truth."

Akilah silently prayed his words would bring no harm to his absent colleague. "Twenty years ago, Tallis was a rising star in Persia's military. Since then, he has expended great effort to bury his past. So should we."

"Why?"

"The Nabataeans didn't like how Tallis and his troops patrolled one of their trade routes at a key junction in Babylon. They claimed the troops interfered with their commerce. They threatened him with force and ordered him to leave. He carried out his orders and stayed. They retaliated by capturing Tallis's wife and infant son."

Rashidi sucked in his breath. "Tallis has a family?"

Akilah's eyes moistened. "He and some of his best men succeeded in rescuing his family from the Nabataeans. But in doing so, he incurred heavy losses. That was bad enough, but the Nabataeans vowed revenge on him—to erase the shame their losses had brought them. To keep his family safe, Tallis sent them far away. Only he knew the location. To keep their whereabouts secret, he didn't correspond with them. He doesn't know if they moved on from there."

Akilah wiped his face. "He chose to stay in Persia but needed to 'disappear,' so he entered Magi society. That way, if the Nabataeans ever found him, they wouldn't be able to trace his family."

"He can't be with family … ever?" Rashidi's frown deepened. "He sacrificed himself for them …"

"Magi society offered Tallis a measure of peace and protection. But becoming a Magus was more than an escape. Tallis was and is a devoted priest-scholar. For many years, only one person in Magi society knew the truth of Tallis's identity—his sponsor. He pledged to keep Tallis's secret unto death." Akilah paused. "That sponsor was Fakhri."

Rashidi exhaled a shaky breath. His head drooped. "How do you know all this?"

"Tallis confided in me after we had worked together for seven years. By then, he felt he could entrust a second person with his secret in case he or Fakhri didn't … survive.

"Listen well." Akilah forced brightness into his voice. "There's light in this darkness. Although Tallis has been captured, the Nabataeans didn't recognize him. They don't see him as their enemy. To them, he's only a pawn with military fortitude they can exploit. They don't know his real name. At all costs, it must stay that way. It will help keep our friend alive. Understood?"

Rashidi nodded.

Akilah paused. What would it ultimately cost *him* for breaking his oath to his closest colleague? His honorable friend. "If the Nabataeans learned Tallis's true name, his life would be forfeit. And it would eventually lead the Nabataeans to his family, as his wife and son know him only by his true name."

Akilah searched Rashidi's face for signs of fear or regret, but it was as resolute as granite. "Fakhri and I kept Tallis's past and his name secret from everyone. Now you are bound by oath to do the same. For the rest of your life."

"Tell me Tallis's real name."

What Rashidi didn't know, he couldn't divulge. But that would carve a chasm between the two Magi. Akilah's throat turned dry. "It's Adrahasus. In Babylonian, it means 'great intelligence.'"

A thick silence settled between them.

Finally Rashidi parted the silence with a whisper. "I will guard this information with my life, no matter the cost." He met Akilah's gaze with settled resolve.

"Thank you," Akilah mouthed. He prayed he could trust Rashidi's vow.

Chapter 4

Mission

The evening brought no rest for Akilah. Relinquishing his astrolabe may have been a hollow gesture. Without it, navigation was more challenging, but not impossible. Akilah still had his cross-staff, a cruder wayfinding tool. Yet his concern for Tallis eclipsed all other worries. What did the Nabataeans want from him?

Tallis had said Nabataeans "formed no alliances" and "moved like ghosts," taking advantage of situations from a side wind. Recent history bore witness to that. Through deception, they had destroyed a Roman army when it tried to find the source of the Nabataeans' monopoly on frankincense trade. What could they want with Herod that didn't involve a direct, wide-scale conflict?

Nabataeans … Herod … Tallis … military. Akilah bolted upright. Nabataean territory abutted Judaea's southern border. Near that border was Machaerus, Herod's reputedly impenetrable fortress. Its lookouts could see invaders more than a half day before they reached the fortress. If the Nabataeans could seize Machaerus, they could advance their territory far into Herod's kingdom.

The Nabataeans are going to force Tallis to find a way into Machaerus. Akilah's breath strangled in his chest. If Roman forces didn't eliminate his friend, the Nabataeans would as soon as they got what they wanted.

Chapter 5

Tallis

Breathing through a feed sack was hard—and humid. If Tallis let himself think about the hood tied over him, claustrophobia would panic him. He had to focus on facts, not feelings.

He bounced again into the chest of the silent rider behind him. The Arabian they rode couldn't maintain this pace much longer. But if they slowed down, the horse could carry two riders an entire day. Unfortunately for the horse, speed seemed to be paramount. The rider changed the horse's gait barely long enough to prevent the animal's exhaustion, then goaded the horse into a quicker pace once more.

If only Tallis could free his hands. Every jolt dug his bindings into his wrists and waist.

His lungs filled with the unmistakable charred-but-rotting aroma of a trash heap. They must be on a camp's outskirts.

The rider wheeled to a halt. "Get down."

He hauled Tallis to someone who sounded like he was short on time. "Tell me what your colleagues know of the Nabataeans."

"Only rumors." Tallis's muffled voice strained through the feed bag.

"And you?"

"Nothing."

"Liar."

Tallis's throat tightened against the rope binding the feed bag about his neck. Whatever the Nabataeans thought he knew, no matter what they did to him, he couldn't reveal his military past—or his hatred for them. He refused to let the Nabataeans take more from him than they already had.

He arched his neck, searching for a threadbare spot in the feed bag that might offer a glimpse of his captors. The only thing Parthians shared with Nabataeans was their contempt for the Roman Empire. "What do you want?"

"Information about Machaerus."

"Can't help you."

"You spent an evening with Herod. Surely he spoke of Machaerus."

"Only to say it was impenetrable."

"Precisely why you're here. You will infiltrate it for us."

"How?"

"With our help and your ingenuity. Succeed and everyone lives."

Behind Tallis, hurried footsteps drew near. The air grew heavy with sweat, burnt air, and tortured metal. Two men flung Tallis to the ground. Before he could resist, one man sat on his chest and cut his ropes while two others immobilized his arms and legs. Another one slit Tallis's right sleeve. A cool evening breeze kissed his bare arm. An acrid yet sweet smell filled his nostrils. Then the night dissolved into white-hot pain and the stench of seared flesh.

Chapter 6

Shadow

Tallis didn't know how long he'd been unconscious when excruciating pain woke him. Whoever had branded him either didn't know what he was doing or had aimed to inflict maximum agony.

A shadow moved beyond his haze of pain. Tallis closed his eyes and waited for the air to shift. All he needed to sense was the slightest bit of warming. His left hand shot up and closed around the shadow's throat.

The figure could have called for help or overpowered Tallis, but it didn't—even though Tallis tightened his grip.

"I'm here to dress your wound," it whispered hoarsely. "You're no good to the Nabataeans if it gets infected."

Tallis raised his head briefly, surprised at the cushion behind it.

The figure came into focus—a sturdy yet compact thirty-something man, dressed like a rural laborer. The man dipped in and out of a basket, applying salve and new bandages to Tallis's right arm with the speed and precision of a military doctor. "You stay alive, I stay alive, I get paid."

Of course. Tallis was a pawn. How the Nabataeans would

play him was the question. But who was this man tending his wound? Clearly not a Nabataean. His Aramaic dialect placed him in the northern fringe of the Parthian empire, possibly near Edessa in Anatolia.

The man bent lower over Tallis. "I'll be back soon. Show your captors that you're fit for travel." His voice dropped to a whisper. "Nod if you know anyone in Adiabene."

Tallis rolled his head to the left then lapsed into unconsciousness again.

Chapter 7

Power Play

One month prior: Herod's Jerusalem palace complex,
7 days after his death

I f tonight's banquet contained a scrap of authentic homage, Antipas would be surprised. The preplanned excesses of Herod's funeral and the past six days of mourning had been staged farces. Why should tonight's gathering be sincere? His brother, Archelaus, had been entrusted with the arrangements for both.

Antipas balled his hands into fists. A deathbed twist in Herod's will had denied Antipas the entirety of his father's kingdom as well as his title. He hadn't even inherited Judaea. Archelaus ruled it now.

Antipas paused at the entrance of the banquet hall. The last time he'd dined there, he had watched his father regale the Magi from Persia. Although he wanted to leave Jerusalem and tonight's spectacle, his mind nagged him to stay. He had unfinished business here. With his dead father.

As an interminable roll call of guests droned on about Herod's accomplishments, Antipas asked himself what he owed his father. No one knew of the private pledge Herod had forced upon him. Only the gods could hold him accountable for it, and he was fairly sure they didn't care. Why should he still be obligated to fulfill his promise to eliminate the Magi?

He wasn't a killer like his father. On the other hand, following through on his pledge could gain him visibility, demonstrate his decisiveness in exercising authority. On a larger scale, it could cement his stance against false prophets and others disturbing the peace with their talk about an eternal child-king. Antipas would be seen as a strong ruler, even if it was from a throne in Galilee.

Maybe he should have pursued the Magi more ardently. No matter. Eventually they would have to travel Roman roads to return home, and the stationarii remained on notice to apprehend the Magi until they—or someone else—did.

Antipas observed his barely older brother from a distance. Archelaus maneuvered from guest to guest with gusto, his face flushed with schoolboy adrenaline. Tsk. An overeager host with no sense of pacing. Had he learned nothing from their father? At such events, Herod the Great always moved with precision timing—lingering long enough to make each guest feel seen and appreciated, while devoting the shortest possible measure to leave that impression. Herod reserved longer encounters solely for his benefit: to make a point, glean information, gain approval, or woo an unlikely ally.

Enjoy your moment, brother. You're already in trouble with the Jews.

Where was Varinius? One reason Antipas had deigned to attend this event was to persuade the jurisconsult to follow him to Perea, the southern part of his inherited kingdom. Disengaging Varinius from Judaea's plexus would be no small feat, as he was comfortably ensconced in Jerusalem's culture and Herod's court. But Antipas could offer him something that Archelaus couldn't.

Tributes to Herod continued. The adulation soured Antipas's

stomach. He slipped out of the banquet hall and turned a corner into the fountain room that adjoined the festive hall with its twin. In the center of the room, burbling fonts mingled with dignitaries' chatter. Along the room's perimeter, waterfalls plunged two stories from Corinthian capitals. Antipas smirked. Rome had elaborate statue fountains, but only Herod had indoor waterfalls. Their breathtaking beauty was truly an engineering marvel.

Antipas liked this place. Not for its aesthetics, but for its opportunities. The walls and water amplified but distorted sound. When full of people like tonight, this room was a cacophony to most. But for as long as Antipas could remember, he had been able to sift through the sounds. As a child, he would hide behind a fountain or under a bench, listening to intrigues guests thought were safe from others' ears. As he grew, he honed his knack for aural discernment. The practice never failed to stand him in good stead, from exposing classmates' trysts to selectively leaking news of statesmen's covert exchanges.

He moved behind a fountain in the center of the room and waited.

Hmm. This game was fun twelve years ago. Disappointed that he didn't hear any court gossip, he considered leaving. But the jingle of a money pouch stopped him.

"From a benefactor, to ensure your safe passage to Rome." Varinius's voice met his ears.

Archelaus's thanks followed.

Antipas's blood boiled. For almost two years, he had paid Varinius for inside knowledge about Herod's court. If that jurisconsult dared to align himself with another family member, Antipas would make his life so miserable he'd wish for death.

He expected more conversation but heard none. Peeking around the corner of the fountain, he glimpsed two royal guards escorting his brother, robed in purple, from the room.

31

Archelaus wouldn't be wearing purple long if he couldn't quell his trouble with the Jews. Some had been killed when they dismantled the golden eagle Herod had erected at the Temple's entrance, and now the faithful followers were in a frenzy. Archelaus had handled the situation so poorly that scores of Roman guards had been pressed into service to augment palace security during tonight's banquet.

Good.

Let Archelaus crash with his problems. All the more reason for Antipas to contest his father's will. He'd use his brother's failures to show Rome why he should rightfully rule the entire region as king.

Ten minutes later, Antipas located Varinius exiting the banquet hall. "Tonight holds many more hours for feasting and homage. Why leave so soon?"

Varinius sighed. "I must appear in court early tomorrow morning."

"For a criminal case?"

"Nothing so interesting. A boring civil case."

"Hmm."

"We should talk tomorrow after I settle this case. The usual place?"

Antipas squared himself in front of Varinius. "No. We will talk now. Why would you pass money to my brother for a trip to Rome?"

If that challenge surprised Varinius, he didn't show it. "I merely relayed a message from a wealthy but ill Roman citizen who supports your brother."

"Who?"

"You know I can't disclose that." Varinius's voice hardened.

"You would do well to check your speculations, Antipas. Consider your carelessness in talking to me here. You want to arouse suspicion of your activities?"

"I could ask the same of you."

"If you had waited until I could meet you, I would have explained everything tomorrow. Talking with you after the case settlement would have been a logical time for me to 'teach' you more about Rome's legal system—as I have done for two years now."

Antipas shoved Varinius back a pace.

The lanky jurisconsult registered only mild annoyance. "Your father built fourteen palaces beyond Jerusalem. Any of them would be more private than this one."

Antipas crossed his arms. "Time is short."

"More than you know. Walk with me."

Halfway through the palace gardens, Varinius paused behind a bronze fountain in the shadow of a cypress tree. "You are in the race of your life—a race against Archelaus for your father's kingdom. Judaea's status as a client kingdom requires the emperor to approve Herod's final will. But Herod was so close to death when he changed his will that it didn't reach Rome until the king's mourning period had started.

"Like you, Archelaus will go to Rome and plead his case to the emperor regarding Herod's last will. Of course, your brother wants it ratified as it stands. He revels in ruling Judaea. He plans on taking a great number of supporters with him. That requires extra funds for travel. It also limits how and when he can travel. Use that to your advantage."

"Go on."

"Take only a select retinue with you. Obtaining passage for a small group is easier and faster than what Archelaus has planned. Leave now. Arrive sooner. State your case before your brother can."

Varinius searched Antipas's face. "First impressions are everything. So, may I suggest you take Ireneus with you? His rhetorical skills are unmatched. He supports you, and his art of persuasion will aid you greatly as you make your case."

Antipas had already secured Ptolemy's commitment to accompany him. Ptolemy, the keeper of Herod's seal, would provide a firsthand account of Herod's physical and mental state the final time he changed his will. But Antipas hadn't thought about Ireneus. What a brilliant suggestion.

On second thought, the inspired plan sounded almost too tidy. "You would freely offer me this advice?"

"As a jurisconsult, my job is to rule against chaos and restore order. As a private citizen, I dislike chaos even more. Archelaus has ruled Judaea for only a week, and look at what's happened. He's far beyond his depth. You are better suited to rule."

Varinius had said all the right words, but could Antipas trust him? Trust was a rare commodity in Herod's court, and Antipas rarely partook of its fickle supply.

"My lord, if you give Archelaus time, he'll be his own downfall. But don't wait and hope that will guarantee you Judaea's throne. Strike now."

A slow grin spread across Antipas's face. He liked what he heard.

Varinius knelt. "As Mars helped Augustus avenge Caesar's murder, may Mars influence Augustus to rule in your favor—if not now, then in the near future. Only the gods know the right time to bestow good fortune. They will grow what you sow in the emperor's mind and will bring the right events to pass to confirm you should be king. Play the game right, starting with this race to Rome, and you will become the king you were always meant to be."

Chapter 8

Ornament of Galilee

One month later; Sepphoris, in Lower Galilee

Antipas grimaced as his servant handed him a white liquid. Drinking chalk was vile. But every time he thought about Rome and the disposition of Herod's last will, his stomach soured.

By all accounts, the outcome should have been guaranteed. Most of Rome's Senate had voiced their preference for ruling in favor of Antipas. Some of Antipas's family had arrived, unannounced, to endorse him. Both Antipas and Ireneus had delivered compelling arguments against Archelaus's rash behavior in mishandling the golden eagle situation at the Temple. Ireneus had further argued how overstepping such authority threatened Rome's stability in Judaea. Ptolemy's firsthand testimony should have struck the final blow to ensure the last will would be invalidated.

Nothing changed the emperor's ruling.

Herod's will stood as written. Archelaus would rule Judaea, but as ethnarch. None of Herod's kin would be king.

The emperor's loyalty to Herod couldn't have been the

deciding factor. Roman loyalty was contractual. If money had passed under the table to ensure the emperor would approve Herod's final will, the funds must have come from Herod himself.

If Herod could twist fate in his death, then surely Antipas could redirect fate in his life. Even if he had to start by ruling strips of land on either side of the Jordan River.

Varinius could help. And he should arrive in Sepphoris within the hour.

"*Ave*, Antipas," Varinius said in a formal Roman greeting. Antipas grasped the jurisconsult's forearm in response, noting the jurisconsult had traveled in his formal magisterial garb. Good. Antipas was prepared to play that power game.

"Welcome to Sepphoris and my humble palace on a hill." Antipas ushered his guest into a reception hall, its floor inlaid with an intricate geometric mosaic bordered by exquisitely crafted animals and entwined vines. Varinius would no doubt want a tour. It could wait.

Antipas guided his guest to the triclinium where they would dine. Varinius leisurely strolled its length, his toga brushing the floor's tiles laden with scenes of Dionysius and the goat-god Pan. "This room is lovely, as is your view in every direction."

"Yes." Antipas fidgeted, rubbing his fingers together. "Sepphoris has all the comforts of home, including a Roman bathhouse. I engaged it for our private use later today."

Varinius nodded agreeably. "So, how are you getting along?"

"I can't seem to throw a stone without hitting a synagogue or a *miqveh*," Antipas said. "Religious inclinations aside, the economy is good, the land is fertile, and every home in Sepphoris has running water."

Varinius registered slight surprise but gestured beyond their view. "I see you haven't wasted any time starting improvements."

"Yes ... roads first. And a wall around the city."

Antipas moved to a southeastern-facing window. "Strange that lower-class houses sprawl so close to the Upper City. That's convenient for hiring laborers, but I can get workers from Nazareth at lower wages. Do you know they walk almost four miles to work here? We'll see if their skills are as strong as their resolve. Maybe something good will come from Nazareth."

Varinius nodded.

"This area is full of opportunity," Antipas continued. "With time, I can make it the Ornament of Galilee."

Seed planted.

He didn't expect his comment to register a reaction from Varinius. In and out of court, the jurisconsult always cloaked his inclinations in detached impartiality. But nothing escaped him. Varinius's comment about the road work indicated he had deviated from the Via Maris onto lesser-traveled byways to see what Antipas was doing. Additionally, Varinius should have gathered from Antipas's choice of words that the city's future could be more than a crossroad of two major trade routes.

"To honor my expansion plans, I'm thinking of renaming Sepphoris." He turned back to Varinius. "How does 'Autocratoris' sound to you?"

"If it befits what you actually accomplish."

A diplomatic non-answer. No matter. Antipas steered his guest to the dining hall. Carefully planned food and lunch conversation should cultivate Varinius's openness to his proposal. "I trust roast peacock is still one of your favorites. Let me know if it is to your liking."

"Indeed I will." Varinius bobbed his head.

Lunch trundled too slowly for Antipas's taste. Too much idle talk. He should have appreciated Varinius's compliments on the roast peacock and medallions of wild boar. Although the food pleased his palate as well, it didn't dull his edginess. Time with his guest was slipping away. He needed a clear opening to lay out his plans—for they hinged on having Varinius by his side.

Five minutes after the second course was served, a steward approached with a tray of ingredients for custom mixing more spiced wine.

"You're late," Antipas snapped.

Varinius raised an eyebrow. "When did you lose your manners?"

Careful. Court Varinius at his pace.

"Apologies. Matters of state occupy my mind. I'm finding that Jews are difficult to rule, and Nabataeans are practically impossible to ally. No wonder my father retreated to his outlying palaces so often."

Varinius steepled his fingers. "You know what you can do about the Nabataeans."

"Stop."

"Have you learned nothing from me? Marry the daughter of their king. The arrangement will please Emperor Augustus greatly. You know how he favors creating alliances by joining Roman officials with foreign princesses."

Antipas rolled his eyes.

"If the Emperor endorses you, he will reward you by expanding your territories. But he can snuff out your career just as quickly." Varinius punctuated his point with a finger snap.

"Take a delegation to King Aretas. Express your desire for peace along your shared border. Grant the Nabataeans some good-faith gesture, like a compromise with trade or tariffs. Then ask the king to pledge his daughter to you. That's how to keep peace in Perea and quiet along your shared border."

Antipas groaned. "Aretas's daughter is practically a toddler. She won't be of marriageable age for almost ten years." He slouched on his reclining couch. "Even then, she won't yet have womanly curves—"

"And won't know how to satisfy you?" Varinius snorted. "Don't be arrogant. The Nabataeans love their king. Demonstrate today that you are his good neighbor. Work toward your tomorrow of becoming a well-liked member of his family."

The lawyer flashed an inscrutable smile. "Who knows? Eventually little Phasaelis may become better liked in Rome's inner circles than you are."

Antipas narrowed his eyes. "That is low. My paternal grandmother, Cypros, was Nabataean. You have no idea how my grandfather's court treated her. They pretended to accept her when public appearances mattered. In private, they found endless ways to belittle her."

Varinius shrugged. "Your father loved her enough to name his fortress near Jericho in her honor."

"My father loved *things*, not people. Don't elevate Herod the Great to Herod the father or Herod the son." Antipas clenched his jaw. "He grew up watching how the court treated her. Yet, when he became king, he did nothing to silence those who still found creative ways to mock her or her heritage. He executed family members for lesser offenses—if they threatened his power. Slights against my grandmother didn't endanger his power."

Antipas's anger rose to a boil. "Don't ever mention that betrayer again to me."

Varinius bobbed his head. "As you wish."

"Despite being an 'outsider,' Cypros eventually learned how to wield her own form of power. Maybe her independent spirit helped her survive." Antipas jumped from his reclining couch and paced the room. "Nabataeans. What makes them so ... autonomous no matter how much time or distance separates them from their homeland?" He rubbed his forehead.

Varinius spun his silver fork to the spoon end and waved it at a servant, who obligingly opened a bowl of shellfish for him. "Think of it this way. With your family background, you already understand them better than others. You'll gain more practice every time you meet with Aretas. The Nabataeans may never be loyal to anyone but themselves. But, in time, they may learn to trust you." He stabbed the air with his fork end. "Meet Aretas on his soil. Soon. And remember this above all: *the emperor's goal is your goal.* Territorial harmony."

Varinius drained his wine goblet. "I couldn't have offended you so much as to warrant your silence through the last course of our meal. What troubles your thoughts, my lord?"

"The Magi. They seem to have vanished." Antipas swirled his wine and stared pensively into its ruby depths. "How is it that I haven't heard from my scouts? They're supposed to be the royal guard's elite."

Varinius shrugged.

"My father said never leave loose ends." Antipas idly rolled an Armenian apricot between his palms. "Maybe I should stir up some intrigue about the Parthians and Jews so I can appeal to Rome for more troops. With more men, I could widen the search for the Magi."

"It would keep you in the emperor's sights. That could be good or bad."

"What would it profit elite foreigners to search for a Jew? What does it profit anyone to deal with Jews?" Antipas exploded. "They constantly cause trouble. All Rome asks is that they worship its gods along with their own. But no, they say they can worship only their God. Observing their major holidays never gained my father any respect in their eyes. I need to do more than that, but I doubt the effort will be worth it."

"Jews are inflexible, Nabataeans don't ally themselves, and Parthians are slippery. Leadership does come with difficulties."

This meeting was not going as Antipas had planned.

He needed a stronger appeal. What would tickle Varinius's legal sensibilities—and his ego? Clearly, Antipas needed more proof, more grounds to leverage in a direct bid for his support. Together they would do something Herod never tried—make Sepphoris the Ornament of Galilee. A military stronghold.

Chapter 9

Freedom Ride

Assur, Persia; 7 weeks before Herod's death

Farzaneh reached for the reins of her Arabian, but her head servant clung to them. "Javad, you have your instructions. Give my cousin, Akilah, what he needs when he finally arrives. If necessary, check the contract in my silver lockbox. You know where the key is. And be sure to give him the extra blankets I set aside for him."

He nodded but still clutched the reigns.

"Javad, I can ride as well as any woman in Persia's cavalry. And I'm traveling with security."

In the predawn light, he looked askance at Gushtasp, her most trusted protector. "Yes, master, you are a highly skilled horsewoman. But your attire—"

"As a postal relay courier." Farzaneh's eyes twinkled. "In case anyone asks our business or tries to slow us down." She patted her sealed bag, identical to what Persia's postal relay system used. "If anyone stops us, the documents in here will prove who this mail is for, and that we are en route to deliver it. No one will argue with that. Nothing will disrupt my trip."

Noting Javad's frown, she added, "Don't worry. We'll ride dawn to dusk, switch horses as the relays do, and lodge in a *chapar-khaneh* as needed."

Javad gulped. "Many pardons for my boldness, but unless you travel the Royal Road—"

"The Royal Road is on the route to my destination." In truth, it ran straight through Farzaneh's destination of Arbela. But, for everyone's safety, she wouldn't tell Javad where she was going—or that the trip was short enough to not require overnight lodging. What he didn't know, he couldn't divulge.

"Master, it's not appropriate for you to stay in a post office that doubles questionably as an inn for couriers."

"I'll be careful." Farzaneh tugged the reins from Javad's clenched hand.

He forced a weak smile. "So, you are a courier in training?"

"Today I am." In one fluid leap, she mounted her Arabian. "But you need not pretend you're overseeing my household. You have that charge in writing. I trust you'll execute your duties well."

Javad bowed deeply. "As you say it, so shall it be done. Safe journey, master."

Although the recent loss of Farzaneh's husband weighed heavy on her heart, the notion of travel lightened it. Nothing compared to the freedom of riding a thoroughbred at full gallop. This would be an adventure.

She needed a new perspective. In her home, memories suffocated her. Her faith endangered her. Ironically, her husband's death had triggered both, as well as this trip. Adiabene had changed him. Would it change her?

Chapter 10

Arbela

F arzaneh's instructions from her late husband, Ihsan, were to find the home of a Jewish holy man, a Levite named Elyakim, on the outskirts of Arbela. She didn't know what a Levite was, but she was to stay at his home while she carried out her husband's final wishes. Uppermost in that charge was to deliver a small, locked cylinder to the Levite. Its key dangled from a pale blue ribbon underneath her tunic.

She dismounted near the city's gate. "I take my leave of you here," she said to Gushtasp. "Return home tomorrow. Tell no one of my location."

"But—"

"Thank you for accompanying me this far. My husband would not have entrusted me with his final wishes if he thought they would place me in harm's way. I will return home as soon as I can."

Doubt clouded Gushtasp's face, but he nodded. "As you wish. May your time here unfold as planned."

Farzaneh didn't have much of a plan and even less assurance

of what this trip would yield. She nodded her farewell and hurried through a small courtyard, hoping it was the home of the person her husband had described.

Thankfully, it was.

Elyakim's home was smaller than she expected. Maybe Levites didn't wield as much influence as she'd envisioned. The dwelling and its tasteful furnishings wore their signs of age comfortably, much like Elyakim himself. Even the well-used scarf about his neck and the wrinkles that framed his features were soft. His age was difficult to gauge, as nothing harsh etched his face. He bore his past with grace and dignity. Whatever hardships he had endured, they had not gained entrance to his soul.

Farzaneh quickly realized she should not assume anything about her visit. When she addressed a lady about ten years older than her with a servant request, she was abashed to learn the lady was Elyakim's wife, Eliana. A young man performing steward duties was Eliana's son, Raphael, but he was not Elyakim's offspring. Eliana seemed largely unconcerned with Farzaneh's missteps and ignored her discomfort as she made them. She said little, but her actions—such as her motherly attentiveness toward Farzaneh—spoke volumes. Despite the foreign surroundings, Farzaneh slept straight through the night for the first time since her husband had fallen ill.

The next morning, when Farzaneh started to mention the cylinder she needed to give Elyakim, he interrupted her. "Business later. We shall eat first meal in the garden, yes?"

He guided her through his house to a walled garden many times the size of his home's courtyard. The garden bore no fruit, vegetables, or herbs, but the space burst with flowering bushes and trees. Pine, tamarisk, carob, and eucalyptus aromas encircled Farzaneh like long-lost friends. It felt a bit like home, minus the ache of being home.

He motioned to two stone benches along the garden's flagstone paths. Someone had set a tray of flatbread, sour cherry jam, and *kaymak*, a thick clotted cream, on one bench.

"We eat this today in honor of your husband. He was partial to this meal." Elyakim winked. "I think it was because of Eliana's jam." He prayed then tore a flatbread and gave half to Farzaneh. He lifted his chunk. "To friendship."

"To friendship."

If this foreigner knew such a detail about her husband, what else did he know? Before she could ponder more, something rustled then thudded behind her. She bolted from her seat.

Unconcerned, Elyakim addressed a cluster of quivering tamarisks. "Helena, have you been visiting the merchant stalls again?"

His scolding, fatherly tone drew a teenage girl out of the bushes' dense shade. Despite being dressed as a man, she carried herself with grace and elegance as she crossed in front of Farzaneh and pulled leaves from her rough-hewn garb.

She hugged Elyakim without pretense or apology. "Ananias tells such wonderful stories of Jewish history. They're far more interesting than the rest of my day."

"You shouldn't be in the marketplace without a court escort."

The girl turned down the corners of her mouth yet fell short of managing a pout. "I wouldn't be in the marketplace at all if I remained tethered to an escort. But a country villager needs no escort." She triumphantly plucked her handwoven tunic.

A growl rumbled in Elyakim's throat. "The marketplace is no place for a queen."

Farzaneh choked on her drink. "Queen?"

The teenager tucked wisps of bronze-brown hair back under

her cloth headpiece. "Yes. It's insufferable to have your entire life planned out for you."

"Farzaneh, meet Queen Helena, wife of Monobaz, King of Adiabene."

"One of his wives," Helena said in quick correction. She waved aside Farzaneh's hasty bow. "Please, don't. I am my brother's wife. Supposedly his favorite wife. Whether that is truth or politics, I do not know. But there are worse fates … like marriage to a stranger speaking in a tongue you don't understand."

Farzaneh's hands shook so hard that she lost her grip on her cup. Her vision blurred. Then, with perfect clarity, she saw her twelve-year-old self standing next to her guardian, crushed by Akilah's refusal to agree to a temporary marriage—a protective measure he wanted no part of. She watched, helplessly, as her guardian took her by the hand and joined her with a distant relative instead.

Horrified, she watched the relative's pretense of protection grow into a spiky hedge that bent and rigidified into a barred cage forged by her first husband's dictates. Yes, Farzaneh understood all too well the captivity that others' decisions could create.

Light scraping drew her back to the present. Stooped at Farzaneh's feet, Elyakim was collecting the shards of the ceramic cup she had dropped. She made a mental note to compensate him for the loss. But instead of apologizing to him, she locked Helena in her gaze. "My queen, if I may be so bold, your life still offers endless possibilities."

Helena's eyes widened, but her shoulders sagged. "I'd rather race a wild horse than attend court."

Elyakim chuckled. "Many similarities exist between those two activities."

Farzaneh leaned forward. "The kind of queen you will be is still up to you, yes?"

"Precisely what I have told her since she was old enough to walk." Elyakim stabbed the air with a fleshy index finger. "You are destined for greatness, my queen. Because of you, the world will remember our little country for something far more enduring than being a Roman-Persian battleground."

"Elyakim fancies himself a prophet." Helena's delicate laugh lilted across the garden, much like the wind chimes that tinkled across Farzaneh's private courtyard of her home.

He grunted as he finished his cleanup. "I don't need to be a prophet to know you will change the world someday." In a lighter tone, he added, "Farzaneh is an accomplished rider and has business in Adiabene for a short while. Perhaps you and she could meet in an officially authorized way and share a morning of riding together."

Helena's eyes brightened. "Yes! Would you come?"

"Of course." Farzaneh leaned forward and winked. "I like to ride fast."

"So do I. We can try to outrun my escort."

The women laughed like friends sharing a secret.

Chapter 11

Digging for Answers

Day 2 in Arbela

"There you are." Elyakim's perturbed voice hovered behind Farzaneh.

Flustered, she straightened and backed against a Zagros field elm near her. She wasn't sorry for what she'd done, even though she might have broken an unspoken rule.

Elyakim surveyed Farzaneh's hands and the ground next to the elm. "Were you ... digging in the dirt?"

"I woke at dawn and didn't want to disturb anyone. Gardens remind me of home. I have many of them. Each one brings me joy." She ran her dirty hands under the noisy, bubbling fountain in the center of the grounds and dried them on a towel hanging from her sash. "The soil here is rich. It's been tended, but it doesn't grow food. May I ask why?"

"The land isn't mine." Elyakim clipped his words.

"Oh. Many pardons, I didn't know. Does it belong to a neighbor? The city?"

"No." Elyakim headed toward the house.

"Wait. Ihsan insisted I bring this to you." She pulled the silver cylinder from her sash and handed it to Elyakim.

He turned the small cylinder over in his hands. "What is it?"

"A gift. I do not know its contents." Farzaneh removed the ribbon from her neck and held out its key to Elyakim.

He unlocked the cylinder and withdrew a scroll no larger than his generous palm. A smile smoothed many of the wrinkles in his face as he read. "Thank you for delivering this. Your husband ... so thoughtful and kind, even now."

"Yes," Farzaneh said unevenly. She ached to know what the scroll said, but Elyakim had already locked it in its cylinder and slid it into the thick sash about his waist.

He lifted the ribbon over his neck and let it fall inside his tunic. Clearly, the topic would not be discussed further today. He motioned her indoors. "Come, have first meal with me. You'll need it if you want to see the *qanats*. The parts that are easiest to see are a long walk."

She did desire to see the water systems her husband had rebuilt while here, but ideas for the garden consumed her thoughts. "Would you allow me to buy the land for you? I would like to do something to honor your friendship with my husband."

Elyakim shook with a deep belly-laugh. "The owner would never sell that land to anyone—including you." He stopped and turned to Farzaneh in all seriousness. "But I appreciate your kind intentions. A Levite doesn't own land. In fact, where I live and what I eat all come from the Hebrews in this community. That is the way of Adonai's Law for Levites, no matter where they live."

"You own nothing?" Farzaneh almost choked on her words. How could one live totally reliant on others? Her childhood had been one painful lesson after another in learning that she couldn't trust provision from others. During her bleak youth, her only security came from mastering the skills of appraising, buying, and managing land. Her sole hedge against poverty or worse. When everyone failed her, she could always rely on herself. "I don't understand. But there are many things about your Law I do not know."

"Adonai's plan for the Levites goes all the way back to our father Jacob. His twelve sons became the twelve tribes of Israel. One of those sons was Levi. When the Israelites entered their Promised Land, each tribe received their inheritance—a territory, a land to settle and steward. All but the tribe of Levi."

"That doesn't seem fair."

"Adonai charged the Levites to care for the Hebrews' spiritual health. The Levites were scattered and assigned to live in designated towns throughout every territory. That way, they could help ensure everyone remembered and followed Adonai's words. What some might see as a disadvantage was, in fact, a great honor."

Elyakim's words barely registered with Farzaneh. How could it be an honor to follow an eternal charge to rely on others' generosity for basic provision? What little she knew about this God was a puzzle, so counterintuitive it made her head hurt. Did everything about the Hebrews need a sacred purpose? Or perhaps a secret purpose, like the garden behind Elyakim's house?

"Come, eat." Elyakim beckoned. "Eliana made stewed figs and eggs steamed with onions and greens."

Farzaneh obliged, but her mind wasn't on the savory food or the elegant spoon served with it. Her years of business dealings had made her an expert in negotiations but not casual conversation. She groped for an engaging starter for table talk. Anything better than spoons.

"So, Elyakim, how long have you served as a Levite?"

"I'm technically retired, although Levites never stop serving Adonai. We help the community in ways less physically demanding for our age." Elyakim punctuated the last word with a grimace.

How should she respond to that comment? Farzaneh stirred her bowl of stewed figs to hide her discomfort. She desperately wanted to learn about these people, their beliefs, and Ihsan's involvement with them. Without being intrusive or obvious, she needed a reason to stay in Arbela longer than the few days it would take to conduct her husband's final business.

"My husband rarely talked about the work that brought him to Adiabene. Can you tell me what he did here? It would help me feel … close to him … now."

Elyakim glanced at Eliana. Was it Farzaneh's imagination, or was her answer of a slight head tip some kind of warning?

"Well, the Persians would fight the Romans. One or both sides would try to destroy our water supplies to gain a military advantage. After the fighting would end, Ihsan and his teams would repair or rebuild every damaged qanat." Elyakim threw up his hands. "His work was so technical I couldn't understand it—only appreciate it. But his meticulous efforts were … lifesaving to our community."

Eliana set her serving tray on the counter so roughly that the dishes clanked. She hurried from the room, mumbling something Farzaneh couldn't understand.

Elyakim remained seated but turned to Farzaneh. "Please excuse Eliana. She's a good woman, but she's had a difficult life."

His description of Ihsan's activities in Arbela didn't tell Farzaneh anything beyond what she already knew, and she wasn't ready for a long walk into the heat of the day. Switching topics might prove more fruitful. "My husband was very fond of writings by your prophet Isaiah. He urged me to read them. I mean no disrespect, but I found Isaiah confusing and disturbing. Words of hope mixed with doom, talk of the past mingled with foretelling events to come."

Elyakim's face lit with a warmth that seemed to rise from the bottom of his heart. "Ah, Isaiah. Court official to four kings. Devoted to speaking Adonai's words. Wept when our people didn't heed him. Yes, he wrote many important things about Israel's past, present, and future."

He steepled his fingers and pressed them to his lips. "But perhaps his most profound passages are his predictions of the birth of a child who would also be born an eternal king. One who would be the Savior of the world."

A stone dropped in Farzaneh's stomach. Ignoring all customs and formality, she reached for Elyakim's arm. Realizing the error of her impulsive action, she drew back. "My cousin Akilah who serves in Persia's Magi society saw a star that he believed heralded the child's birth. He risked his reputation and more to find the child. I … helped him finance his trip."

Elyakim's eyes widened. "Did he succeed?"

"I don't know. No one has heard from him since he left."

Elyakim's ample hands gripped his knees. "My dear, I don't mean to cause you distress, but he is in grave danger."

"What do you mean?"

"More than 700 years ago, Isaiah prophesied Adonai would give a miraculous sign of His love when a virgin would give birth to a son and call him Immanuel—meaning 'God with us.' Isaiah further described the child as Mighty God, Everlasting Father, Prince of Peace. An eternal ruler of a government without end. Imagine how audacious—and threatening—that would sound to anyone in power. Especially if it came true."

"Do you think it has?"

"According to our prophets' predictions, the time is right. Consider what any ruler would do if he thought he and his kingdom would be replaced by another—forever. He would justify any means necessary to snuff out that child's life—and the lives of all who knew of the child."

That should have terrified Farzaneh, but waves of vicious speculations pounded the coastline of her heart instead. Why should Akilah have the honor of finding that child? Had he stopped to count the consequences of his actions? Her cousin was always so sure his way was right.

"Forgive me, but my hearing isn't what it used to be. What did you say?"

Farzaneh coughed. Had she actually voiced her thoughts? "I said my cousin was sure he would find the child." Suddenly Akilah's guardedness in talking with her about his findings made sense. The puzzle pieces of Sassanak's sanctions against Akilah and threats to her fell into place. As Head Magus of the Lower Council, he had the power to appeal to the king to eliminate such threats. She shuddered. "Surely local Jewish authorities would offer my cousin protection, yes?"

Elyakim frowned. "He was traveling to Jerusalem?"

"Yes. To talk with the Jewish priests about the prophecies. He needed more information to pinpoint the location of the child's birthplace."

Elyakim sighed. "Hebrews are united in their belief of Adonai, but they are divided on what our holy writings say about this child. Jerusalem's religious authorities spend more time worrying about relations with resident Roman authorities than rightly divining Adonai's words. Roman and Jewish authorities are oil and water—unless they unite against a cause that benefits both sides." He slapped his knees. "I'm a terrible host, talking of history and religion and politics."

How much danger was Akilah in? Farzaneh had to know. "Tell me. Is there no one who can help my cousin?"

Elyakim paused, his face somber. "We will try."

"We?" She couldn't hide her incredulity.

"We have ways of finding your cousin."

"How?" The word escaped Farzaneh's lips as a demand.

"First we pray. Then we act." He waved his index finger at the sky. "My dear, I have no doubt that Adonai has brought you here at precisely the right time. I will explain more later. For now, all you need to know is that this community is a sanctuary, one of several that protect God-fearers who need it. But your cousin needs more than we can provide."

"I don't understand."

Elyakim rose. "After we pray for guidance, I will send word to friends in the north to listen for news of your cousin's whereabouts. We have ... connections ... people adept at learning of plots against God-fearers. If your cousin made it to Jerusalem, he must have crossed paths with Herod's guards— and his spies. They're everywhere, including the city gates."

Farzaneh grabbed her knees to keep them from shaking.

"Tell me everything you know. Your cousin's plans, past or present threats against him or yourself. Any detail may provide a clue for finding him."

Her knees drummed.

"Let me say this plainly. This is a safe place for everyone who comes here. Including you."

"Safe." Farzaneh savored the word like a rare, delicious fruit she had only hazy memories of tasting.

"But, for this visit, I suggest you not tarry in conducting your husband's final business," Elyakim added briskly. "Otherwise, people in Assur will rumor about your absence so close to your husband's death. If you need to send a message to your household or a trusted friend, avoid Persia's postal relay service. One of our private couriers will deliver a message for you."

Farzaneh nodded, but her head swam. Could she trust these people? Once again, she had no one to rely on but herself. And maybe this God that her husband had learned to trust implicitly. "I have so many questions ..."

"Yes, of course. Your husband, Ihsan, was a good friend to

this community. I look forward to sharing that with you. But first we must attend to this news of your cousin. It is a glad tiding as well as a great concern."

Elyakim paused, gauging Farzaneh's confusion. "When Messiah comes, the world will never be the same again. He will reveal what's in people's hearts, and many hearts are dark indeed. Kings who believe they alone deserve their throne ... Jews with their own ideas of what the Messiah should be instead of what the holy writings say He is. All those people have much to lose from Messiah's coming. Religions—even empires—will shake or crumble."

The weight of those last words hit Farzaneh as hard as if she'd fallen off a runaway horse.

What had Akilah done? If he hadn't seen the star or hadn't pursued it when the Council tried to dissuade him, his career would be intact. Maybe Magi society would have dismissed his assertions.

What had she done? If she hadn't aided him, he'd still be safe in Persia, and Sassanak wouldn't have dug into her family affairs.

Her heart galloped like a bolting stallion. Akilah had escaped threats at home only to walk into greater threats abroad—that she'd enabled by her financing.

On a larger scale, what else was in jeopardy? Had Ihsan tried to tell her something between the lines when he talked about Isaiah's writings?

"I don't mean to overwhelm you," Elyakim said. "We can visit the qanats another day." He motioned to Eliana, who had reentered the room.

A dam burst inside Farzaneh's heart. Torrents of loss, grief, anger, and remorse rushed over her. She stood to excuse herself but stumbled as her eyes filled with tears. "Everyone I care about gets taken from me. First, my parents. Then my intended husband. Finally I joined with a man I could love. Now he's gone. And my cousin ..."

A sob burst from her chest. She wasn't close to Akilah, but her host would assume that concern for his safety prompted her tears. He would be wrong. What Akilah had done to her by not following his father's wishes still pained her as much as a horned viper's bite. No, something greater moved her to tears. A holy fear—a peculiar dread mixed with anticipation. A sense of a divine plan vaster than she could comprehend.

The floor lost its firmness under Farzaneh's feet. Eliana eased her onto a cushion.

"I deeply regret this day has brought you more distress than you've already endured." Elyakim rubbed his forehead, as if summoning something from a far corner of his mind. "May I share something?"

Farzaneh nodded numbly.

"The prophet Isaiah wrote, 'Do not be afraid ... do not be intimidated ... For you will forget the shame of your youth and will remember no more the reproach of your widowhood. For your husband is your Maker—the Lord of Hosts is His name—the Holy One of Israel is your Redeemer; He is called the God of all the earth. For the Lord has called you back, like a wife deserted and wounded in spirit, like the rejected wife of one's youth, says your God."[1]

Elyakim's words, soft and low, washed over her soul.

"Forget the shame of your youth ... No more reproach of widowhood ..." Farzaneh shook her head. "My husband and redeemer is your God?"

Elyakim's kindly gaze pierced Farzaneh's heart. "Isaiah's words speak of Adonai calling His people back to Him, but they have meaning for you today as well. Adonai sees your wounds,

---

1. Isaiah 54:4-6 (BSB)

Farzaneh. He has not deserted you. I pray you will draw strength from that truth."

He rose. "Rest now. You and your cousin are in the care of El Shaddai, God Almighty."

Chapter 12

Straddling a Secret

The countryside beyond Arbela

Farzaneh fell in love with Adiabene during her first ride with Helena. Verdant plains touched majestic mountains. The country's beauty was matched only by its people's resilience despite the Roman-Parthian battles waged on its lands.

"What a glorious ride." Helena's face glowed, buffeted by the wind and flushed with the sheer delight of riding fast. She dropped a blanket on the ground and motioned for Farzaneh to sit with her.

In her official capacity of entertaining a guest, Helena didn't try to outrun her escort. But she commanded him to stay at a distance sufficient for her and Farzaneh to talk freely. They chatted about everything from horses and customs to commerce and careers. Helena was wise beyond her years. Farzaneh was wise from her life experiences.

The morning sun shone warmly on the two. Farzaneh couldn't remember ever feeling so comfortable with a friend.

Certainly not one she'd known for barely a week. Especially not one who was twenty-five years younger than she.

As Helena looked toward the mountains, she grew pensive. "Farzaneh, do you remember what it was like to be a child?"

Snakish dread slithered up Farzaneh's spine. She had buried her early years deep in her heart. Did a royal request require her to unearth them?

Helena sighed. "I never had a proper childhood. No spontaneity. As part of the royal family, everything was scripted for me. I want to hear what being a normal child was like."

"I'm not sure I can answer that."

"You must remember. You aren't old yet." The sparkle in Helena's eyes dimmed at Farzaneh's agonized look. "What happened?"

Farzaneh's pulse galloped with anxiety. If she said something, could it be used against her in the future? Life had taught her to be cautious. "I ... didn't have much of a childhood."

"Go on." Helena's voice was so entreating Farzaneh couldn't resist. Without naming anyone, she briefly explained how she became an orphan, her guardians' conditional support, and her unhappy first marriage. She omitted all mention of Akilah and his failure to agree to a protective temporary marriage.

Helena listened intently.

"The only people still living who know that much about my past are Elyakim—and now you," Farzaneh admitted. "Perhaps talking about it is the first step in healing. Adiabene has drawn that out of me. I'm grateful for that."

Helena took Farzaneh's hands in hers. "You will always have a place at my table."

Farzaneh jerked away and bowed her face to the ground. "My queen ..."

"Please, get up. I may not be a God-fearer, but I respect the customs of the Hebrews living in my country. Ananias has been teaching me about King David. To the Hebrews, saying 'you will eat at my table' is more than a dinner invitation. It confers the equivalent of a Magi pension and housing to your family—that is, if I understand Magi society correctly." Helena's eyes brimmed with compassion.

"My queen." Farzaneh prostrated herself and kissed Helena's feet.

"That's enough formality." Helena pulled on Farzaneh's shoulders. "Your friendship is a rare gift. You've shown me that I can be all I'm intended to be without losing who I am along the way. That truth will stay with me wherever I go. I pledge you this: no matter what distance separates us, you will always have a place at my table."

Something indescribable blanketed Farzaneh—a feeling she had resisted for years in her husband's kindness. *Can it be that I am loved?*

Farzaneh didn't want to spoil yesterday's euphoria, but a question burned inside her. As queen, Helena had everyone at her command. Why sneak off to the marketplace to hear stories from a Jewish merchant when she could simply summon Elyakim to her palace? Farzaneh resolved to ask Helena at the end of their next ride.

The question seemed simple enough, but Helena dodged it. "It's a thrill. I love to outsmart my escort." She rummaged in her leather pouch. "Want some dried figs? They're from our royal orchards."

Farzaneh's years of business dealings had honed her expertise in reading people. Helena may have a rebellious streak, but it was not her main reason for visiting Ananias.

"Many pardons, my queen, but would you care to try that answer again?"

"No, I would not. Not as queen."

Farzaneh smiled. *"Helena,* why do you visit Ananias, really? Why not call Elyakim to your court to teach you the Hebrews' ways? That would be more reliable … convenient … and safer."

"Elyakim is a friend. I want to keep it that way," Helena said obliquely.

"Surely you could summon him on the basis of an intellectual or cultural exchange—"

"Farzaneh, you don't know our ways," Helena said, her voice uncharacteristically cold and strong. "Besides, Elyakim is busy with many things."

Farzaneh had ventured into uncharted territory and needed to make hasty amends. "Many pardons. I spoke insensitively. Of course you know what's in the best interest of all your subjects. But, if I may ask as a friend, does this merchant interest you otherwise?"

Helena's now-familiar lilting laughter shattered the tension. "A thousand times, no. At least not in the way you imply. He's three times my age."

Farzaneh resolved not to talk about the matter again. At least, not with Helena.

Chapter 13

More than Qanats

End of Week 2 in Arbela

F arzaneh was running out of reasons to remain in Arbela. She'd seen Ihsan's handiwork with the qanats and heard enthusiastic stories of how he'd brought life-giving water back to the war-torn area. But rebuilding qanats was his job. The residents acted grateful for more than that.

She finally asked Elyakim about it.

His lips tightened into a thin line. "Life here in Adiabene is not like what you enjoy in Persia. We have endured much war and hardship. Armenians to the north, Romans to the west, Nabataeans to the south, and Persia's changeable support in protecting us from those who would take all we have from us."

"Many pardons. I didn't mean to presume anything." Farzaneh wasn't sure how geopolitical strife related to her husband, but her mind raced. Government contracts financed most of his work.

"My people's struggles are not your concern, my dear."

"But they are—because they mattered to my husband." Farzaneh studied her hands as if the right words might magically appear on her palms. "He said little about it, but I could tell he bonded with your people in a way that was stronger than family ties. It seems the feeling was mutual. I don't know the best way to describe it."

She straightened her spine. "Ihsan changed his beliefs during his time here. He came to believe in Adonai … and so do I. At least I'm trying to. It was easier when Ihsan was alive."

Farzaneh nervously folded and unfolded her hands. "This bond … his belief … seemed to come with a great cost but also great joy. That gave him peace, especially near his life's end."

Elyakim's face crinkled into a smile tinged with sadness. "Ihsan said you were the smartest person he knew. He was right."

Her forced laugh didn't convince even her. She summoned a deep breath. "My belief is costing me. I'm not safe at home. The head of Persia's Lower Council wants to arrest me. He knows Ihsan abandoned Persia's official religion, and he suspects I've done the same. I don't know what awaits me when I return home. I have everything to lose"—she lifted her chin—"but I refuse to lose something I could have gained by your telling me more about my husband. If you're withholding that from me, tell me what it is."

Elyakim's face clouded with worry. "The less you know, the safer you are."

"Tell me. I won't leave until you do."

"I see." He stroked his beard. "Then perhaps you're ready to hear what Ihsan wanted you to know. What he couldn't speak of in life, we can share in his death. We will talk tomorrow morning, yes?"

Chapter 14

Connections

The anticipation of what Elyakim might tell Farzaneh stole her sleep. Restless throughout most of the night, she finally dozed off—until a strident exchange seeped through the floor below her while the sun was still weak in the morning sky.

"How dare you question my loyalty to Persia or the Parthian Empire? I am descended from the Levite Pethahiah, Persia's deputy of Jewish affairs and royal commissioner to Judaea—the same Pethahiah who sat at the right hand of King Artaxerxes I."[1]

"You have nothing to fear if you answer the allegations by accounting for all the Jews in Arbela within two weeks—their names, addresses, and occupations." A vaguely familiar but muffled voice continued. She pressed her ear to the floor.

"If I must personally retrieve this information, you will regret it."

A door slammed.

---

1. Nehemiah 11:24

Who would want to threaten Elyakim? Farzaneh crept down to the first floor. In the kitchen prep room, Eliana fiercely kneaded bread dough. In the main room, Elyakim seemed lost in thought.

"How can I help?" Farzaneh said.

Both her hosts startled at her voice.

"Perhaps it is time for you to leave, my dear." An unusual heaviness weighted Elyakim's words.

"No." Farzaneh shocked herself and her hosts with the force of her reply. "Who was that man?"

"Someone from the Lower Council who claims he's the acting Head Magus."

"Acting?" Sassanak no longer held that position? Farzaneh could only hope.

"Yes. A disagreeable man named Azazel."

Sassanak's right hand. From what Farzaneh had heard, Azazel was worse than Sassanak—if that was possible. "What did he want?"

"Census information. An accounting of people, foodstuffs, and the number of wells in the area. He was here two years ago as well."

Eliana punched her dough so hard that a nearby cup clattered to the floor.

Farzaneh crossed the room and planted herself in front of Elyakim. "I've spent most of my life dealing in land acquisitions. Persian census-taking is not that frequent, even when calculating land grants. My late husband's work included assessing water sources he had to report to the government. That isn't due now either. What aren't you telling me?" Farzaneh's voice brimmed with fear-laced insistence.

Something inside Elyakim sagged, adding years to his weathered face.

"Many pardons, but everything I've learned since coming to

Arbela raises more questions than it answers. My husband's involvement with this community. Helena's involvement with the Hebrews. Your involvement with …" Farzaneh fanned the air in front of Elyakim. "I'm not sure what all you're involved with." She winced. She must be breaking a dozen rules of protocol in talking so boldly to a holy man.

Elyakim winced as if in physical pain. "My orchards," he moaned.

"Orchards? You own no land. The closest orchards grow within the walls of your king's palace. Speak plainly."

Eliana shot a withering look at Farzaneh, but she couldn't stop herself. Rude and demanding as her words were, she was determined to uncover at least some of the mystery surrounding this place.

She knelt in front of Elyakim. "Please, tell me everything."

Elyakim's face creased with worry lines. "Do you believe Adonai directs the ways of man?"

"I … don't know." Farzaneh had spent her adult life trying to direct her own steps down a good path. The notion of the Hebrews' God taking an active part in it was foreign to her. But if Elyakim's question was indeed fact, then Adonai had directed Ihsan's path to Arbela—and was directing her path even now—in ways beyond her understanding.

"Adonai brought Ihsan to Arbela precisely when we needed help. But it was for a purpose beyond restoring the city's water supplies," Elyakim said.

She held her breath. Would she finally get some clarity?

Elyakim explained Adiabene had experienced war for so long that Arbela had become a place where refugees sought a fresh start. Many came from areas where the fighting had taken its greatest toll. But with them came people who had been persecuted for their beliefs. He didn't say who did that but alluded to a high-ranking official in the Lower Council.

He dubbed all those displaced people "his orchards" because he "replanted" them, gave them the chance to flourish in a new place. But he couldn't hide or relocate everyone fast enough. Certain officials used the chaos of war to cloak their hunt for religious dissenters, capturing them or worse.

"Your husband worked in Arbela long enough to see what we faced," Elyakim continued. "He saw an opportunity to increase the amount of people we could handle."

"How?" Farzaneh moved to the edge of her seat in anticipation.

"He used his knowledge of qanats to build a hiding place for them. A refuge where soldiers wouldn't think to look."

Most of a qanat was underground and hazardous to construct. Farzaneh imagined details Elyakim hesitated to share. Regardless, what her husband had done was doubly dangerous.

"Ihsan poured his soul into building something that would outlast him … that would help people for generations to come."

If Ihsan had worked himself to exhaustion to help this refugee effort, was that why he returned from Arbela ill and never recovered? She couldn't let that ugly accusation take root in her heart.

"Show me."

"For now, that must remain a secret—to protect the people we're housing. But I can tell you we are growing as Ihsan hoped we would. We've connected with like-minded people who are aiding others under duress for their beliefs. For example, our Edessan friends learn information through the military and rescue military captives when they can. In fact, one of our Edessan contacts sent me word about someone who was with your cousin."

Farzaneh's palms grew sweaty. *Was?* Had the caravan been attacked? Who had survived?

"Do you know someone named Tallis?" Elyakim's question punctured her thoughts.

"Yes." She tried to steady her voice. "He's a priest-scholar in the division of Magi society that my cousin Akilah serves in. Tallis and a younger Magus were with Akilah in their search for—"

"The prophesied eternal child-king." Elyakim's voice dropped to a reverent whisper.

"Is my cousin alive?"

"We don't know. We continue to hope for the best. Were you close to him?"

"No."

"Yet you supported him, yes?"

"Financially. For his trip to Jerusalem." She couldn't tell this holy man her reasons for helping Akilah had virtually nothing to do him.

"He must be greatly indebted to you for your generosity."

Farzaneh wanted to unburden her whole story behind why Akilah needed the funds, why she chose to help him, and how she'd forced him into signing a *stūrīh* in exchange for her assistance. In this house, her motives were glaringly self-serving. What could be more out of place? She was sitting with an exceptionally kind man who had shared his hospitality with her for three weeks.

She cleared her throat. "You were going to say something about Tallis."

"He was captured. Someone we trust is trying to help him escape to safety."

"Where is he now?"

"We don't always get details. They would be too dangerous for everyone involved."

"What of the rest of the caravan?"

71

"It hasn't been located yet."

Farzaneh's breath caught in her chest.

"That's a good thing," Elyakim added quickly. "Raiding parties like to brag about their exploits and handle their spoils loosely. Attentive ears and eyes can learn much information that way. Our contacts haven't heard anything about your cousin's caravan." He paused and studied his hands.

"What?"

"Herod is dead. But word among his troops is that his son Antipas will not stop searching for your cousin and his colleagues until they are found … and disposed of." Elyakim raised a hand heavenward. "Your cousin must be a very wise man if he can evade the royal scouts."

Maybe so. No one should be hunted like prey.

She cleared her throat. "Thank you for telling me this. I won't burden you with more questions that you're not free to answer. But could you please speak more about how my husband helped your community?"

"Yes." Elyakim's forehead wrinkles deepened. "And no. Ihsan was very specific about what I would tell you. He chose to help us—but he insisted that no one, including himself, should ever make you feel you needed to do the same."

"I don't understand." Farzaneh's frustration bled through her voice. Grass could grow beneath her feet before Elyakim spoke plainly.

"While Ihsan was here repairing qanats, he got the idea for building an underground refuge for people we help. Carving rooms into rock, mostly underground, was similar to how he would prepare a qanat. That's how he avoided curious eyes. Everyone assumed he was simply doing his job—only taking longer than usual. One entrance to the refuge is hidden at the back of the garden behind this house."

No wonder Elyakim didn't want her digging in the garden or asking questions about it.

"We reclaimed the garden's land on the city's outskirts as a beautification project, but we did everything at Ihsan's guidance to shield his work. The garden makes it easy to move people from the refuge to locations beyond Arbela. Also, a tunnel connects the refuge to a secret entrance in Arbela's synagogue where I serve. That's another way we move people around. Roman soldiers are usually so superstitious they shy away from holy places."

Farzaneh's mind sped faster than a weaver's shuttle interlacing yarn on a loom. "Is Azazel demanding a census because he suspects more people are consuming food than are paying taxes?"

"If we grew fruits and vegetables in that garden to feed the people we help, locals or military forces would raid it, putting our refuge at risk. Even if we could avoid that, it would soon become clear we were feeding people who didn't pay taxes. So we don't grow edibles in the garden."

"Did my husband ... do anything to government records to cover up 'excess consumption'?"

Elyakim's laughter scattered the room's tension. "Your husband was an honorable man. He never altered any records. But he told me his reports documented how generously both Roman and Parthian invaders took from our land—and how difficult *their* excess consumption was to calculate."

"Who owns the garden?"

"Ihsan."

A dead person can't own land.

Elyakim seemed to read Farzaneh's thoughts. "The scroll in the cylinder you delivered to me contains Ihsan's instructions for maintaining the garden."

"But someone has to own it. You said Levites don't own land."

"True. Ihsan's instructions included a short list of people

who could legally assume the deed to the land upon his death. People he could trust to carry on this work."

"Like Queen Helena?"

Elyakim stiffened. "The queen's job is to fulfill her position as ruler."

What about her destiny? Elyakim said Helena was fated to achieve something grand and enduring. Wouldn't this work fit his prediction? His non-answer didn't sit well with Farzaneh, but it could explain why Helena didn't summon him to her court. Maybe she had to distance herself from him to avoid accusations of favoritism toward any religion or people group.

But what of Helena's meetings with Ananias? Were they a distraction while Elyakim hid people in the merchant's caravan? Or was Ananias a messenger, connecting Elyakim with outside contacts? Either way, Ananias's travels and transitory life would be a perfect cover. For a moment, the thrill of becoming privy to such intrigues swept Farzaneh away.

But her musings didn't tell her which names Ihsan had penned. "Am I on the list?" She held her breath.

Elyakim enclosed Farzaneh's hands in a warm but firm grip. "Ihsan made it clear that he didn't want you to ever feel pressured to choose between your life in Assur and something you would not have considered otherwise. He wanted you to live fully—regardless of where and how you chose to do it."

Farzaneh's eyes welled with tears. Yes, it would be presumptuous to assume she would want to take on a cause that her husband had never divulged to her. Yes, it would be preposterous to walk away from her work, her lands, and all she had built for herself over the past twenty years. To know that Ihsan had already considered and accounted for those things made her feel closer to him than ever. Cords tugged her heart in opposite directions.

"My dear, you need time to heal. I think you should return

home. But know this: you will always be welcome here, no matter what."

"Thank you," she whispered.

Wait. Was she on the list or not? She asked again.

"May Adonai go with you, surround you, and fill your dwelling place. *Shalom shalom.*"

Chapter 15

Stumbles

Somewhere in the Arabian Peninsula

The Wilderness of Paran gave way to less mountainous, but still desolate land. And new challenges.

Suhail, an older pack camel, stumbled and almost dragged down the camels hitched directly to him. Camels screamed and servants shouted as gear spilled from Suhail's saddle framework. The caravan pitched to a halt.

While servants scrambled to retrieve the gear, Abdul and Obadiah, the caravan's two animal healers, rushed to Suhail to see if he was strong enough to continue. Akilah read the verdict in Obadiah's face.

Rashidi plucked Akilah's sleeve. "We should check all the animals. I can feel a difference in my camel's sway."

Akilah cringed. Changes in a camel's sway signaled nutritional deficiencies. Shrinking humps spoke to low energy stores. Carrying heavy loads over rocky land further taxed their bodies. Leaner bodies made the saddle frameworks unstable on the camels' backs.

The frameworks needed adjustments to fit securely, then the

loads redistributed and lightened. Otherwise, the animals could sustain serious injuries.

Under Abdul and Obadiah's supervision, the servants thoroughly examined every camel for signs of problems.

Akilah paced as he waited for Abdul's report. It couldn't be good.

"Bites, scratches, tendonitis, swollen feet," Abdul said. "We can treat all that. But we must rest the camels."

"How long?"

"At least several days." Abdul shifted uncomfortably before Akilah.

"There's more?"

"The cushions underneath the camels' loads."

"What about them?"

"The combination of miles, the gear's weight, and the camels' sway have ground the straw cushioning into chaff. That's causing pain and chafing over their humps." He sighed. "Replacing the padding would mean sacrificing some of our teben. The camels would have less to eat."

"Attend to their injuries first. Then we'll decide how to repack everything."

Abdul nodded but looked away.

"What now?"

"If Suhail doesn't make a miraculous recovery, we'll have to leave him behind."

Chapter 16

Bandaged Royally

Akilah called for three days of rest to tend to the camels.
"It's always about the camels," Tahrea complained to fourteen-year-old Hasrat, the youngest servant in the caravan.

"They're taking us to our destination," Hasrat said timidly.

"No, the Magi are," Tahrea growled. "But where *is* our destination? We could die out here in the wilderness."

Hasrat's eyes grew big as dates. "Don't say that. I want to go home."

Akilah started toward Hasrat, but Abdul and Obadiah intercepted the servants.

"More salve and cloths over here," they said, motioning.

Tahrea hmphed but headed toward the healers with supplies in hand.

One by one, the healers hobbled each camel requiring medical attention and lassoed it to the ground. Amid the camel's fearful cries, Abdul held its head to calm it while Obadiah wrapped a leg or foot in cloths. Hasrat cringed and turned away, tears in his eyes.

Akilah rested a hand on the young servant's shoulder. "It's

for their good, even if they don't understand it. Gifts can be hard to recognize when one is in pain."

Hasrat smiled weakly, but his eyes were blank. Akilah sighed. Hardship diluted the potency of teachable moments.

"I've never seen bandages this nice," Abdul commented. "Such a fine weave, cloth bleached to perfection. It's so white it almost looks like royal tunic material—not bandage cloths."

Obadiah shrugged.

"Where did it come from?" Abdul said.

"Some private reserve the Magi had. When Akilah gave them to me, I didn't ask questions. Let's use these bandages for leg wounds. We'll wrap the camels' feet in surplus tent material."

Akilah grinned and turned away. What would Herod think if he knew the clothes he'd given the Magi had been repurposed as bandages?

"Tahrea, I have a special assignment for you," Akilah said quietly.

"What?" Travel and hardship had not blunted his surly tone.

"A pack camel named Suhail."

"What about him?"

"He's not doing well with the miles. Suhail needs more attention than either healer can afford to give one camel right now. Obadiah is our most experienced animal healer. He can teach you what to do for Suhail. He will be your charge for a time. Come."

Although Tahrea shrugged Akilah's hand off his shoulder, he dutifully walked across the campsite with him.

Akilah raised his hand. "Obadiah, I've brought you extra help."

"Glad to have it," the healer replied.

Tahrea approached the camel carefully from the front. "What's wrong with Suhail?"

"Scrapes, bites, arthritis, tendonitis, a stress fracture. And age."

"I already know what to do for scrapes and bites. Show me what else to do."

Obadiah nodded. "I'll gladly show you what medicine can do. But I can't show you everything beyond that."

Akilah prayed Tahrea would learn the latter.

Chapter 17

Praying to an Incomprehensible God

A few minutes later, Akilah slipped away from camp. Beyond everyone's sight, he dropped to the hardened ground. "Are we on a fool's journey?" he asked the sky.

No caravan traveled this far or long at one time. Even along the Silk Road and Spice Route, travelers and their wares switched caravans at way stations, getting fresh supplies and rested camels for each leg of their journey.

They were nowhere near Egypt yet. Akilah thought of the tired legs carrying them. The rugged territory behind them. The uncertainties ahead of them. The griffon vultures that seemed to follow them.

How can we get to Alexandria?

Akilah's heart buckled under the weight of the question.

Reason and logic had always served him well. If his first plan didn't work, he found an alternate strategy. Yet, despite all his education and capabilities, despite rationing food and finding hidden water, he couldn't see how this would end well. They were still far from villages and farmland. They didn't dare travel on Roman roads. Herod's sentries would surely overtake them.

Akilah replayed Bethlehem in his mind. After they'd found Yeshua, the angel's message had been the same to all three Wise Men. Don't go back through Jerusalem. Don't talk to Herod. Don't go home the way you came. Their flight was a group decision. Yet, as lead Wise Man, the full weight of that responsibility rested on Akilah.

He longed for easier decisions. Rest. Safety. Guidance.

Oh, to see the star that had led them to Yeshua. The memory built momentum, welling from his inmost being until it burst from his lips. "God of the Hebrews, I don't have the strength to carry this burden. Lift it from me!"

He fell to the ground in despair. "When we traveled to Jerusalem, You gave us a star of hope. We saw a child the prophecies foretold. Your prophet Isaiah called Him the hope of the world. But in this wilderness, I can't see hope. Please show me some hope!"

He stretched his hands skyward, agonizing pleas pouring from his heart.

"Haruz says the Hebrews don't speak Your name aloud. How can I call upon You so You will listen? How can I understand You? Haruz says You are with us. *Where are You?*"

He'd never prayed like that before. As a priest in Magi society, Akilah had prayed many kinds of prayers, mostly prescriptive. This was effortless. Unrehearsed. Gushing from a wellspring in his soul.

For the first time, he wondered if he really knew how to pray. Or to whom he should pray. He dropped to his knees, his hands covering his head.

Akilah didn't remember all he said. He didn't know how long he stayed crouched on the ground. He didn't understand the peace that washed over him when he finally got up. He hadn't solved any problems. But somehow, he felt different. Calmer. Hopeful.

Chapter 18

Winds of Change

Early the next morning

Akilah's first view of the day was Tahrea outside the Magi's tent flap.

Legs wide, arms akimbo, the servant's face burned with anger. "Why didn't you tell me Suhail is dying?"

Akilah gathered his cloak about him and noticed Tahrea was without his. "Why would you say that?"

"Is this a cruel joke?" Tahrea's voice rose. "Suhail is too old and too injured to go on. You knew that, didn't you?"

"I knew he didn't have a good chance of continuing this journey. That is all," Akilah replied.

"Then why assign me to him?"

"What do you think you can do for Suhail?"

"I did what Obadiah told me to."

"But what do you think *you* can do for Suhail?"

"I don't know what you mean."

"You'll figure it out."

"Do all Magi talk in riddles? Or only you?" Tahrea spat each word from his mouth as if it were poison. "You want to teach

me something? Make it useful—like how to win a knife fight."
He stomped off.

Akilah peered skyward, praying help would rain down on him. This vast wilderness and endless sky reminded him how small a creation he was. How ineffective his best efforts could be.

As he exited the Magi's tent, an unusually strong gust of wind hit his face. Drawing his cloak tightly about him, he quickened his steps to find Hakeem.

The servants clustered near the fire, waiting for his signal to break camp and load the camels. But should they?

Blasts of cool air whooshed through the caravan, stirring the fire's embers into an anxious dance. Everyone scrambled to don their outer cloak.

Akilah dove into the Magi's tent for another layer of clothes.

Rashidi paused from rummaging through his clothing trunk. "Are you well, Akilah?"

No, he was not. He wondered about the servants. Their extra cloaks or mantles were often their bedrolls. Did they have more than one extra? Why hadn't he considered that until now?

He walked out of the tent and glimpsed lightning in the distance. *Good. The storm is far ahead and traveling fast. It'll wear itself many parasangs ahead of us.*

As Akilah joined Hakeem, another gust of wind blew their cloaks. Jagged streaks of light sliced the sky.

The wind shifted strangely. A harsh gust pushed their backs. Then another. And another.

"Haboob!" Hakeem yelled.

Chapter 19

The Storm

Everyone raced to grab their waterskins. Within seconds, they'd doused their headscarves and tied them tightly above their ears.

Roaring wind drowned their frightened chatter.

A dense dust cloud barreled toward the camp. Raging billows gobbled loose dirt in their advance.

Akilah looked frantically for the safety of higher ground. It was too distant. The storm moved too fast.

With their backs to the dust storm, the caravan could only huddle together, heads down, scrunched against the sides of the camels for protection. In minutes, a wall of sediment engulfed everyone. Vengeful winds shrieked and howled about them. Churning dust doused, scratched, or tore at everything it touched.

Akilah clutched his camel's neck and pressed his head deeper into its curly mane. Oh, to be a camel at a time like this. They didn't need wet headscarves; they could seal their nostrils and mouths shut. The dust wouldn't burn their eyes; their three sets of eyelids protected them. The storm wouldn't scald their skin; two layers of thick hair covered it. He vowed that, if he survived this storm, he would show more appreciation for these sturdy animals—and the brave servants with him on this journey.

Mangling sounds filled the air. The dust storm ripped through the camp for what seemed like an eternity.

The suffocating cloud moved on after fifteen minutes, but a choking haze lingered. Everyone remained huddled, waiting for it to disperse.

After an hour, Hakeem tapped Akilah on the shoulder and relit the fire. Although it was still morning, it was impossible to tell through the haze. The fire's light tinged the tan haze with orange, but it was enough illumination for Akilah to get his first glimpse of the damage. Torn tents. Dents, dings, and splinters in the camels' saddles. Dirt-filled gear. And waterskins—their precious water containers—full of mud.

Another gust of wind caught everyone's cloaks. Servants screamed, still crouched and frozen in fear. But Hakeem called them to the fire.

This wind was fresh, clean, pure. Within half an hour, the air was renewed. The haze dissipated so completely that the shrieking storm almost seemed like a dream—except for the devastation around them. Hakeem stoked the fire and started a story to quell the servants' jitters.

What a day of extremes.

If this was what one got from praying, Akilah wasn't sure he should do more of it.

Then he remembered something God said through the prophet Isaiah. *Do not be dismayed, for I am your God. I will strengthen you and help you; I will uphold you with my righteous right hand.*[1]

He exhaled softly. "Words written so many hundreds of years ago. But also a message for us—for me—right now. This is a sign. We can do this. We *will* get to Egypt."

---

1. Isaiah 41:10 (ESV)

Chapter 20

Impossible Decision

Akilah walked with resolve through the campsite, silently inventorying the damage while offering encouraging words to the servants. Cleanup from the storm would take a full day. Repairs, at least two more days. Some tents were beyond mending, but their intact parts could be salvaged to patch other tents. Other remnants might work as bandages for the camels—if they could wash the fabric. Fewer tents meant overcrowding the servants' sleeping arrangements. The camels would get three days' rest, but there was no water for the human contingent faced with backbreaking labor.

"Akilah, you'd better get over there." Obadiah pointed across the camp.

"Is someone hurt?" Without waiting for an answer, he sprinted past the healer toward a figure huddled in a corner of the campsite.

Akilah approached it gingerly.

It was Tahrea, his arm and flimsy cloak flung over Suhail's back.

"It's not fair." Tahrea choked on his words. "The storm … a wood shaft pierced … I tried … it wasn't enough." As Akilah knelt near him, Tahrea lifted his hand, sticky with congealing mahogany blood. Dirt-caked, dried blood coated the length of his arm. His soaked cloak, stiff on the bloodied side of Suhail's chest, rose and fell with the camel's labored breathing.

"You stayed with Suhail."

Tears carved trails through the dirt on Tahrea's face.

"Everyone deserves a friend who will stay with them through a storm."

"Poison of a snake!" Tahrea shoved Akilah to the ground, bloodying his cloak. "I know what happens to camels like Suhail. They're left alone to die. Then vultures eat them."

The heavy-handed insult cut Akilah's heart. "That doesn't have to happen. But we do have a difficult choice to make."

"We? What—"

"A choice to show compassionate leadership." Akilah stood up and dusted himself off.

Tahrea sniffed. "I don't know what you're talking about."

"Tahrea, you could be a leader if you knew how. Here's your first lesson. Most of leadership is servanthood, putting others' needs before your own, knowing that your decisions affect everyone."

Tahrea stared as Akilah continued. "If Suhail can't recover enough to carry a load or keep up with the caravan for the rest of our journey, what would you do with him?"

"My master owns Suhail."

"Yes. And I must make restitution to her if I don't return him."

"Let him stay with the caravan but not carry a load."

"We can't afford to do that," Akilah said, his voice low and gentle. "All our extra camels were stolen near Susita. Every camel must bear a load."

"Then you should have bought more camels in Ayla." Tahrea's voice shook through his unconvincing bluster.

"We didn't have money for that."

The surly servant heaved a stone that barely missed Akilah's ear. "Decide what you want."

"Tahrea, you have a stake in this decision. You were with Suhail in Assur. You took care of him some of the time, yes? And again here. But the decision can't be only about you, your feelings, or the camel. Think."

"I'd never leave him behind."

"A tired, hungry caravan needs extra energy to make repairs before continuing its trip. What would you do?"

His eyes wide with terror, Tahrea backed away from Akilah. "*No*. People don't eat camels. It isn't right."

"True, we revere our camels. But, in dire circumstances, people resort to that—even drink their retained water. Is our caravan in dire circumstances?"

A wild abandon flickered in the depths of Tahrea's eyes. Shuddering, he turned as if to bolt.

Akilah grabbed him by the shoulders. "Don't run from hard decisions."

"It's not mine to make." Tahrea struggled in Akilah's grip.

"Step back from your feelings," Akilah ordered. "What would be most merciful and yield the greatest good for everyone?"

Tahrea sagged in the Wise Man's arms, sobbing and mumbling.

"Brave answer," Akilah said, pulling him close. "The ultimate decision does rest on me. I would have chosen the same. You've taken your first step in leadership. Now you know what it feels like."

Lana Christian

That evening

After a long, dusty day of cleanup, the cook served a piquant stew laced with spices, garlic, and dried fruit. Everyone gratefully filled their belly. Except one. Akilah watched Tahrea slip away to the far edge of camp. Stooping by a boulder, he doubled over and heaved.

Chapter 21

Orchard Secrets

Assur

Farzaneh halted her horse on the ridge that overlooked her land. After three weeks in Arbela, she was home.

Home had been such a source of pain that she hadn't realized it could also still be a source of comfort. The faint rush of the waterfall reassured her it would forever shield Ihsan's tomb in the hill's depths. She pulled her knees up, legs tight against her horse's sides, and bid him into a gallop.

Without waiting for her horse to come to a full stop at the stables, she alit and called to a stable boy. "Tell Javad his master is home and needs to see him immediately."

Javad appeared at a run. "Master, welcome home. I trust all went well." His voice, though warm, seemed tinged with unease.

"Thank you, it did. What news since I've been gone?"

"There is little to tell."

Farzaneh's eyes narrowed. "You are a terrible liar, Javad. What happened?"

"I handled it."

95

"Handled what?"

"Just some mischief, I think." Javad faltered in his reply. "Minimal damage."

"Damage to what?"

"Some trees in your orchards. Workers had tended your apricot trees earlier that evening. A few were still in an adjacent orchard when it happened, so we were able to put out the fire before it spread."

Fire. Arson? Farzaneh seethed. "Show me."

"What's of most value has not been touched."

That didn't make any sense. Some of her trees had burned. All her orchards were equally valuable. Any damage was an expensive loss. Especially her apricot trees—the most difficult to grow and the most labor-intensive to maintain.

Her heart sank as she walked down a blackened row. "How many burned?"

"Maybe a fourth of the apricots."

Hot tears stung Farzaneh's eyes. If she could coax the trees to survive, it would take years for them to grow back. Even then, they wouldn't produce fruit like they did before. When would the world stop taking from her everything she loved? The cares of life were relentless in overshadowing sweet, fleeting moments like Arbela.

"Who did this?" Her words were more a demand than a question.

"Based on a couple servants' descriptions of his clothes, it was a vagrant. They saw only his back side as he fled. I'm not sure how or where he gained entrance to the grounds, but he may have scavenged for food then tried to make a fire for the night. We had more wind than usual that night." Javad sped through his explanation. "But master, there is good news in the midst of this destruction."

"You caught him?"

"No."

"The local magistrate caught him?"

"Better news than that." Javad lowered his voice. "It's intact."

"I have no idea what you mean."

He led her halfway down a row of singed trees, then pointed at the ground. "It's safe. Down there," he whispered.

"Speak plainly."

"Before you left for Adiabene, your last order to me was to burn the contents of a certain trunk in your room. I carried out most of that order." He cringed. "Many pardons, but I couldn't burn the Isaiah scroll that sir was so fond of. So I wrapped it in an oilcloth, placed it in an amphora, sealed the lid with resin, and buried it here among the apricot trees. I thought no one would notice because we turn the soil so often to nurture the trees."

"Oh ..." Tension drained from Farzaneh's body. She should have punished Javad for his disobedience, but she couldn't. Her fear of Sassanak's investigation had prompted her to order Javad to burn all the household's scrolls of Hebrew writings. Instead, he had risked preserving something dear. A scroll that linked her with her husband and her new friends in Arbela.

Tears flooded her eyes. "I have never been so glad to have someone defy me. You saved what I thought I'd lost." She cleared her throat. "When the moon wanes to its slimmest crescent, we will rescue it from its hiding place."

Chapter 22

Hidden Wounds

The next day

Amorning breeze kissed Farzaneh's cheek. She closed her eyes to the merry serenade of her tinkling wind chimes. Spending time in her private courtyard was always a treasure.

A discordant clank broke her reverie. Javad ducked, then fumbled to straighten the chimes. "Many pardons, master."

Bowing, he held out a scroll at arm's length. "This just arrived."

Her blood ran cold as she broke the unmistakable administrative seal of the Lower Council. The last time she'd spoken with Sassanak, he had threatened her with arrest and more. But she shouldn't assume anything. Politics could change the world in a wink. "Thank you," she managed in an even tone.

The scroll was an invitation—no, more like a summons—signed by Azazel as Head Magus. What a far cry from him being under investigation. The scroll's message urged everyone to come to the Great Hall of Audiences in the central Magi complex to attend a remembrance ceremony. Flowery words paying tribute to Sassanak overshadowed the sorrowful note that he had drowned during a goodwill trip to Macedonia.

Farzaneh didn't believe the "goodwill trip" story in the least. Sassanak was an isolationist, particularly regarding religion. Macedonia was almost as far as one could get geographically and philosophically from Parthia.

"Javad, wait. Can you confirm what this dispatch says?"

Unfortunately, he could. He supplied details of how Sassanak had been on his way to Macedonia after the Chief Megistane had sentenced him to exile—when the ship carrying both of them was crushed in a storm. Sassanak was presumed dead because the ship's captain and the Chief had seen an enormous wave wash him overboard. Javad had few details about the Chief other than he had sustained serious injuries. If he survived, he was either convalescing abroad or in Persia, if he was able to travel. In the interim, supposedly to maintain order, Parthia's new king had hastened Azazel's appointment as Head Magus of the Lower Council.

All that had happened while she was in Arbela? Farzaneh inhaled sharply. She desperately wanted to close the fearful chapter of her life titled "Sassanak." Maybe now she could. But the Chief was another matter. She didn't know whether it was possible to write a chapter that could finish her business with him. But she could start by confirming whether he was alive.

Farzaneh approached the arched stone entrance of Ctesiphon's place for the sick with trepidation. Her husband, Ihsan, could have been treated in a facility like this, but he had chosen to remain home, surrounded by all he loved. Those raw memories halted her steps. As much as she had cherished her final months with him, the burden of caregiving had often eclipsed her closeness to him.

She braced against the archway, drawing deep breaths to ease the squeezing in her chest. This was different. If her former guardian, the Chief Megistane, had survived and was recuperating in Persia, he would have been brought to Ctesiphon. Megistanes were the governmental elite of Magi society's Upper Council. They served the king, so it was logical for the Chief to convalesce here in the royal capital.

Prudence and fear had kept her from approaching the Council to confirm anything about the Chief. If Sassanak's threats of punishment for her religious practices had outlived him, then she was still under scrutiny. She couldn't afford to draw attention to herself or disadvantage the Chief because of their family connection, strained as it was.

If he was alive, if he was here, if he was well enough … and if she could bear to talk with him long enough, maybe he could shed more light on recent events. That was a lot of ifs.

Suppose he was here. How should she address him? By his Magi title, his name, something else? He was the Chief Megistane, the highest-ranking member of the Upper Council. He was Gadiel, her uncle. For seven years, he was also her guardian. But she hadn't called him "uncle" or spoken his name since she was twelve. Not since the day he thrust her into an unwanted marriage and early adulthood.

Acknowledging him as a blood relative was beyond her sensibilities. Even so, she owed him much.

She slipped down the main hall, a silent gray shadow in her nondescript outfit and soft leather shoes. If he were here, he would be in the ward for internal injuries. She would find it on her own.

Maybe she should have planned her visit more thoroughly. What if he was alive but grossly disfigured from his injuries?

Her fluttering stomach belied her confident strides down another hallway.

"Your herbs are fetid." Like a beacon, the Chief's commanding bellow echoed down the hall. "I don't need more divine words recited over me. And I assuredly do *not* need a surgeon. *Leave.*"

Farzaneh pressed against the room's entrance as a flustered attendant fled down the hallway, muttering something about the questionable virtue of that man surviving. She passed through the doorway and bowed. "Chief Megistane. It is ... I'm pleased to see you are alive."

She lifted her eyes and met his steely gaze, the same piercing look she'd squirmed under as a child. Suddenly she felt ten again. He raised himself up on one elbow. She recoiled, expecting a rebuff.

"Thank you. Please, sit." Though his words bordered on kind, they were strangled. He suppressed a cough.

"Are you well?" *Of course he's not. He wouldn't be here otherwise. But he looks good for someone who almost drowned.*

"My physicians disagree with my opinion about my body and spirit."

She opened her mouth but couldn't form a response.

"Farzaneh, neither of us is good at casual conversation, so I'll be brief." A weariness she'd never seen pleated the Chief's brow. "Whatever you think of me, I have always had your best interests in mind. I still do."

I don't believe you. She swallowed hard.

"Time is short. Maybe one reason I survived that shipwreck was so I could warn you."

"Of what?"

"Parthia's government is about to change. Radically. Rumor is that Phraates IV died from poisoning—not old age. The Megistanes are investigating, but as long as I'm here, I'm not privy to their findings." He snorted in disgust.

"His wife, Musa, is likely behind the poisoning. I know your disdain for government intrigue, but this affects everyone. Despite the Megistanes' efforts, her son, Phraates V, now sits on the throne. Musa rules by his side." Something feral rose in his throat. "That Roman whore."

The Chief's eyes darkened with unbridled loathing. "If Phraates V survives his first year as king, Musa will marry her son to solidify her power. She is the most dangerous person I know." He paused and pressed both hands to his chest.

Alarmed, Farzaneh rose from her seat. "I'll call for—"

"No." The force of his command drove her back to her chair. "Sit and listen. Time is short."

Fear overcame her annoyance at his tone. She sat and waited.

"Phraates V never should have been a candidate for king. But seven years ago, as soon as he was eligible for the throne, Musa sent his older half-brothers to Rome. Magi always trained Persian princes on how to lead and govern—until now. Phraates V received no Magi training. I assume Musa was behind that too. That seventeen-year-old half-breed has no moral convictions about government or religion. He isn't fit to rule."

The Chief turned his head toward the window and its view of the royal palace in the distance. "That's exactly what Musa wants. She has the power to destroy the Parthian Empire from the inside—then hand it over to Rome."

Farzaneh stiffened. She was much younger than seventeen when the Chief had handed her over to a self-absorbed, heartless man. "I don't involve myself with politics."

The Chief groaned. "Spoken like Akilah." He pushed himself upright. "*Listen* to me. I know Sassanak threatened you. He was a religious zealot, but Azazel is diabolical. He doesn't care about upholding Magi values. He cares only about power. He won't hesitate to ruin people if it serves his purposes. And he's garnered Musa's favor to ensure he has a clear path to his goals."

A bead of sweat formed on Farzaneh's hairline. "I don't understand."

"Azazel is capable of doing far worse to you than Sassanak ever threatened. Could you survive if you lost all your lands?"

The Chief's bluntness stole her breath. No one should be able to take her holdings from her. Not unless the law changed dramatically.

"I ..." She fought to answer. Only one option came to mind. "There is a place I could go." Her voice gathered strength. "It would be difficult, but I would survive."

She diverted her dread of the unthinkable by focusing on the Chief. "What about you? If you're not privy to the Megistanes' proceedings, have you been—"

"Stripped of my position? No. But it's coming. Even if I could resume my work, the government is finding ways to silence ... dissenters."

"Then we must get you the very best care so you—"

"Farzaneh, stop. All of Persia's doctors report to the chief physician, who reports to the Head Magus of the Lower Council. That's Azazel. The system is against me." He lowered his voice. "I plan to leave here before they say it's safe to go."

"Then we mustn't wait," Farzaneh blurted. "Stay with me while you decide your next steps."

The words tumbled from her mouth before her brain could sift them. The Chief had caused her years of pain. She shouldn't invite him under her roof.

She had to act fast, or she'd lose her nerve. "Are you well enough to ride?"

"Yes."

"Tell me which herbals they give you and their schedule. Do they prepare them at your bedside or in the pharmacy?"

The Chief raised an eyebrow but rattled off the particulars.

Farzaneh smiled. He must have forced the attendants to tell

him everything they administered. Thanks be to Adonai for the Chief's unfailing attention to detail—and his interrogation skills. "I'll return tomorrow. Be prepared."

Chapter 23

Getaway

The next day

The Chief seemed to grasp Farzaneh's plan until he had to execute it.

She cracked open the door to his room. "No one's in the hallway. Hurry." She watched, alarmed, as he struggled to walk on weak, uncoordinated legs. She half-dragged him to the window then yanked a sheet from his bed. "Straddle the sill. Wrap yourself in this to protect you if you fall. Whether you climb or jump, aim for the bushes. I'll create a distraction."

"Do you still throw like a girl?"

"I'm not ten anymore," Farzaneh hissed. "Go before I renege on helping you. My best protector, Gushtasp, is directly below with his horse and mine. Ride with him. I'll be right behind you."

"You'll get caught."

"Not as fast as I ride."

She withdrew two small vials of herbs from a pocket in her sash, medicinary ampules the same size as all Persian pharmacies carried. She tossed both on the bed, placed one

107

under the pillow to muffle sound, and smashed the vial with a bedside drinking cup. Picking up the largest shard, she dragged it diagonally across her left temple, toward her hairline.

That hurt far more than she'd expected.

Pain seared her forehead as she turned to make sure the Chief had made it through the window. She shook the vial's shards onto the floor and hurled the other vial down the hallway.

"Somebody help me." She pressed her hand into the fresh cut, then dropped to the floor. "Oh, my head. Help!"

Shouting amplified the cut's throbbing sting. Kneeling, she gripped the bed linens and called out again. An attendant came running, then stopped, horrified. "Who did this to you? Where is the patient?"

Farzaneh held her head. "He became agitated … We struggled … I tried to stop him but couldn't. He went that way." She pointed with her bloodied hand down the hallway. "I think he took some medicine with him." The attendant dithered between the bed and the doorway, then called for help.

Attendants crowded the room. Without touching her bloodied hand or head, one gingerly guided Farzaneh to another area so her wound could be cleaned and stitched. Another investigated the hallway. A third remained in the room, presumably to clean the floor and remove the bloodied bed linens.

Everyone's guarded actions spoke to how strongly Persia's religion still influenced its science. Religion said blood was defiling, so everything it soiled needed cleansing. *That should occupy them for a while.*

An attendant holding a vial entered the alcove where a physician stitched Farzaneh's cut. "I found this in the hallway. It's one of the herbals you prescribed to the Chief Megistane."

The physician nodded without pausing but looked sternly at Farzaneh. "We need to monitor you in case you become nauseous, dizzy, or have unusual head pain. You may stay here for the evening."

He was distractingly handsome, but she had to concentrate on her task. "Thank you, but I'm not dizzy. I need to return home to warn my staff about this patient in case he heads in my direction."

"You know him well?"

"*Knew* him. Long ago. I came here simply to pay my respects. I had no idea he would be unsettled."

After more convincing, the physician reluctantly discharged her with bandages and a dark glass vial containing a slightly syrupy liquid. She sniffed it. Poppy juice. Ironic. Ihsan had adamantly refused that medication, despite his intense, terminal pain.

The physician insisted on walking her to the building's front entrance. "Do you live far? I can provide an escort to see you safely home."

"Thank you, but I have no need to be accompanied."

She ran lightly down the steps to prove her point. A drumbeat sounded in her head, but she maintained the ruse until he disappeared behind the facility's arched entryway.

That was close.

Time is your enemy. Keep moving.

She found her Caspian stallion grazing, loosely tied to the bushes where Gushtasp had left him. "Good boy, Dalir. You are as smart and brave as your name." She yanked the reins free from the bushes and swung into her saddle. The sudden motion tilted her world. She prayed that would not last. She leaned into his crest. "Take me home, Dalir."

Farzaneh entered her home from the rear, hoping to speak with Javad before she had to confront the Chief. Unfortunately, both sat at the cook's prep table. The Chief scowled at her bloodied bandage.

Javad scurried to his feet, his mouth agape. "What happened?"

"I'm happy to see you survived the drop, Chief."

"Don't coddle me." He huffed. "How did you get injured?"

"It was part of my plan to gain you more time to escape."

"We didn't discuss that part of your 'plan.'"

"You wouldn't have agreed to it if I had."

Noting Javad's agonized expression, Farzaneh said, "It's not a deep cut. I had to make the Chief's exit more convincing. It will heal. I received expert stitching. It should barely leave a scar, and I can style my hair over it."

Turning to the Chief, she added, "My house. My rules." She ignored his perplexed stare.

She pivoted to Javad and his palpable shock. "I need a word in private with my guest." She waited until his steps faded in the hallway.

"Chief, as soon as you're rested, tell me everything that's happened to you since you left for Macedonia."

Chapter 24

Night Terrors

Ever since the storm, Gadiel had slept fitfully.

Sleep brought no repose, only troubled dreams of his fateful trip to Macedonia. Escorting Sassanak into exile … their ship capsizing somewhere near Crete … a huge wave engulfing the ship … Sassanak's final look of panic and hate as the hull split and threw Gadiel onto the ship's deck, away from the wave.

His clear memories ended there, but his mind conjured endless variations of new, tormented scenes to continue the dream.

Gasping, Gadiel forced himself awake and freed himself from his tangled mass of sheets.

The ship's captain had said the dreams would abate with time, as would the intermittent blurry vision. The doctor who treated both of them said broken bones and Gadiel's waterlogged lungs would heal faster than his head injury. Whether he'd fully regain use of his legs was questionable. In due time, most everything could mend. The mind would take the longest.

Dense clouds hid the moon, shifting the shadows in Gadiel's room.

But one shadow didn't shift.

"You failed." A throaty, strangled voice emanated from the darkness.

Gadiel turned his head toward the voice.

Moonlight fell on a bloated, freshly scarred face. A contorted mouth, one side twisted and drawn, sneered before racing clouds swallowed the feeble light again.

"The once-high-and-mighty Chief, brought low. I'll bet you can't even get out of bed."

Gadiel's walking infirmity was a closely guarded secret. Unless …

"No one is here to save you now." With animal-like fury, Sassanak hurled himself onto the bed. Gadiel rolled off the other side and landed on his feet.

Standing wasn't a problem. Walking was.

Sassanak's knife glinted in the moonlight as he circled the bed. "You took everything from me. Time to even the scales."

Gadiel's only hope was to keep himself out of the knife's strike zone. He grabbed Sassanak's upper right arm and drove the flat of his other hand hard into Sassanak's face. In that momentary stun, Gadiel stepped back and ran his left hand down Sassanak's arm to immobilize his wrist. With the back of his other hand, he smacked the flat of the blade, dislodging the knife. It grazed Sassanak's arm.

Yowling in pain, he dropped the knife.

Gadiel kicked it across the room.

Sassanak dove for the knife.

Gadiel launched himself onto his attacker's back. He couldn't keep fighting on his feet, but fighting on the floor might work. For a bit.

The two rolled over, crashing into furniture. Pain daggered Gadiel between his broken ribs, reducing each breath to a gasp.

Sassanak rolled on top of him. "No power ... No possessions ..." With each tortured phrase, he squeezed his knees harder into Gadiel's ribs. Pain seized his fractured chest, giving Sassanak the moment he needed to scoop up his knife. "Your niece is next."

With a roar, Gadiel punched Sassanak below his diaphragm. He lurched but kept his grip on the knife.

Every breath wracked Gadiel with pain. With all his strength, he stayed Sassanak's arm. The shaking knife drew closer to his chest. He felt Sassanak's arm tense for a thrust.

A crash, a twang, and Sassanak jerked upward. A second, almost musical twang, and he dropped his knife, crumpling across Gadiel.

Drained of all the fight in him, Gadiel inched out from under his attacker but couldn't get up.

Scraping sounded from the window. A shadowy figure approached. Panting and helpless on the floor, Gadiel closed his eyes and prayed for a quick death.

A faint wet animal smell reminiscent of fresh bowstring sinew nudged his nose. He opened his eyes. "Gushtasp?"

The protector shouldered his composite recursive bow and thrust his arms under Gadiel's shoulder blades. "We need to get you into bed before Farzaneh sees ... all this."

"You—"

"I was assigned to do more than bring you from Ctesiphon to Assur. Your niece is very particular with details."

Chapter 25

Confessions

J avad had alerted Farzaneh about the struggle in Gadiel's chambers, but when she arrived, the only sign she saw was blood spatters on the rug and Gushtasp waiting in the doorway.

"Go back to bed, Farzaneh," Gadiel said wearily.

"This is my home. Your orders carry no weight here." She pulled her night robe tighter around her. "We need to talk. Unless you'd rather try to sleep ... which seems unlikely."

"If you don't find it improper to sit in my chamber, then I will entertain a conversation with you." Gadiel winced as he pushed himself to a sitting position in bed.

"Gushtasp will remain nearby in case you try anything." The corners of Farzaneh's mouth turned up ever so slightly.

"You are quite the planner." Gadiel grimaced and held his ribs.

"You taught me caution. Attention to detail. And how to outthink my opponents."

Farzaneh lit a globe lamp and glanced around. "Where is ..." She couldn't bring herself to say the name.

"On its way to a mass grave for beggars," Gushtasp said. "No one will ever find the body." He bowed. "Unless you have further questions, I will take my post in the hallway—or outside the window—whichever you prefer."

"The hallway, thank you." She wanted to savor the closure, but her concern for Gadiel and her household overrode the urge. "I don't know whether to—"

With great effort, Gadiel held up his hand. "Farzaneh, let me speak. I have always tried to protect my family. Sometimes it didn't transpire as planned. I couldn't force Akilah to marry you when you needed protection, but I couldn't bear the thought of you enduring a life with Sassanak. Even when he and I were classmates, his zeal tempted him down a dark path. A privileged life with him would have become a cage." He stopped to catch his breath. "I knew Sassanak's heart … but not the heart of the relative I pushed you to wed. I saved you from one cage but forced you into another. I didn't realize that for many years."

Was that an apology? If so, it would be worthy of recording in Persia's annals. Farzaneh bit her trembling lip. "You … compensated. Taught me land management and how to stand on my own. Over time, I was … grateful … for the skills I learned." She turned away from his gaze. "I'm glad to hear you considered me family."

"I still do."

He'd have to prove that for her to believe it.

"I have a bit of news about family as well." She forced lightness into her voice, but her hand trembled as she ran it across the storage chest next to her. "When I was in Arbela attending to my husband's final affairs, I learned that one of Akilah's colleagues had been captured by Nabataeans. Akilah and the rest of his caravan seem to be safe."

Gadiel sat up straighter. "Where is he?"

"No one knows. That's good news," she hastened to add. "It means Herod's men haven't found him. But Akilah is in more trouble than we can imagine."

Farzaneh paced as she related all Elyakim had told her about the Hebrew prophecies of the child-king Akilah had tried to find. She explained why any king, especially Herod, would be relentless in silencing the child and anyone who found him.

Gadiel's unflinching stare and the weightiness of the moment forced her to sit. She paused, wary of the danger in saying more. "This was more than an academic pursuit for Akilah. When I talked with him, I saw his passion."

Aware there was no turning back from what she was about to say, she plunged ahead. "When you investigated Akilah, you questioned me at length about funding his trip to Jerusalem. I had to give you all my financials—and reasons for choosing to help him. But I kept the true reason from you."

He raised an eyebrow.

"My husband, Ihsan, became a God-fearer late in life. So have I. I thought assisting Akilah would pay tribute to Ihsan's belief in the Hebrews' God and would bolster my new faith— especially if Akilah found the child, and He was all the prophesies said He'd be."

She braced for backlash.

"There's more." She had to bring everything to light before Gadiel's stony silence completely unnerved her. "I ... made Akilah sign a stūrīh as a non-negotiable condition for accepting my financial aid. Ihsan was dying. Without his protection, I feared I'd be harmed for my new beliefs. I thought the stūrīh would secure some measure of safety for me. I knew Akilah would agree to its religious obligation, even though he would sign it against his will. I should not have forced that upon him."

She waited for some acknowledgment. Any reaction would be better than silence. "Whether you approve or not, I—"

Gadiel exhaled the start of a laugh, but it triggered a cough that sent pain skittering across his face. "You did what I could not. You two will finally marry. At least contractually. Even if only for protection."

Farzaneh looked askance at him. She hadn't trusted him for years, and she didn't even like Akilah. But she admired her cousin's convictions about finding the eternal child-king.

Gadiel waved the air as if it could disperse another coughing fit. "You and Akilah are more alike than you know. Pacing helps you think, you walk faster when frustrated, and you both hate governmental affairs."

Common threads don't stitch wounds. Farzaneh's lips tightened into a thin line.

"In the past month, I've learned a bit about the Hebrews' God." Gadiel grimaced. "I didn't want to, but I couldn't get away from it. The captain who saved me prayed over me and prayed with the people who cared for me. He told me about this God he believed in. It was annoying. But what could I do? I was bedfast." He flicked his wrist.

"Then he explained all the reasons why we never should have survived the storm. Said he'd captained ships for fifteen years and was convinced God had intervened … rescued us for a purpose. I have my doubts, but I respect his beliefs. The same goes for you and Akilah." Gadiel trailed off, seemingly lost in thought. "I may have misjudged my son."

Relief flooded Farzaneh's heart. The sweetness of his words almost overwhelmed her. "Where is your brave captain now?"

"Headed home. Said he needed time to reevaluate his life choices. I think he's considering a different line of work. In Edessa."

Chapter 26

Laughter

Gadiel needed rest and a doctor. Farzaneh didn't quarrel with his refusal to see one. Keeping his whereabouts a secret for now seemed best, but his broken ribs and the fullness in his lungs greatly concerned her. With Javad's recommendations, she picked four servants to attend to his needs every hour of the day and night.

She was behind in her business affairs since she'd returned from Arbela, so she locked herself in her study to address the most pressing matters. Normally she'd attack her work with zeal. But not today.

She meandered the grounds with her Persian mastiff, Hadi, until they reached the steps by the waterfall. Without hesitation, he ambled ahead. She paused on the first step. The last time she had sat on the bench at the top, her husband had died, and she had promoted Javad so she could leave for Arbela.

She took another step. How odd that her life had split into "before and after Arbela." She wasn't sure how to sort that. But reaching the bench at the crest of the waterfall didn't hurt quite as much as it did before. She stroked Hadi's head. "That's a good sign, right?"

In response, he pawed her leg and nuzzled her hand. She filled her lungs with the exceptionally fresh air. The waterfall's constant tumbling always renewed the air. Maybe it could renew her spirit too.

She drank in the scenery around her, its perennial beauty marred only by her scorched apricot trees.

After ten minutes, she cradled Hadi's head in her hands. "I suppose we should get back to work, yes?" The mastiff growled a throaty dissent. Farzaneh laughed out loud—for the first time since she could remember. Maybe the fetters of her pain were loosening. The loss of her husband, her childhood shaming from Akilah, and her past with the Chief felt more tolerable than before. She was finally able to call the Chief "Gadiel" again. She wasn't quite ready for "uncle."

As Farzaneh and Hadi neared the house, Gushtasp met them in the courtyard. Gadiel, looking pale but determined, limped behind, leaning heavily on Javad.

Gushtasp bowed deeper than usual. "I found something." He handed Farzaneh an elegant silver tinderbox. "I think this was used to set fire to your apricot trees. I found it this morning while patrolling the grounds. Yesterday's rain may have uncovered it."

Farzaneh turned it over in her hand. Nothing could steal her moment of laughter at the waterfall. "I see. The vagrant must have stolen it—and undoubtedly more—from a rich person." She handed it back.

Gadiel pointed to a wedge-shaped *alif* symbol on the underside of the tinderbox. "This is more than some nameless rich person's property. This belonged to Azazel."

"How ..."

Gadiel took Farzaneh's hand, a gesture she barely remembered him doing. "Your vagrant may have been Sassanak. He certainly looked the part when he attacked me. I'm not sure how he survived the shipwreck, but he must have made his way here while you were in Arbela. He would have had time to scout your property. Observe the schedules of your servants and protectors."

"He wouldn't have known you were here."

"He would if he had contacted Azazel. I left Ctesiphon without medical authorization. That would have been reported to the chief physician, who reports to Azazel. Even with Sassanak gone, you are in danger. Maybe you should leave for a while until this gets sorted."

Farzaneh pulled away from Gadiel. "No."

"There's more." Gushtasp nodded to Javad, who pulled a scroll from his sash. "This dispatch just arrived."

She recognized the seal from her rides with Queen Helena. Adiabene's royal seal was embossed on the horses' saddles. Farzaneh's heart hammered. Why would she receive an official communication from the queen?

Gadiel awkwardly touched Farzaneh's arm. "Double reason for you to travel to Arbela?"

She broke the seal. She hated to admit it, but he was right. "The queen has summoned me to Adiabene's court."

She motioned to Javad. "Prepare a reply. I will be there within a week."

Turning to Gadiel with a penetrating stare, she added, "That is, if you can satisfy me that you are mending."

His jaw tightened. "You don't keep royalty waiting."

Javad stepped forward. "Master, delaying is not an option. A royal escort awaits you in your stables."

Chapter 27

Trial by Fire

Thankfully, Farzaneh's escort was a single rider, dressed in plain clothes but riding a horse bearing Adiabene's royal seal on its saddle and the colors of its standards on the horse's braided noseband. Arriving without fanfare at the royal stables, the escort whisked her through a back entrance of the palace. An attendant showed her to a spacious bedchamber and bade her don the lavish clothes and jewelry laid out on the bed.

She had an hour to prepare to meet the king and queen. A royal dinner would be a world apart from riding horses and sprawling under a shade tree with Helena. Silver teardrop earrings danced in Farzaneh's shaking hands as she fastened them. She slipped the last adornment over her head—an exquisitely painted mother-of-pearl teardrop set in a silver pendant necklace.

The formal affair was a rather intimate gathering of the queen, king, and a handful of people Farzaneh assumed were court officials. In this setting, Helena appeared older, wiser, more serious. Gone was any vestige of the irrepressible teenager Farzaneh had ridden with.

The queen introduced Farzaneh as a valued acquaintance and new advisor.

Advisor for what? Why am I here?

A stately, elderly lady seated to Farzaneh's right managed an almost-friendly smile. "What special skills are you lending to our queen?"

"Whatever the queen requires." Farzaneh grabbed her wine goblet and feigned drinking deeply to avoid further conversation.

The dinner guest tilted her head, her brows pinched together. But she said, "May you serve Adiabene well."

Farzaneh nodded her acknowledgment.

The older lady rose. "My queen, it would please the court to hear from your new advisor."

A man three seats to Farzaneh's left also rose from his seat. "Her briefing and credentialing ceremony are tomorrow. Until then, she is in no position to expound on any matter."

"Are we so tied to tradition that we can't hear informally from this valued advisor tonight?" The woman flashed Farzaneh a simpering smile.

Farzaneh silently pleaded across the room to Queen Helena for a reprieve.

She rose in a commanding stance. "Proceed, Farzaneh. Until tomorrow, you will not act in any official capacity, so everyone in this room will refrain from drawing any conclusions or acting on what you say." Her gaze swept the room with absolute authority.

Farzaneh rose and bowed. *Think fast. Use what you know best.*

"My queen, my king, honored guests, thank you for this

early opportunity to address you. Rome and Parthia's repeated battles waged on Adiabene's land have created hardships for everyone in this beautiful country. We need to improve that lot while showing Parthia your hardships hurt them too."

She smoothed her hand across the pendant gracing her neck. "The Greek historian Xenophon considered land management as crucial to developing leadership as it was for increasing one's wealth through farming. He said 'if a military commander does not sufficiently protect the country, it is impossible to work due to the lack of protection.'"

Farzaneh paused. Every eye fastened on her like fish hooks.

"Parthia needs to protect the countries under its reign to ensure their lands are productive. In particular, the empire should provide adequate protection and provision for Adiabene's safety and rebuilding. Delays negatively impact crops. Lower crop production negatively affects the empire's treasury revenues. At times, Parthia has seized land to recoup those lost revenues." A few nods of approval punctuated her sentence.

"Parthia should not be allowed to seize land based solely on economic hardship after conflicts. Instead, a two-year period of Parthian-assisted rebuilding plus one full year of crop production should be instated. Only after that time elapses could Parthia consider repossession of any land affected by a conflict in which it participates."

She scanned the room for growing interest but detected only a modicum of active curiosity.

"Furthermore, individuals should not be taxed for crops taken from them—only crops they can sell. I propose land allotments designated solely for feeding soldiers. This would prepare your country to serve the empire's military needs during conflicts so individuals' lands would not be raided. A lower, fixed land tax rate could be set for the people who work those lands. This governmental oversight would avoid unfair taxation.

And accountability with a country-wide tax auditing system would ensure tax collections followed those rules.

"Finally, if Parthia circulates notice of any change to taxes, it must be accompanied by information on the right to petition the king regarding the changes—and the assurance that informing the king of any potential abuses could be filed without fear of reprisal."

She bowed. "Thank you for allowing me to voice my thoughts in an unofficial capacity."

Silence continued to blanket the room.

Farzaneh had never been so relieved to sit down. She dried her moist palms on her lap. If that was some kind of test, had she passed?

The man three seats away rose and placed his hand over his heart. "It is fitting. May Ahura Mazda grant it."

Queen Helena rose. "The king and I thank you for your presence tonight. We look forward to seeing all of you tomorrow at the credentialing ceremony."

Farzaneh wasn't sure what credentialing entailed, but she needed to find out fast. She dallied so she would be at the end of the line to bow and exchange pleasantries with the royal couple as they wished everyone a good evening.

Helena whispered something to her husband then dipped her chin to acknowledge Farzaneh's bow. "Walking after dinner is a pleasant way to end to the evening. Would you like to join me for a stroll?"

"It would be an honor, my queen."

Helena slid her hand through the bend in Farzaneh's elbow. "This way."

As always, a guard followed at a respectful distance. "I find a nighttime walk in the gardens enchanting. When darkness limits one's sight, the other senses heighten." Helena inhaled deeply. "The smells are glorious. Especially in the orchards."

Orchards?

The guard rolled his eyes. Farzaneh smiled. Walking outside at night must be another way Helena perturbed her escorts.

Damask rose, jasmine, orange blossoms, and scents Farzaneh couldn't recognize embraced her as they walked in silence.

Helena slowed near a row of orange trees. "You cultivate orchards, yes? How are they faring this year?"

Orchards again. "They're doing well, my queen. I'm trying a new cultivar of cherries. I planted mulberries around the trees to protect the cherries. Hopefully the birds will gravitate to the mulberries more than the cherries."

"A wise move. Protect what's cherished and vulnerable. What of the rest of your orchards?" Helena turned her back to the guard so she was directly between him and Farzaneh.

"I had one mishap. A vagrant made a fire for the night in my orchards. The fire got out of hand and burned some apricot trees."

"If you desire advice about orchards, I know a person on the city's outskirts who should be able to advise you on how to reclaim what you've lost."

Elyakim?

Farzaneh's heart skipped like a flat stone on a calm lake. "Thank you. I'd very much like to meet that person."

Helena resumed walking and chatting about nothing of importance while Farzaneh's brain buzzed with questions. The evening seemed to be over as Helena steered her back to the palace, but then the queen directed her to a private chamber.

Chapter 28

A New Charge

Woodsy citrus-spice tones from the room's cypress beams greeted Farzaneh. The ample but not opulent room must have been built or renovated recently. It suited Helena. She wasn't one to worship the trappings of her station.

She ordered the guard to wait outside the doorway then turned to her guest, her eyes bright and warm. "Tonight's silence after you spoke was a high sign of approval. I knew you'd be equal to the task."

What task? Farzaneh swallowed hot, embarrassing words that threatened to leap from her throat.

Helena took Farzaneh's hands in hers. "I brought you here to be more than an advisor. I want you to be an envoy. Tonight you more than proved your capacity for that."

Farzaneh wanted to pull away, to distance herself as far as she could from that word. *Envoy.* A silky wrapping for governmental activities she wanted no part of. Negotiations. Treaties. Who knew what else. Ihsan had navigated those murky waters with skill, but she had no desire to dip her toe into them. Farzaneh's expertise in land management could carry her only so far. Dealing with civilians was a world apart from dealing with contracts.

"You want me to serve you as a diplomat?"

Helena's eyes sifted Farzaneh's face. "It comes with privileges. Certain protections. Free movement between countries." Her description coursed with undercurrents.

"My queen, may I speak freely?"

"In this room, yes."

"What do you need that requires my expertise?"

Helena circled her desk and met Farzaneh in the center of the room where a six-sided, star-shaped mosaic dominated the tiles. "Your instincts are as strong as your skills. Tonight you rightly divined some of what Adiabene is facing. Parthia appears intent on requiring more censuses as justification for levying higher taxes and seizing lands—but not uniformly across the empire. Adiabene is among its main targets."

She moved to a window with a breathtaking view of the Zagros Mountains, now etched in charcoal against a sapphire night sky. "Rome and Parthia want control of Adiabene for many reasons—its location, land, the trade route through Arbela, the minerals in our mountains. But the empire's protection for my country is wavering."

Helena's graceful shoulders drooped slightly. "Parthia's new king and his sympathies to Rome are endangering us. We cannot be made a pawn." The resolve in her words pulsed like a drumbeat. "I need to use every means at my disposal to ensure that doesn't happen. Who better to speak for Adiabene than someone who loves this land and lives in Parthia's administrative capital?

"Besides ..." Helena slid three fingers under the painted pendant Farzaneh wore and brushed her thumb across the bird scene. "I need your help in discerning who is friend"—she flipped the pendant over to the hunting scene—"or foe."

Farzaneh's stomach pitched like a small ship on high waves.

Most of the time, Parthia's expanding presence had caused few ripples in the lives of the people whose lands it had conquered. Vassal states, including Adiabene, had been granted independent rule. The government shouldn't be able to seize land from those countries.

She studied the floor and its star, studded with arcs of peacock plumes, a symbol of Persian royalty. Her next words could change the course of her life—and others'—forever. "I'm honored you've chosen me to aid you. But may I suggest someone with greater skills who can help you in many matters beyond land disputes?"

Chapter 29

Credentials

"Too risky." Helena shook her head.

"He'd be perfect. He's dedicated his life to serving the Magi's governmental arm."

"By your admission, he'll be dismissed from it soon. You made things worse by taking him into your home. Now the Megistanes—and possibly Parthia's government at the highest levels—will assume he has secrets to hide. They could target him for persecution or worse."

An annoying, prickly fear in Farzaneh urged caution, but she pressed her point. "He has a brilliant mind. He knows the inner workings of the king's court. He knows the hearts of the people influencing Parthia's new king." She drew a deep breath. "And he's ... my uncle."

Helena's expression clouded. "Your recommendation is fitting. Your intentions are noble. But once a Magus becomes a Megistane, he is forbidden from engaging in other governmental positions—for life."

Farzaneh silently scolded herself for her shameful stumble. Although she lived in the empire's administrative capital, she knew practically nothing about the Megistanes. Her biases that had distanced her from her former guardian during his early years as a Megistane were returning to haunt her.

"Are you fluent in Akkadian?" Helena continued.

"Yes."

"Good. You will need it on occasion for sensitive correspondence and legal documents. We'll give you details tomorrow. That is, if you accept the position I've offered you."

"Yes, my queen. I do accept. Thank you." She bowed deeply before Helena.

Farzaneh offhandedly added, "If I'm to see how Parthia handles land holdings, perhaps my first task should be to buy a parcel of land here, build on it, and see what comes of it."

Helena looked up sharply. "As my envoy, you would reside in the palace while you are here."

"Of course."

"Do not let haste or emotions cloud your thoughts, Farzaneh. Sometimes family concerns must be set aside for a greater good. Including when one is an envoy."

The queen pulled a small parchment from a chest by her table. "Tomorrow morning you'll meet with the court to present your credentials. Emphasize the advantages of your living in Assur. Mention you are an *arashshara*. Everyone will be impressed with your status as a great chief in business. After the court's private vote, which will assuredly rule in your favor, you will meet with my most trusted advisors to learn particulars about Adiabene's status and needs. Before dinner, we will formally announce you as our new envoy from Assur. The court and all royal advisors will attend the ceremony bestowing the standards of your position on you. A celebratory dinner will follow. The next day, you'll be free to explore our capital city. As time permits, an escort will take you to the man who can help you with your orchards. Here's his name."

Helena jotted something, beckoned Farzaneh closer, then held the parchment over a flame. Its words seared her heart as the fire consumed it. *Orchards in danger.*

Chapter 30

Food or Fuel

The Wilderness of Paran

Unforgiving barren land loomed before the caravan. The ground didn't even support bushes or thorns. Both would have been welcome food for the camels, but they found only scant tufts of parched grass to graze on. They half-heartedly nosed at the meager fare. Akilah ordered the camels' legs hobbled with leather thongs to prevent them from wandering too far to forage.

The decision when to feed the camels teben rested solely with Akilah. Although he was reasonably sure they were headed in the right direction toward Egypt, it was impossible to predict how long they'd traverse this rocky wilderness.

"We can't find enough wood for a fire," Hakeem said to Akilah in private. "And we don't have enough camel dung to fuel a fire all night."

The caravan needed a fire for both protection and warmth— even if they didn't cook over it. Nighttime temperatures dropped drastically in this area. Akilah wasn't sure which wild animals lived nearby, but he didn't want to find out. He had little choice regarding what they could burn. He had hoped he'd never face the decision he faced now. Especially so soon.

Akilah could entrust only Hakeem with the task. "Burn some of the sacred bundles of camelthorn, juniper, and chenar. If that won't last until morning, wake me. I won't burn any teben unless we have no other choice."

His faithful servant nodded and vanished into the darkness.

Akilah looked to the sky. *God of the Hebrews, deliver us out of this hardship or show me a way through it. I'm not wise enough to choose the right way all the time. No one is.*

That night, cheery firelight danced across the tent walls, but the campfire burned without smoke and smelled sweet instead of woody. If the servants noticed, they were too hungry or tired to wonder why.

Chapter 31

Wisdom and Discernment

Arbela

Morning couldn't come soon enough. Farzaneh was escorted to Elyakim's door as Helena had promised. While the escort remained within earshot behind her, she said, "Thank you for seeing me. I hear you might be able to remedy a problem I'm having with my orchards."

Inside the privacy of Elyakim's home, Farzaneh broke into an unabashed smile. What a joy to see him again.

Eliana served them breakfast with a side of warmer demeanor. Elyakim blessed the food then asked Farzaneh how she was faring.

"Queen Helena appointed me as her envoy from Assur. But I suspect you already knew that."

"Yes." Elyakim beamed. "A fitting installation."

"I don't know if I'm equal to the task."

"Adonai has chosen you for this. He equips those He calls."

"How can you be so sure?"

"Do you think it's coincidence how Ihsan had the skills to help Arbela ... how you and he met and married ... how you

139

met Queen Helena … and how you are here, now, in this capacity?" Elyakim chuckled and shook his head.

Farzaneh scanned her hands as if she'd dropped a morsel of food. Every inch of ground she'd gained in life had been based on her merits, not some divine hand.

This wasn't the first time Elyakim had shown her a string of providential circumstances. If Adonai truly was the Great Architect of people's lives, then happenstances weren't random but rather connections with something else—even if only she could see the connection. Settling that in her mind gave her great comfort. But she wanted answers to connections she suspected.

"Since you know my purpose here, perhaps you could clarify a few things for me."

"I will try."

"I want to help your refugee efforts, but I'm unsure whether I'll have the freedom to do that now. Queen Helena clearly is aware of your dealings with them, but I don't know to what extent she's involved. If I understood that—and Ananias's role —it would help me navigate this new territory."

"She's not involved. Not as queen."

"But her sneaking off to talk with Ananias—"

"She had two reasons to visit him. She does deeply desire to learn more about Hebrew teachings. But she used that to learn about Ananias's travels and his loyalties. When she told me what she found, it helped me decide whether he could be trusted to help us smuggle people to other areas."

"Is he trustworthy?"

"For as much as we know of him, he seems to be. I've arranged for a young couple to travel with him to a place where he trades regularly. They will appear to be new hires, assisting with loading his caravan before he leaves. If they arrive safely at their destination, we may try other transfers with him. If they don't, their youth will give them the best chance of surviving."

Elyakim rubbed his beard. "Helena's visits to Ananias were becoming too dangerous. Even in disguise, someone could recognize her because her duties as queen are requiring her to be more visible. She won't chat with him again any time soon—unless she calls him to court to discuss trade or tariffs."

"May I still visit you?"

"Yes, my dear. As Assur's envoy, you have certain privileges and protections that allow you to move about unimpeded. But take care what you discuss and where."

"Elyakim, I need your wisdom on so many matters," Farzaneh blurted. "I need to understand more about the Hebrews' writings and their ways. Are you allowed to teach me, or does my new position as envoy endanger you if you do so?" Her words tumbled faster from her lips. "What if I err in relaying Adiabene's concerns to Parthian officials? Yesterday I was briefed on everything from water rights, land excavations, and trade treaties to border security and religious issues. No one person has the wisdom to deal rightly with all of that."

"From what you've told me, several people in your life could guide you in those areas."

"They're not here—"

"But you know them, yes? What would they tell you if they could?"

Gadiel would say to pay attention to everything and start problem solving. He'd say much of life was common sense if one stopped to think long enough about the matter at hand. She'd ask him which Megistanes were trustworthy. She wasn't sure what Akilah would say about religious harmony. Within Adiabene's borders, Ashurism, Zoroastrianism, Manichaeism, and Judaism coexisted. She silently prayed for Akilah to return —then scolded herself for her double-sided, self-serving prayer.

Her spoon clattered to the floor. If Akilah survived the wilderness and Gadiel survived his injuries, Magi from both the Lower and Upper Councils would be living under her roof.

Assuming they'd be willing to share their collective wisdom with her, she could assuredly be an astute envoy. But could she live with the two people who had hurt her the most?

The risk might be worth the cost. With a jolt, she realized the great risk Akilah had shouldered—and the high price he'd paid for following his convictions.

"Will this envoy position and its possible dangers be the next chapter of my life?" She whispered the prayer skyward. "It would be impossible alone, but asking Akilah and Gadiel for advice is beyond my abilities. Adonai, I can't do this without You. Guide my steps. Protect me from harm—and harmful thoughts."

Chapter 32

Planked

Farzaneh had intended to stay longer in Arbela to visit with Elyakim, but a dispatch called her home. Javad was waiting for Farzaneh in the stables when she returned. His sober face spoke before he did. "I regret to say your uncle is worse."

She dashed to Gadiel's quarters, with Javad close behind. She burst through the door as Gadiel crumpled forward in a fit of coughing. She thrust a wash basin under his chin barely in time to catch the blood he spat.

"Javad, how long has he been like this?"

"A thousand pardons, master. The blame is mine. I felt I couldn't interrupt the ceremonies of your new appointment, and he still refuses a doctor."

"You did everything you could. Thank you. I'll call for you presently."

Worry and grief streaked Javad's face as he bowed and left.

She turned back to Gadiel. "Don't you dare die on me."

He gripped her arm. "Too much of the sea stayed in my lungs. They're rotting. Tell Akilah I'm sorry. I judged him wrongly."

"Tell him yourself." Farzaneh wrenched out of his grasp. After all that had happened, she refused to entertain the notion of more loss. As a child, she couldn't save her parents. She couldn't save her husband, Ihsan, from the *carcinos* that had consumed him. She had no control over Akilah's fate. But this was different.

She shook Gadiel's shoulder. "Listen to me. You still have work to do. More than you know. Don't give up hope. Live so you can greet Akilah when he returns." She forced more strength into her voice than her heart held.

Adonai, this can't be happening. Not after we've come this far. I don't know how to be an envoy. Spare Gadiel so he can show me how. Spare Akilah so we can learn how to be a family again. She couldn't untangle her selfish wishes from her prayer. But she meant every word.

Anger and worry wrestled in her thoughts. Gadiel would die without proper care. She couldn't trust any doctor to keep his location a secret.

If only she could turn him upside-down and shake the contagion out of his lungs.

Maybe she could.

She'd heard how children in Greece played on a plank that pivoted on a rock or a log. An up-down rocking motion might drain his lungs. She called for Javad.

His face clouded as she outlined her plan. She expected her head steward's skepticism. Her odd orders must have sounded like lunacy, but she trusted he'd carry them out.

Constructing a plank long, thick, and wide enough to hold Gadiel's weight was simple. Finding a log at least two cubits wide and thick was another matter. The oldest date palm tree on her property fit that description. She charged Javad with recruiting help to cut it down. She'd need at least twelve more strong servants, working round the clock in pairs, four hours per shift, to tilt Gadiel on the plank.

Amid his protests, she cleared space in his room for her experiment.

"It won't work," he said flatly.

"If that's how you talked to Akilah, it's a wonder he ever accomplished anything." Farzaneh should have curbed her anger, but letting a bit of it bleed out felt good.

Chapter 33

Grand Plans

Antipas stared out a south-facing window of his palace, imagining he could see all the way to Jerusalem. Localized revolts bespattered Herod's now-divided kingdom, but Antipas welcomed them.

Sepphoris had endowed Antipas with a curious clarity. Far from his initial disdain of Galilee and Perea as an inferior appointment, now he appreciated why Herod had altered his final will. Of course his intentions were unspoken, but the result was brilliant. Herod didn't want any of his sons to be king. Yet. But he'd set up Antipas for success by assigning him the most important military defense base in Herod's kingdom—plus prime territory for another.

Couple that with recent events surrounding a nearby revolt headed by Herod's high-ranking slave, and Antipas had ample ammunition for talking again with Varinius. Forget an indirect approach. Outlining his intentions plainly should work—especially now.

"Master, your guest awaits you in the gardens."

Antipas nodded to his slave and grabbed a map from a shelf behind him. Now maybe Varinius would see the ingenuity of his plan.

"*Ave.*" Varinius bowed deeply to his host. After commenting on the weather and the tediousness of his job, he added, "Traveling always gives one opportunity to gain a fresh perspective. You've rebuilt with amazing speed since Simon's brief uprising. Wasn't he from your jurisdiction, somewhere in Perea?"

Antipas's nostrils flared. Varinius didn't ask a question unless he already knew its answer. Herod's exalted but rebellious slave hadn't lived in Perea for two decades. *Turn this to your advantage.* "You may have heard how the Pereans aided Jerusalem's guards and a Roman contingent in stopping Simon's failed attempt to gain control of Judaea."

"Pereans." Varinius stroked his beard. "Reportedly a rather unruly lot. Good fighters, though."

Despite the sideways compliment, it was the opening Antipas needed.

"Simon's failed takeover is a prime example of why Sepphoris should become the Ornament of Galilee, a military stronghold. My capital is the perfect site for it. Look." He unrolled a map on a bench.

"I'm the only one of Herod's kin who rules lands in both the northern and southern parts of the kingdom. Southern Perea's military jewel is the impenetrable fortress of Machaerus. From there, troops can see as far as Jerusalem and Jericho. We can create the same here in the north. In Sepphoris."

Antipas fanned his fingers over the Galilee section of the map. "Picture Sepphoris as a stronghold *and* a base for military training and deployment. Upper Galilee offers the rigors of endurance training in the mountains. Lower Galilee's wide valleys are ideal for training on choke points and flanking attacks. Troops would become proficient fighters on all terrains.

A signaling system like Machaerus's would alert and dispatch troops on short notice. Sepphoris can become to the north what Machaerus is to the south—and more. It's a perfect plan."

Varinius arched one eyebrow. "And your brothers would obtain military assistance from you?"

Antipas cocked his head. "Admit it. They need help. Archelaus doesn't know a *spatha* from a *gladius*. He had worn his crown less than a week when he failed to mobilize his forces from Samaria—the military base in his own realm—to quell trouble in Jerusalem. Instead, he turned to Rome for help. Rome has a low tolerance for outstretched hands begging the empire to solve their problems. On the other hand, my insipid brother Philip sits on his hands as unrest washes over his lands."

Antipas clapped Varinius on the shoulder. "Think big, Varinius. Move to Perea. I'll give you power over both governmental and military concerns. Together, we will build this Ornament of Galilee. We'll show Rome why they should copy our tactics on a grander scale. Then we'll oversee its replication beyond my kingdom. Our work will bring peace to the region— and beyond." He cocked his head. "Of course, the economic benefits from such an addition would be immense ... for all of us."

He studied the jurisconsult's impassive stare. "Come with me to Machaerus. I'll show you what I envision for Sepphoris."

Varinius's eyes glinted. "Who would build this complex?"

"Local workers, plus laborers from Jotapata, Cana, and Nazareth."

"You'll need long-term loyalty for such a large project. Villagers will respond more readily to their kind, not overseers living in the shadow of your palace."

"Yes ..." Antipas rubbed his thumb and forefingers together. "I could use a good principal workman. Who knows? Maybe one will come from Nazareth."

149

Chapter 34

The Acacia Grove's Surprise

Somewhere in the Wilderness of Paran

Akilah couldn't ignore how loose everyone's clothes hung on them. Every day he wrestled with whether to push ahead or allow everyone extra rest. Rest for the camels meant unrest for the servants.

"If we don't get more food soon, simple scrapes won't heal. Infection can set in," Obadiah said. "For camels *and* people."

Akilah could barely remember what a full stomach felt like, and he didn't care to recall which wild animals had passed for a meal in this wilderness. Although Haruz's food had lasted longer than expected, it was long gone. Hunger, heat, and fatigue were the caravan's constant companions.

He rubbed his eyes. Far in the distance, a yellow blur interrupted the land's brownness. His mind had tricked him before, so he had taken to keeping his strongest ocular in the inner pocket of his sash. His hand trembled as he held it to his right eye.

Could those be acacia trees? If they were, a stream bed would be nearby.

Shade and water. He imagined its coolness and fresh smell. But he didn't dare say anything. He nudged his camel straighter in that direction.

Ten minutes later, Akilah gazed through the ocular again. Caution tempered his enthusiasm. It *was* an acacia grove, and dots amid the yellow were people camped near one end of it. Friend or foe? He signaled Rashidi. "Keep everyone back a hundred paces until Hakeem and I return."

As Akilah approached the camp with his head servant, whiffs of an intoxicating smell roused his empty stomach. Roast goat. When was the last time the caravan had savored a meal like that? *Stay sharp. The caravan's welfare depends on it.*

He slowed his pace, wondering how he should greet these strangers. Despite his linguistic skills, he didn't want to give away who he was or any information about the caravan's travels. The wrong greeting could do both.

He approached an authoritative-looking man sitting under a tree. Hopefully he was an elder or tribal leader. "Good day to you, sir. I bow to you."

"Have you eaten since sunrise?" the man replied.

The man's dialect and question caught Akilah off guard. He couldn't quite place the language origin. But the question … In some cultures, "have you eaten" meant nothing more than "welcome." Or it could be an actual invitation to dine.

"Our camels are thirsty, and so are we. We would like to stop here for a short while," he said. Perhaps avoiding the question was the safest choice.

"A stream is over there." The man gestured toward Akilah's right. "But have you eaten since sunrise?"

"No."

"Then join us," the man said. "I am Waqilu. My servant, Zabin, will show where everyone can wash."

Akilah froze. Those names were uniquely Nabataean.

Refusing the kindness offered would be an insult. But it could be a trap. It felt so different from Petra, but still …

A fire pit sizzled with two whole goats roasting on it. The smell wafting from cooked flesh told Akilah the goats must have been old. But he was so hungry, their age didn't matter.

Zabin pointed to Hakeem then to the goat. "You like?"

"Very much," Hakeem blurted.

Zabin picked up a pail and motioned beyond a tree. "Water there."

Hakeem glanced at Akilah. He nodded his approval.

Waqilu scanned Akilah's dingy clothes and filthy sandals. "You have been traveling far."

"Mmm."

"Come. Sit." Waqilu waved toward a spot in the shade.

"Thank you, I will. But I would like to attend to my friends first."

"Friends." Waqilu mulled the word. Then his face relaxed. "Yes."

Akilah bowed again and tried to walk casually to the caravan on the pretense of saying they would stop at the grove for a while.

Akilah told the group to enjoy their time as they paused to eat at this place but pointed to his eye, then his lips. Those were his unspoken signals to be on watchful alert and not say anything about their travels. He nodded to the protectors, a tacit advisory to watch for signs of trouble.

As the camels drank their fill from the stream, the rest of the caravan enjoyed the biggest, best meal they'd had since leaving Lufti's caravansary. In addition to roast goat, Waqilu's people offered soup made from *jamiid*, fermented goat milk. A version of *sabzi khordan* completed the meal—goat cheese, herbs, scallions, and radish slivers rolled into flatbread.

Akilah tried in vain to warn his servants against eating too much too fast. After weeks of meager meals, he worried that many stomachs couldn't handle so much food. Appreciative lip smacking and soup slurping told him no one was concerned about losing his meal.

Akilah mulled whether if this area was Waqilu's permanent residence but didn't want to prompt reciprocal questions about the caravan's home. Instead, he said, "This is a welcoming place. Have you been here long?"

"Long enough," Waqilu responded.

A diplomatic non-answer amid this guarded dance of conversation. "Well, you make excellent roast goat," Akilah said with enthusiasm.

Waqilu's nod prompted Akilah to venture another question. "Might our camels graze somewhere nearby this evening? That is, if it doesn't encroach on your goats' grazing."

"Two ridges over, your camels can eat their fill. We won't take our goats there until after you leave," Waqilu said.

"Thank you. That's very kind of you."

"The land is for everyone," Waqilu replied matter-of-factly. "As is the water," he added emphatically.

Akilah stared at the fire pit to avoid Waqilu's gaze. He was unlike any other Nabataean he'd encountered.

As if able to read Akilah's mind, an edginess crept into Waqilu's voice. "We are our own."

"Yes." Akilah swallowed hard. "So are we."

Waqilu's nod conveyed an understanding beyond their words. As he passed a bowl of dates to Akilah, he said, "You are not far from the Bitter Lakes—if that interests you." Gesturing north, he added, "Villagers near the lakes harvest and sell grain."

Were they that close to Egypt? And farmland and food? "That is welcome news," Akilah said.

Waqilu looked into Akilah's eyes as if searching for a window into his soul. "Everyone is on a journey. The question is whether it is worth the trip."

Although that statement deeply troubled Akilah, he hid his concern with a smile. Touching three fingertips to his forehead, then to his stomach, he replied, "Good words satisfy as much as a good meal."

"Your place will be green," the Nabataean responded.

"What did he say?" Hakeem whispered to Akilah.

"Grass will grow in the place where you sit until you come again," Akilah said. "I think that means 'you will be missed.'"

Murmurs ran through the Nabataeans. Although Akilah couldn't dissect the dialect quickly enough to understand everything they said, he was reasonably sure they agreed the caravan could press on to the grazing land and camp there in safety.

Hakeem had signaled the servants to prepare the camels to leave when Waqilu steered Akilah away from the group. "One from your caravan is missing, yes?" he whispered.

Akilah looked up sharply. The Nabataean had effortlessly switched to an Arabic dialect he understood perfectly. Why now? Akilah's heart thrashed against his chest. He couldn't afford to drop his guard. Maybe he already had. "We've suffered many losses on this journey."

"Then I'll speak plainly. Your colleague, Tallis, was alive a month ago."

"How do you know?"

"That is all I can say." Waqilu's hand on Akilah's shoulder

remained steady. His counterparts smiled, seeming to interpret it as a gesture of friendship.

Akilah bent closer to Waqilu. "Can or will say? There must be more."

"I have no more recent news."

"Who told you about Tallis?"

"In my culture, it is rude to question someone who extends you hospitality."

Akilah bit his tongue and bowed. Every fiber of his being wished to wring more information from Waqilu.

"People on borders of countries or conversations ... hear things. Take what I've offered and move on."

The caravan crested the second ridge to the west as the sun sagged near the horizon. Gravel-strewn ruggedness and scarce, scraggly bushes gave way to a valley of lush grasses, date palms, and other vegetation. Tamarisk trees bursting with pink blooms suffused the valley with their delicate perfume.

This place was either a local anomaly or a sign that the wilderness was yielding to more arable land. The Bitter Lakes could be as close as the next ridge or two ahead. Akilah's excitement soared.

Stumbling upon Waqilu's camp was an improbable, if not statistically impossible encounter. Moreover, a potential enemy had offered hospitality—and hope that Tallis was still alive. Had the Great I AM engineered their meeting?

Despite how restless Rashidi was to leave the area, Akilah let the camels graze for three days. They munched nonstop on the smorgasbord of tasty vegetation.

The verdant valley brought sweet sleep, thanks to the tamarisks. Also called salt cedars, they secreted salt, which absorbed moisture from the air. When their held moisture evaporated, it cooled the air deliciously.

The crisp air seemed to brighten the countless stars blanketing the night sky. Akilah tilted his head heavenward, deep in thought. Waqilu was either a very good *Shatranj*[1] player or a genuinely kind person. Akilah chose to believe the latter. Something or someone had brought the caravan thus far and had given him the strength to persevere. He stretched his arms to the sky in silent thanks to the Great I AM.

---

1. Chess

Chapter 35

Straight Line

The closer the caravan got to Egypt, the more grateful Akilah was for Rashidi's heritage and knowledge of the area. According to their maps, the straightest route lay between the Great Bitter Lake and Lake Timsah, but Rashidi insisted they travel north around Lake Timsah.

"We'll avoid problems with the Canal of the Pharaohs that way," he said.

Akilah wasn't eager to add more miles to their trek. "I thought the canal was finished ages ago."

"Finished, rebuilt, finished, rebuilt … It's been under construction or repair for two thousand years." Rashidi grimaced. "And the blood of hundreds of thousands of slaves attests to it. Who knows which part they're working on right now? Wherever it is, it'll be full of people and questions we don't want to answer. We can avoid those problems altogether if we go around the north side of Lake Timsah. From there, we can head west to On—or Heliopolis, as the Greeks call it. The City of the Sun. 'The mound of creation,' according to Egyptian beliefs."

"What's the best place to stop and camp before then? Succoth?"

"No. That's mostly a mining colony."

"Listen to us … talking about cities in Egypt. How encouraging!" Akilah shook Rashidi's shoulders in glee.

Heliopolis was finally within reach. Somewhere near it should be a place to rest without being noticed.

Akilah finally felt comfortable assigning Rashidi a task he would love. "When we get settled, you can go to Kher-Aha to learn which ferries will get us closest to Alexandria."

Rashidi beamed. "We should travel the Nile's westernmost branch that flows past Naucratis," he said. "That's Greek settled and is a trade city—the largest market port in the area. We can buy our supplies there instead of paying an extra fee to ferry them all the way down river."

Akilah chuckled. "You've had every dusty day of this journey to plan this. Well done."

He pointed to two horizontal lines between the easternmost arm of the Nile and an area near the lakes. One showed a length of the canal; another, a Roman road. "If we avoid the main roads along this stretch of canal, we can camp outside of Heliopolis while we look for something more secluded. Our identity needs to remain unknown."

The caravan barely resembled a Magi entourage now. Saddle frameworks with makeshift repairs … everyone's skin weathered from wind and sun … mended clothes hanging loose on gaunt frames. That and layers of dust effectively obscured the Magi's station and origin. Even so, Akilah couldn't be too cautious.

The caravan desperately needed more comfortable rest than camping—in a place far less populated than Heliopolis. After poring over maps, Akilah and Rashidi settled on Metariyeh, an insignificant-looking nearby dot on one map. Finally, they could attach a name to their destination.

Chapter 36

Dice Roll

The eastern shore of the Great Bitter Lake was easy to locate. Akilah stopped the caravan out of sight of a small village nearby that Hakeem had scouted and reported to be friendly.

"They have plenty of food and grain, just as Waqilu said," he noted.

"Well done. Keep the caravan hidden. We'll buy what we can." *It won't be much, but anything will help.*

Akilah and Rashidi had no sooner entered the village when Akilah espied soldiers approaching from the north. He grabbed Rashidi's sleeve. "Act like you're buying food but tell the villagers to hide what they can of their food. Warn them to not talk to the soldiers."

"Why—"

"That's a scouting party," Akilah tipped his chin in the soldiers' direction. "Auxiliary Roman fighters. They'll take whatever they want."

Akilah and Tallis had encountered their kind before. Lower-ranking soldiers, a boring assignment, and the lust for action were a volatile combination.

He pulled Rashidi close. "Listen well. I need you to be your best Egyptian self as the head of a caravan."

Ignoring Rashidi's grin, Akilah continued. "I am your father. No matter what happens, you *must* act like you can't understand *anything* the soldiers say. Talk only in Egyptian and only through me. Talk fast and passionately. When the time comes, say in Egyptian, 'Our caravan got lost in Arabia while traveling home to Egypt.' Don't embellish. Say you need to get me home because I'm ill."

Akilah paused. "Whatever the soldiers do, act like your father is your only concern. Let me interpret your words to them. As if your life depended on it. Understood?"

Rashidi nodded.

The soldiers alit from their horses and swaggered through the village. Akilah gauged the most cocksure one to be their leader, likely a low-ranking *decurion*.

He sauntered up to Rashidi. "You there. State your business."

Rashidi dutifully continued his food purchase.

"I said you," the soldier barked, spinning Rashidi around.

Rashidi held up a bag of barley. The soldier knocked it from his hands.

He grazed Rashidi's neck with his *gladius* sword. "What are you doing here? You look Egyptian, but you're dressed like ... I don't know what."

Rashidi glanced at Akilah.

"Our caravan got lost in Arabia while traveling home to Egypt," Rashidi said in Egyptian.

The soldier swiveled his head from his colleagues to the villagers. "What did he say?"

Pointing to himself, Akilah said, "*Scio quosdam Latinos.*"

"Huh. The old man thinks he knows some Latin." The soldier strode toward Akilah. In an all-too-loud voice, he said, "We've seen only locals for a week. Why are you here?"

162

"Travel ... Arabia ... lost ... return Egypt," Akilah offered in halting Latin. "Hungry. Food." His knees wobbled. He stumbled to a seat near a villager's hut.

"What's wrong with him?"

"My father has been ill for weeks. I need to get him home," Rashidi pleaded rapidly in Egyptian.

"Home ..." Akilah pointed vaguely beyond the lake.

The soldier pivoted to his men. "We haven't had much fun this week." He pulled a board and a cup with three dice from a side pouch of his saddle. Turning to Rashidi, he leered. "Let's have a game of *Tabula*.[1] You win, you get to pass. We win, we take all you have. Understand?"

Rashidi looked curiously at the game board.

"That's right, Egyptian." The soldier sniggered. "Know how to play this? We'll find out."

Rashidi pretended to comfort Akilah but whispered to him in Egyptian. "They're challenging me to a game. If I win, they'll let us go."

Akilah shuddered and gripped Rashidi's tunic as if a great pain had passed through him. His acting bought a few moments for him to whisper in Egyptian, "The soldiers are experts in gaming. It passes the time when they patrol remote areas. *Tabula* relies on strategy as much as dice throws. Use your math, and pray for divine intervention." In a quavery voice, Akilah begged for water in Latin, but a soldier blocked a villager from bringing him any.

The soldier pointed his sword at Rashidi, then the game board.

"This should be good," the others scoffed.

Rashidi half-smiled as if he didn't fully understand.

The game didn't start well. The soldier outmaneuvered Rashidi's pieces. Sweat beaded Rashidi's brow. Soon one-third

---

1. Tabula is backgammon's ancestor.

of his fifteen markers were off the board. More were blocked. The villagers watched tensely as the soldiers laughed and called for wine.

The celebration was premature. Somehow Rashidi blocked all pieces but one of his own from moving.

He looked innocently at the stunned soldier. "I win?"

Growling, the soldier smacked the board across the grass.

Rashidi bowed. "We go. Thank you."

"Keep moving," the lead soldier ordered his contingent. "Nothing to see here."

The soldiers disappeared down the road.

Akilah exhaled.

Rashidi had so convincingly said all the right words on cue that even Akilah believed him for a moment. With those acting skills, Rashidi could have a future in Persian theatre. Or government.

After a few minutes, Rashidi spread word to the villagers that it was safe for them to leave their huts. The entire village erupted into cheers—and showered the caravan with far more food than Akilah could have bought—enough to get them to Heliopolis and beyond. Even the camels' date pouches hanging from their necks were once again filled to their drawstrings.

Akilah raised his eyes to the sky. "God of the Hebrews, thank you for protecting and providing for us."

Chapter 37

Creation Dismantled

Heliopolis, 2 days later

"We made it," Rashidi exulted.

With their caravan camped safely outside the city's borders, Akilah and Rashidi approached the city on foot. Thanks to the villagers near the Bitter Lakes, the caravan's food supplies were still plentiful, so Akilah focused solely on finding lodging for the caravan. He was as tired of camping as the rest of his group.

Towering needle-shaped obelisks dotted the city. Akilah could only guess what sacred coordinates and holy structures they marked. He stopped and spread his arms wide in front of twin obelisks. "Tallis would have loved this. Abraham, the father of the Israelites, probably saw these more than sixteen hundred years ago. What a witness to this city's march through time."

He pointed toward the city's epicenter, a massive walled area enclosing the Temple of the Sun and the site where Egyptians believed the world was created. "The priests of Ra were reputed to be the greatest historians of their age. I wonder what we could learn from their chronicles."

He dropped his arms. "Pardons, Rashidi. I keep remembering Tallis's love of history."

"Yes." Rashidi smiled, perhaps a bit too brightly. "Let's make an 'Alexandria pact'—to honor Tallis by reading what he would have loved to learn." His smile widened. "Here's an idea. When Ptolemy II was championing Alexandria's Great Library, he somehow persuaded the chief priest of Heliopolis to hand over the city's archives of the history of the ancient kings of Egypt. Those records should reside in Alexandria's library."

Reading those historical records would be a touching tribute to Tallis, but Akilah wasn't ready to concede Tallis was gone. He clung to the hope of what Waqilu had said but dared not repeat it. Hope could be a tricky thing. He cleared his throat. "The high priest of Ra also was the Chief of Observers and head of astronomy. I wonder if that's still true."

He clapped Rashidi on his shoulder. "The city's engineering feats must be a paradise for you. I read that a corner of each Great Pyramid directly aligns with Heliopolis's Temple of the Sun or another structure in the city. What a grand engineering puzzle to solve."

Akilah and Rashidi grinned at each other like boys playing in mud puddles.

They circled the city's outskirts. Street after street revealed Heliopolis's past splendor, but the city clearly was no longer the religious and intellectual center it had once been. In fact, it had more than declined. It was being dismantled. Chatter on the street soon told the Magi why. Stones from the city's grand edifices were being moved to other locations for new construction projects.

Heliopolis's questionable future seemed to bruise Rashidi's spirit. It did seem unfair, even sacrilegious, to foster the dissolution of the city where Egyptians believed all creation started. But the circumstances suited Akilah. Amid the throng of temporary workers and the chaos of deconstruction, no one should notice or care about new strangers in town. Obscurity was good. Housing would be even better.

Chapter 38

A Place to Stay?

Akilah mulled the lodging issue. If Heliopolis had a caravansary, he'd be tempted to stay there. He dismissed the idea. Too public. Too easily noticeable.

"This place might direct us to lodging." Rashidi pointed to an official-looking building. "Maybe this is a magistrate's office. The door is open."

Sunlight turned to haze in the dusty, cluttered interior. Scrolls in disarray littered shelves, baskets, and a table. "Pardon me," Akilah said to the back of a man standing over a desk. "Could you direct us to the nearest public inn?"

The man, in official Egyptian garb, turned only halfway around and laughed derisively. "I could, but I wouldn't stay there if I were you. Unless you don't mind losing your reputation."

"Ah. Perhaps an open place near town where we may camp for a fee?"

The official waved Akilah off. "Come back when I finish my business."

"Yes …" Akilah shuffled awkwardly. "We will wait outside."

Another man, his face obscured from shouldering planks of cedar, passed Akilah as he paused in the doorway.

"Good. You found Lebanon cedar. Just what I need to impress my superiors. Finish the project in two days, or I'll cut your pay," the Egyptian called to the man.

"You will have your shelves on time," the worker said.

Akilah stopped. Something about that voice …

"Go around back," the worker whispered to Akilah.

Akilah tried to act casual as they rounded the corner of the building.

"Are you sure this is safe?" Rashidi said. "Now what?"

"We wait."

A few minutes later, a murmur came from beyond the corner of the building. "A landlord owns a house that will be vacated in two days. He can help you with lodging."

Akilah shaded his eyes to see who was speaking. But against the sun's glare, all he could discern was a partially hidden silhouette. "That's very kind of you, but a house won't fit all of us. Or our animals."

Akilah laughed inwardly. In his dirty, worn clothes, he didn't appear to be a man who owned servants and camels.

"The landlord also owns an abandoned farm next to the house," the man whispered. "He'd likely discount the rent if you agree to make some repairs."

Akilah caught his breath. "Can you take us to this person?"

"Sorry, no. But if you go straight down this street and turn right at the metalworker's shop, the landlord's home is next door on the second floor." The shadowed man vanished from the alley.

The Magi rushed around the corner to learn the identity of

their kind informant. But all they saw was a crowd of people, many with white tassels and blue threads on the hems of their garments. Haruz's people. Akilah's pulse quickened.

He wasted no time in finding the building next to the metalworker's shop. Garlic and cumin smells almost overwhelmed him at the top of the stairs. In response to Akilah's tentative knock, a burly man filled the doorway.

"What?" The man scratched his back side.

Akilah bowed. "We want to inquire about the house and farm you own. We'd like to rent both."

"I need a month's advance. Can you pay?" The oversized man eyed the Magi with suspicion.

"We will pay you the first *two* months' rent in advance," Akilah said firmly.

"Really." The man snorted. "Right now?"

"Now," Akilah said with finality. "Please pardon the state of our travel attire."

"Do you have the money with you?"

"No, but it's nearby. We can bring it back within the hour."

"If you're not back by then, I'll rent it to someone else," the man said gruffly.

That likely wasn't true, but Akilah didn't want to risk losing the opportunity to rent a whole farm of privacy.

The large man paused with the door halfway shut. "You can rent the farm for a third less if you fix the roof. Most tenants don't fix anything, and the latest ones didn't stay long enough to try. You'll have to sign a lease. Can you read?"

A growl squeezed through Rashidi's gritted his teeth. Akilah surreptitiously laid a restraining hand on his arm.

"Yes," Akilah said evenly. "We'll return within the hour. How close are the house and farm from here?"

"You'll find out when you bring the money," the landlord said. "The properties will be available in two days. The name's Basa. Talk only to me about the rental."

"Very well. Thank you." Akilah bowed again and hurried down the steps.

"How could you promise that?" Rashidi hissed. "We're camped almost an hour from here."

"I have a plan."

Chapter 39

A Greater Good

Akilah strode down the stairs and walked next door into the metalworker's shop. "Sir, do you work with gold?"

"Yes. All kinds of metal." The sweating man mopped his brow.

"Do you ever purchase gold to make it into something else?"

"Yes."

"Then please tell me what you would pay for this." Akilah pulled the ring from his right pinkie finger and held it up to the sunlight. "This is pure gold surrounding a Persian diamond."

The man wiped his hands then eyed the perfectly faceted champagne-colored rock inside its elegant setting. "Let me weigh it."

"First give me an estimate," Akilah said. "You have an eye for metal. Working with it every day, you should get close."

The man scanned the Magi as if trying to decide whether they were thieves or people pressed by hard times. Akilah didn't care. He knew the old market trick of altering scales to shortchange buyers. An accurate estimate would likely yield a more equitable transaction. He met the man's gaze.

As the metalworker turned away, Rashidi grabbed Akilah's

arm. "What are you doing?" he whispered. "That's your family's Magi heirloom. You've had it since your induction ceremony."

"Yes. And today it's being used for something greater than adornment."

The metalworker handed Akilah a scrap of papyrus. "I could give you more if the ring was silver. But that's a nice stone."

Akilah glanced at the papyrus and nodded. "Good enough for me. No need to weigh it. Money for the ring, yes?"

The man handed Akilah the money; he relinquished the ring.

"Thank you for the fair transaction." He bowed. "I knew I could trust a Kushite metalworker."

"How?"

"The quality of your work. And the meteoric metal you're working with over there." Akilah gestured toward the forge. Several chunks of shiny, metallic-looking rock with a distinct crystalline structure glinted on a nearby workbench.

The worker opened his mouth but nothing came out.

"Good day to you, sir."

Rashidi hustled Akilah out of the shop. "I can't believe you did that," he sputtered.

Akilah shrugged. "We had no time to get back to camp."

"I'm not talking about your ring. Why did you spout about meteoric metal? Hardly anyone knows what that is—or how it's used. What happened to remaining anonymous?"

"I simply showed the man respect. Few people do."

"Do we have enough money to get to Alexandria?"

"Let's secure our housing before we count that cost." Akilah's mind churned. The Magi's money pouches were almost empty. His Magi ring had just become a thing of his past. But the future of his caravan was uncertain. After rent, food was the next priority. Then they'd need to earn more money—or sell more possessions—to get to Alexandria. After that …

"I don't want to appear too eager to pay the landlord. Let's split up and walk the streets, listen and learn what we can about

Heliopolis. Meet me in the market square in an hour. I'll go directly there after I pay the rent advance."

"You're the expedition leader," Rashidi said.

Akilah wasn't so sure. They had weathered too many circumstances beyond his control. The God of the Hebrews had brought them this far.

As Akilah browsed the main street's market, he idly wondered if Joseph and Mary had to travel and rent housing during the last Roman census. That would have been near the time Yeshua was born.

Against the backdrop of Heliopolis's eroding beauty, its market flourished. Temple employees, construction workers, and other residents clamored at the stalls for goods and prepared food. Akilah pushed through the crowds, brushing against a donkey tethered next to a camel. The donkey shuddered and let out a high-pitched bray.

"Easy, my friend," a kind voice said in soothing tones.

Akilah whirled around. That voice. *Joseph?*

Chapter 40

Lost in the Crowd

Oh, to see Joseph's family again! But where did he go? He was practically beside Akilah a moment ago.

Akilah scanned faces as he weaved his way through the crowd. "Pardon me. Excuse me."

Outstretched hands waved wares at him. Insistent vendors tugged on his cloak.

"You need protection." A woman shook a glass vial of herbs at Akilah.

"You need real protection," a wizened man said. "Spells and amulets here." He pressed Akilah with a cheap Eye of Horus painted on wood.

"No, thank you." He knew what would come next—offers of greater protection from more costly faience or ceramic amulets.

"Grave goods," another vendor called, beckoning Akilah with a *shabati* statue. "Buy these, and I assure you will reach the blessed Field of Reeds in the afterlife."

Akilah's polite refusal provoked promises of curses from the vendor. His condemnations continued to ring in the air as Akilah passed stalls of live and dead animals and leather goods.

Halfway down the street, he doubled back. Surely he could find Joseph or his family. Why were they in Egypt?

"'Artichoke.' Say the word and the letter it starts with."

"Ar-ti-choke," a toddler-sized voice parroted.

"Beet. Cabbage."

Wonderful mother, teaching her child his letters already.

Akilah walked past, his thoughts divided between Joseph and lodging.

Wait. He'd heard that gentle voice before. As he pressed through the crowd to listen more intently, he knocked an eggplant from a woman's hand.

She yelled a string of words a seaman would use.

"Many pardons." He slid past her as she stooped to pick up the vegetable.

"Dates." The tender voice sounded closer.

Months ago, a kind teenager with a voice like that had offered Akilah a bowl of dates, saying, "Please, noble lords, have some refreshment."

Mary?

If it *was* Mary, then Yeshua was with her!

Akilah pivoted to double back, but an angry shopkeeper cut him off. "Stop those thieves," she shrilled.

"Where?"

She wagged a finger opposite of where Akilah was headed. "Street urchins. Faster than lightning, always stealing food. A bigger menace than the pests I battle to grow this food." Her rant pitched higher. "Where's a magistrate when you need one?"

Akilah shrugged and shook his head.

"Want some radishes? Artichokes?"

"No, thank you."

She pawed his arm. "I have fresh cucumbers."

"Not today." He pulled against her two-handed grasp.

"Now I need to sell twice what those troublemakers stole. You don't want my husband to blame me for what those thieves took, do you?"

"I must go." He fled, retracing his steps. Who would most likely have seen Mary and Joseph? He hailed a stable boy. "Did you see or talk to someone who might be the master of the donkey that was tied next to a camel here?"

"Maybe." The boy, less than half Akilah's height, held out his hand. Clearly, only money would loosen his tongue.

Akilah pressed a small coin into his open palm.

"I overheard two people talking, like they were going on a trip. A man said something about 'farther than they had ever imagined.' What does that mean?"

Akilah wasn't sure.

"And the woman said, 'We trust ourselves to the unknown because we know the One who knows all things.'" The boy extended his hand again.

What a hustler. Akilah held up another coin. "I'll shake this and more out of you unless you have something further of value to say."

The boy's eyes grew big as saucers, but he grabbed the coin. "Then the man said, 'The great I AM will guide our steps.'"

Akilah inhaled sharply. Haruz had said that too.

Was this great I AM the One who made the Magi's hearts burn when they studied the Messianic prophecies? The presence Akilah had felt guiding them from Persia before they saw the star again above that tiny Bethlehem house? The One who'd spoken to the Magi in their dream? Had the great I AM spared the Magi's caravan in its flight from Herod? If Joseph was fleeing Herod like the Magi were, had I AM spoken to him in a dream too?

Akilah had no more time to reflect. The obelisks' shadows testified the sun had advanced an hour. He raced to Basa's.

Chapter 41

Housing

The landlord counted Akilah's money twice. "This is more than two months' rent, so I'll write a credit to your account." He snatched a reused papyrus from a disorderly stack on his desk. "If you find anything has been left behind, consider it yours. People leave things all the time. I don't want to deal with it."

"Indeed." Akilah watched Basa scribble. "Do you know the current tenants well?"

"They paid me. That's what matters," the burly man answered.

"Any idea where they're headed?"

"People come and go. I don't ask questions."

"I see. How many people lived there last?"

"Why do you care?" Basa growled.

"No reason. Just making conversation," Akilah said.

"Rent is due the first of each month. Pay *me*. No one else." Basa waved two sheets in front of Akilah. "Your receipt and directions to the properties in Metariyeh. I expect the roofs to be fixed in a month. If they aren't, I'll increase your rent."

181

Basa's mention of roofs was lost on Akilah. Metariyeh was exactly where they had hoped to stay.

Chapter 42

News of Herod

Metariyeh. The word rang in Akilah's head. An answer to prayer. Seclusion and access. He could hardly contain his excitement as he left Basa's garlic trail and found Rashidi.

With all the work sites scattered throughout the city, Akilah had no trouble spotting a public place where workers bought food. He slapped Rashidi on the back. "Today is a very good day. We should toast to it, yes?" Akilah winked and pulled three coins from the folds of his cloak.

"I'll have Egyptian honey beer." Rashidi grinned in anticipation.

Beer was abundant in quantity and variety, both as refreshment and laborers' wages. Everyone was eager to claim their ration.

The months of travel and struggle for survival ebbed as Akilah waited in line. Doing something normal like ordering a drink was an overwhelming luxury.

If Tallis were here, he'd ask if they could make sahlaab. The hot milky drink flavored with orange blossom water was best suited to winter months, but it was his year-round favorite. Probably because it was topped with pistachios.

Akilah shoved thoughts of his colleague to a far corner of his mind. Waqilu's scanty information about Tallis was more than a month old. He couldn't bear to think what might have happened to his friend since then.

As he sipped his honey beer, more people with white tassels and blue threads on their garment hems wandered past. More of Haruz's "people."

A cluster of them paused near Akilah and Rashidi.

"Egypt is so much better than Judaea. I'm glad I left when I did."

"What Herod did was unspeakable."

"He should be cursed forever, ordering death by the sword to all babies and toddlers in Bethlehem."

"Can you imagine losing your only son that way?"

A shudder passed through Akilah. The angelic being that told him to flee Herod had a sword. When it touched the hilt, the blade turned crimson. Mothers' screams issued from it. Then it dulled to mahogany. *Like dried blood.* The angel had delivered more than a warning. It had shown Akilah the future —exactly as those people near him described it.

"Where is this child destined to be a king, anyway?" one continued.

"Do you think Herod's men are still looking for him?" another said.

"Adonai won't let that bloodshed go unpunished."

The conversation faded as the group moved on.

Adonai. Akilah mulled the word. A plural of the Hebrew word for "lord," meaning "lord of lords." Now he knew a name of God that His people uttered aloud. He could pray that name.

News of Herod overrode that thought. Akilah grabbed Rashidi's sleeve. "We would have given away the child's location if we had returned home the way we came," he whispered.

Another epiphany bubbled to the surface of Akilah's consciousness. Haruz had warned the Magi of more than they realized when he said to hide in their hearts what they had seen until the right time.

Akilah leaned close to his colleague's ear. "If we learn anything about this child or his family, we must keep it to ourselves. Agreed? His life and ours depend on it."

Chapter 43

Moving Evidence

Metariyeh, 2 days later

As Akilah had hoped, Metariyeh was little more than a wide spot in the road northeast of Heliopolis. A long dirt path parted lush countryside rustling with reeds and Halfa grass, then emptied into two secluded properties. To Akilah's delight, the area included a spring with unusually fresh, sweet water. No more searching for water or hauling it a distance.

That victory was short-lived. The farm must not have been operational for years. Pastures overgrown. Fruit trees choked with weeds. The barn full of debris and bird droppings. The farmhouse's interior desperate for scrubbing and limestone paint. Both roofs needed repairs. So that's what Basa meant about roofs—plural.

"We'll clean the barn first," Akilah said. "Everyone can stay there with the animals or in tents until the farmhouse is fixed." The servants' faces fell, but chagrin changed to cheers when he tossed his outer cloak aside, rolled up his sleeves and breeches, and grabbed a shovel. Rashidi reluctantly followed suit. Hakeem started an inventory of the farming tools in the barn. Akilah hoped some still worked or could be sharpened.

The day ended around an open fire, just as before. Tents went up in a circle, just as before. They'd have to eat and camp under the stars a while longer.

After the evening meal, Akilah motioned for Rashidi to walk with him. They paced the perimeter of the land according to Basa's notes until they found a tiny house, perhaps once a groundskeeper's home, tucked in a far corner of the property. Akilah hesitated to open the door, but Rashidi pushed through it.

"It's almost bare but very clean."

Akilah wandered out back. A partial enclosure for animals abutted the back side of the house. Not a proper stable, but a shelter, roofed and fenced, its bare ground strewn with straw, much like the back of Joseph's house on Bethlehem's outskirts. Akilah ran his hands over the rough fencing. The Magi's camels could fit in it.

Thinking of how this tiny house would finally offer some true privacy for the Magi was bittersweet. Tallis wasn't here. Only his camel was.

The stone cottage was a far cry from Magi accommodations in Persia. Yet, in this moment of exhaustion and elation at arriving in Metariyeh, it was equally as splendid to Akilah. For the first time since leaving Bethlehem, he felt safe. "Adonai, thank you," he whispered.

Rashidi must have seen enough. He headed toward the campfire. "Coming?"

"Soon."

Akilah paced the width of the small stable, reminiscing about Bethlehem. "Kani was over there. Our box of gifts was—"

A glint of light caught his eye.

It could be anything. A bit of quartzite. A shard from a mirror. In the moonlight, Akilah couldn't be sure. On impulse, he knelt to look closer.

He picked at its corner. Barely protruding from the dirt, it was too small to grip firmly. He grabbed a sturdy stick and trenched around the object. His energy soaring like a child convinced he'd found treasure, he finally extracted the heavily caked object. With a satisfied laugh, he scooped a bucket of water from the trough and swished the item until he freed it from its muddy shroud.

It couldn't be.

Glistening in his hand was one of the gold pieces the Magi had given to honor Yeshua.

Akilah grabbed his head in glee. Joseph and his family had stayed here.

Chapter 44

Dangerous Talk

In Akilah's excitement, he forgot his charge to Rashidi when they were drinking beer. With his fist closed firmly around the gold piece, he headed to the campfire.

The gold piece was unmistakably from the Magi. Not a coin, but rather a rectangular wafer, cast expressly for them. The shape was deliberate. Rectangles fit more efficiently into a box than round coins did, making the gold easier to transport in smaller containers over long distances. Unlike currency that had to be exchanged, the gold wafers did not.

Akilah traced the rectangle's edges with his thumb, imagining how the piece might have fallen out of its box. Had Mary and Joseph left this place in haste? If so, why? Where were they now?

"Rashidi." Akilah motioned him into their shared tent.

"You look like you just ate a plate of *sarshir* drenched in date honey. What's excited you so?"

"We are staying in a holy place. Look what I found." Akilah reverently held up the gold piece.

"No." Rashidi's eyes widened.

Akilah nodded. "Yeshua and his family stayed here. I think

Joseph was the man in the alley who told us to talk to the landlord about this place."

"Do you think he recognized us?"

"Hard to say. But from what we heard on the street today, I can see why he didn't want us to know who he was. They had to flee from Herod like we did. They must have come here because Egypt is friendly to the Hebrews. In fact, about half of Heliopolis's population seems to be Hebrew."

Akilah palmed the gold piece to Rashidi.

Clutching it, he thumped his chest rhythmically, as if doing mental math. "This should be more than enough to cover our fare to Alexandria."

Akilah snatched the wafer back. "This was never meant to be ours."

"How do you know? Maybe it's a good omen. Provision for the last leg of our journey." Rashidi's voice notched higher in defense. "Haruz said to hide what we have until it's the right time. Besides, didn't you say that the landlord said we could keep anything the previous tenants left behind?"

"Lower your voice," Akilah shushed. "Since we left Jerusalem, we've received many blessings despite many perils. I believe this house and farm are the blessings we're intended to receive now. Not the gold."

Chapter 45

Burial

The tent's air thickened with Rashidi's palpable ire. The only way Akilah could end the day on an amiable note was to tell Rashidi that he'd consider his arguments. That was at best a stall tactic. Akilah needed discernment. What appeared to be good fortune could, in fact, be neither good nor fortuitous—like the dates from Susita. That "gift" had hindered, not helped the caravan. Did this gold piece pose a far greater risk? If it wasn't meant to be a gift, using it might reveal who the Wise Men were—and, by extension, could endanger Yeshua's family.

He couldn't sell the gold wafer to the metalsmith. Its uniqueness would raise more questions with the Cushite than when Akilah sold his Magi ring. With dismay, he wondered if the gold posed the same burden for Yeshua's family. He never intended that. But he couldn't have anticipated any of these circumstances.

A still, small voice sounded in his mind. Unobtrusive but insistent, it said don't keep the gold. Was Adonai exhorting Akilah to trust Him more than financial security?

Akilah spent a sleepless night on his side, clutching the gold wafer in his hand thrust in his pocket.

Early the next morning, he told Rashidi he was still considering all he'd said. That wasn't true, but it eased him into suggesting Rashidi travel with his head servant to Kher-Aha and inquire about ferries down the Nile to Alexandria.

Rashidi offered to go alone, saying Kassim's time would be better spent working on the barn. "For safety, we never travel alone—especially now," Akilah replied. "We don't know anyone here. Besides, it'll be more pleasant for both of you than doing cleanup, yes? You've more than earned an overnight respite in the city. May Adonai lead you to the information you need and bless you with a safe journey."

Akilah watched until they reached the road that took them southwest toward Kher-Aha. As soon as they were out of sight, he ran to the stable behind the tiny house where his camel, Dain, was tethered.

"This will look like madness to you, but I need your help," he whispered to the animal. "You'll get fresh water and extra dates for your effort."

Akilah bailed all the water he could from the water trough, then dragged it out of place. Fetching buckets of water from the spring, he poured one bucket on the ground where the trough had stood and plunged the gold wafer into the mud.

"Come and drink," Akilah cajoled, holding a second bucket of water in front of Dain. He despised drinking out of a bucket, but he reluctantly stepped forward. Akilah weaved the bucket back and forth in front of him until Dain thoroughly trampled the mud.

Akilah repositioned the trough then poured more water

around its perimeter to sink it slightly. As he pressed down on the trough to seal what it concealed, his hip pain remined him time never stopped its march.

"Good job, Dain. Here's a whole bucket of fresh spring water. Drink your fill." Dain guzzled the water then wet Akilah with his nuzzling. "Maybe I deserved that." Akilah chuckled as he palmed a handful of dates to his camel.

"Our secret," he whispered.

Chapter 46

To Machaerus

A month prior

Tallis had been moved about for weeks, hooded each time so he'd remain disoriented. When he wasn't being transported, he was isolated so he couldn't identify a camp's location, people, or their patterns.

The specter of his task loomed large when he overheard they'd entered Judaean territory. Herod's men, Roman sentries, robbers, mountains, and desert stood between them and Machaerus. Yet his captors kept moving, seemingly unimpeded. Either the Nabataeans paid off those men or knew of a secret route that circled south of the Dead Sea to reach Machaerus.

The final leg of the journey was not on horseback but in a metal cage of a cart driven by a sullen, burly driver, built like the Thracian mercenaries Tallis had encountered in his military past. The driver was preoccupied with two things—wedging more shackled human cargo into the rectangular cage and muttering unintelligible syllables, perhaps about getting his fee upon delivery.

Within a day, the grunting driver had picked up so many

people that they fit only by standing, facing each other, three deep. Tallis pitied the men sandwiched in the middle, wedged on all sides like fish in a barrel. Some men, like Tallis, were branded as slaves. Regardless of who they were, if their destination was Machaerus, their lot would be jail or conscription to the fortress's work detail. Herod had never-ending expansion plans for Machaerus.

The driver saved his full-throated syllables for the horses as they labored against the groaning cart. His harsh, guttural outbreaks weren't quite words, so his whip often spoke for him.

"Adonai, help us," one older captive cried as he swooned from thirst and fatigue on the second day. Other captives screamed as they crushed each other to hold him upright. The driver's whip maintained his cargo's silence the rest of the way.

Tallis busied his mind to block out distractions. What was the Nabataeans' larger objective for their vested interest in Machaerus? Gaining ground in Judaea would be an obvious coup, but their timing in taking Tallis to the fortress seemed calculated. Why? Without that insight, he may miss vital information they wanted, and his life would be forfeit. It might be, anyway—but he would die by his own hand before letting them take more from him than they already had.

Tallis craned his neck to glimpse the stunning yet stark desert mountains framed by the cage's bars. In the distance, a cone-shaped hilltop dominated the landscape. The path snaking up its ridge confirmed Machaerus was about a half-day journey away.

The Nabataeans hadn't shared extraction details with him—only their expectations. Tallis had a week to infiltrate Machaerus then escape and deliver his news to them. Somehow he'd have to find their camp in a wadi across the border in Nabataean territory. An effective hiding place this time of year, but "meet me in a deep ravine near Machaerus" was scant directional help for one on the run. The Nabataeans might leave him to his own devices to escape but would undoubtedly comb the area to find him.

His thoughts turned to his branding and the Edessan who had dressed his wound afterwards. He had taken more care than necessary in attending to it and had appeared two other times during Tallis's transfers. But unlike a traveling field doctor, the Edessan seemed to do more than handle medical needs. Whether he was working for or merely with the Nabataeans was impossible to discern. The enigmatic man had exposed Tallis's branded arm like presenting a passport when the mercenary arrived to cart him away. While shoving Tallis into the caged cart, the Edessan had whispered, "One week—or all will become waste."

Tallis didn't trust the words or who'd said them.

The cart slowed, turned, then tilted. The final ascent to Machaerus began. Partway up, the cart passed a series of openings like caves, possibly prisons. Tallis's skin prickled. Every sense heightened. Every nerve sharpened to razored edginess. Like it or not, he had to let his past tactical training and battle readiness reenter his life again—or he wouldn't survive.

Chapter 47

Assignment

Machaerus remained hidden during the cart's winding climb. Fog shrouded the lower elevations, suspending the cart in eerie isolation between desolate earth and an unseen summit. Tallis continued to mull how to get an assignment that would gain him access to the most areas in the fortress. He had no inside contacts. He'd have to manage with whatever came his way.

"Trust me." The command invaded his thoughts almost audibly.

The wilderness and Tallis's capture had rekindled his past career's survival mentality. Gone were his daily rituals. Self-preservation had supplanted prayer until he'd almost wholly forgotten it. With shame, he recalled a few months prior when he'd been so sure of the Hebrew God's preeminence. He had silently pledged his life and future to Him. He had brushed aside Akilah's questions of faith as he confidently talked about trusting what they'd learned and the One they'd seen. How quickly he'd let his hardships erode his faith and demote prayer to a last resort during an emergency. *Forgive me. If You are with me, show me a way through this. I can't do this on my own.*

Jangling chains interrupted his prayer as the driver unlocked the cage and hurled one captive after another at a line of sentries stationed on either side of a desk where some sort of foreman sat.

"Can you read? Doesn't matter." The foreman grabbed a stack of *titili*. Dangling them by their leather thongs, he shook the plaques in front of the captives' faces. "This is your assignment." He draped one over the nearest person's neck, pointed at the writing on it, then poked the person with his finger. "South courtyard. Garden. Dig and trench." A sentry pulled the person aside before he could respond. Clearly, workers were to be seen, not heard.

The foreman turned to the next person in line. "North wing. *Miqvehs*. Dress or clean stone." Next. "East wing. Bathhouse. Lay tile if you know how. Otherwise, scrub the baths after people bathe." He grimaced then moved on. "West wing. Food. Taste it, serve it, clean it up after guests eat. If the food hasn't been poisoned, you'll live long enough to serve workers like yourself. Steal food and you'll live without it—in prison."

He doled out half a dozen more assignments. "Wear this, be where it says you should be, do your work, and all will go well." He approached Tallis last. "You get the honor of waste disposal." The foreman swatted the titulus on Tallis's chest. "No one will let you sleep near them, so you'll stay in 'the inn.'" He laughed derisively. "One of our nicer prison cells."

The Edessan's words rang in Tallis's ears: " … or all will be waste." What a peculiar—or perfect—answer to prayer.

Day 3 in Machaerus

The palace complex was a wonder, invisible until one scaled the hilltop's highest point. Its main building, courtyards, and bath complex wooed royalty as a grand getaway. Four watchtowers, imposing bastions anchoring each corner of the fortress, told another story.

Snatching bits of conversations from tower sentries and prison guards, Tallis pieced together news of Herod's death, rumored revolts throughout his divided kingdom, and who ruled each region. Antipas now controlled Perea, which included Machaerus.

The fortress gloried in its astonishing water collection and distribution system. From people working on the miqvehs, Tallis learned the palace complex had two separate sets of plumbing—one for everyday use and another for ritual bathing, per Jewish standards. In addition, high-level workers and guards living on the hill's lower elevation openly boasted that they also had plumbing. The city's housing was likely an exchange for their loyalty to Herod and his dynasty. But not every part of the fortress enjoyed the luxury of waste removal.

Tallis's daily labor was to collect waste from the watchtowers and prison. His task started in daylight with climbs to the top of each bastion and ended in darkness, in the bowels of caves ensconcing the prison cells. He invented ways to linger at each spot, hoping to glean information. He offered to lend a hand removing food trays in the prison. He plodded through his task in each watchtower and bore the consequences of appearing slow or clumsy.

From the watchtowers' heights, Tallis discerned six lines of sight to other fortresses—southwest to west, then north, Masada, Herodion, Hyrcania, Cypros, Doq, and Alexandreion. If he looked hard, he thought he could see Jerusalem. Each bastion was well equipped to relay signals with fire or smoke. Any warning would be visible to all those fortresses.

Herod's ambition and paranoia had pushed him to build "bigger and better" all his life. Why would his son, Antipas, feel the need to do more at Machaerus—especially now? His closest enemies were the Nabataeans, but they were careful and crafty, outwitting their enemies rather than assaulting them. Strengthening this already impenetrable fortification for a full-on attack seemed unlikely.

Something didn't feel right. Tallis had three more days to figure out why.

Chapter 48

The Ferry

Day 5 in Machaerus

"Back again, urine carrier?" The west tower sentry fondest of harassing Tallis feigned relieving himself in the Wise Man's direction. Tallis dodged the imaginary stream while the sentry doubled over with laughter. Enjoying his joke with the other sentries gave Tallis enough time to pivot westward.

Unless his eyes deceived him, a boat bearing royal standards was approaching across the Dead Sea. When it docked, it would be less than three parasangs from Machaerus. Its passengers would undoubtedly have horses waiting for them and could reach the fortress in less than an hour.

Tallis hurried as best he could down the watchtower steps without slopping the buckets of waste he carried. The palace complex swarmed with frenzied activity. Guards streamed in every direction. Foremen shouted orders to workers. One guard barked at Tallis to dispose of his load and stay out of sight. He nodded and headed to the sink basin, a cesspool where solid waste settled to eventually become manure.

Tallis returned to the base of the west tower and looked for the guard assigned to him. On any other day, he would escort Tallis to the prison to complete the other half of his assigned task—collecting waste buckets from each cell. But in today's commotion, the guard was nowhere in sight.

Tallis weaved through the chaos. Making his way to the southern courtyard, he ran to the garden and ducked behind a large cluster of oversized ruta shrubs. Their musty, bittersweet scent should disguise his acrid aroma. If not, their new layer of soil would. Enriched with compost, it didn't smell much different than he did.

He burrowed a few inches into the soil and tucked himself flush against the biggest bush.

His gamble would either be his salvation or destruction.

The sun had advanced a cycle when the lowest branch of Tallis's hiding place rustled. On high alert, he watched the hem of a purple robe brush past. *Stop,* he silently prayed.

The robe paused at the end of the row by a cluster of date palms. "Look around you." A young, steady version of Herod's voice spoke with barely contained swagger. "We'll use the best of Machaerus in Sepphoris. As the Ornament of Galilee, Sepphoris will supply enough military strength to the region to decisively end every uprising. Every country will fear us."

"Avoiding war by showing strength is good. Fighting opinion is harder," an older, softer-spoken voice replied.

"I don't fear the Pharisees' prophecy. It's rubbish."

"Still, they—and their words—hold great sway over the people."

"Herod's government didn't cease when he died, and those who rule it now have not been deprived of its posterity as the

Pharisees predicted. Their empty words came to nothing—other than to inflame my father's madness."

"As you say, so may it be."

"My road improvements in Galilee are almost complete. Sepphoris is poised for greatness, and its blueprint is Machaerus."

Tallis strained to hear more as the voices faded.

"Every detail of this place defies all odds, Varinius. Even this garden flourishing on top of this desert fortress shows us there's no limit to what we can do," the Herod-like voice said.

Tallis waited until the voices were no more. He scrambled to his knees and brushed as much dirt from his body as he could. Ducking behind columns, he made his way toward the west tower.

But not fast enough.

"You." The guard assigned to Tallis grabbed him. He'd be beaten or lashed. But he had gotten what he needed.

Chapter 49

Dying to Live

Day 6 in Machaerus

Tallis had to get out.

If he took the Edessan's whispered words literally, he had to leave today or tomorrow. But how? The guards watched his every move. He couldn't escape their sight, let alone the fortress.

His wounds from yesterday's whip were raw. Every jostle and stumble while carrying waste reopened a welt that shot pain down his back all the way to his toes.

His daily tasks complete, he was locked back in his cell.

What now? God of the Hebrews, help.

He couldn't muster more of a prayer. Heat and fatigue overwhelmed his body. His skin burned. His tongue numbed. His thoughts flew to his family that he'd always hoped to find again. He curled in a corner of his cell and waited for the inevitable.

Tallis must have slept because the cell's stone floor felt colder than before—although it didn't quell the fire in his skin.

Arguing outside his cell door forced its way through his veils of fatigue and pain.

A key clanked in the lock. The cell door creaked open. "This one isn't dead."

"Stay back." A shadowy figure pushed into the cell. Tallis recoiled, expecting to be dragged to his feet. But familiar hands gripped him. "Stay down."

Tallis obligingly slumped on the floor.

"This one and others *will* be dead, if we don't get him out of here." The voice near Tallis sharpened with accusation. "How do you expect workers to be productive if you let this happen? No one attended to this person after he was lashed. His wounds are infected. He's also developed some type of plague. He needs immediate medical attention—more than I can offer here. The warden will not be happy if you allow an outbreak of disease."

"You're lying."

Tallis recognized the guard's voice, laced with anger and fear.

"See for yourself." The man gripping Tallis held up his blistered arm.

"Get him out of here," the guard bellowed. "I can't have that on my watch. Shroud him so no one gets sick."

"At once." The man pulled white cloths from his backpack.

"Don't move," he whispered to Tallis.

Stunned and in pain, all he could do was obey. Soon he was cocooned. A face cloth shrouded his vision. Hefty but clumsy arms lifted him, banging his feet against the cell door.

Tallis was plunked into a cart, atop rigid bodies exuding the pungency of rotting meat. He had succumbed to thinking he'd die before he left Machaerus. In a sense, he had. He was being transported with the dead.

Chapter 50

Excess Baggage

The cart stopped briefly at a guard's barked command. Someone replied, "They're dead. One has contagion. Stay back."

Clearer air reached Tallis's lungs. The cart must have exited the prison through one of the caves halfway down the hill from the palace complex.

A silent, bumpy drive commenced, punctuated only by guttural sounds. Was that the same driver who'd brought Tallis to Machaerus?

The cart finally stopped. Burly arms shoved Tallis aside. Grunts ensued. The cart listed as its load lightened. Thuds followed. Bodies were being disposed of in the dark.

Soon a knock and a voice sounded on his side of the cart. "We need to clean you, dress your wounds, and attend to your blisters." Someone pulled Tallis's face cloth off of him.

His jaw dropped. His rescuer was the Edessan.

"I have plague. Why would you risk coming in contact with me?"

The Edessan laughed. "You aren't sick. But nice touch to get blisters that look like plague."

"I don't know how that happened."

"Did you hide somewhere for a long time?"

Tallis nodded. "Under a cluster of ruta bushes."

"Ruta can cause severe skin reactions, especially if you're in the sun and sweating. You saved me the trouble of making you appear infected with plague."

Over the warmth of an evening fire, the Edessan told Tallis as much as he was willing to share about his connection with a Levite named Elyakim. Their efforts to help displaced, captured, or persecuted people. How Elyakim met Akilah's cousin and learned of the caravan's efforts to find Yeshua. "You're alive because Farzaneh confided in Elyakim about her cousin's intentions. Then Elyakim contacted me. I tracked you to Machaerus through my military contacts."

"We haven't found any trace of Akilah and the caravan yet," he continued. "That's good news. They may still be alive."

Tallis winced as the Edessan dressed his back wounds. "How can I thank you? I don't even know your name. Or his." He nodded toward the driver, sitting a distance apart from them.

"Don't thank us yet. You still have to appease the Nabataeans. We'll take you to them. If we all survive, you'll learn our names and more. Until then, this is safer. You can't divulge what you don't know."

Tallis nodded. "What next?"

"Assuming we live beyond tomorrow, our next job is to reunite you with your caravan. You know where they intended to go. That's our only lead for finding them."

Like a locust storm, questions swarmed Tallis's mind. How could this unlikely trio cover that much territory quickly? What if Akilah and the caravan hadn't reached Egypt? If they made it there then heard of Herod's death, had they left already? How could they finance their return to Persia? They were low on funds months ago.

The Edessan patted Tallis's shoulder. "Done with your back."

"Your friend over there. What happened to him?"

"Got part of his tongue cut out when he dared defy a Thracian ruler."

A shiver ran down Tallis's spine. Persian torturers did that too.

"His anger is a good cover. No one knows whose side he's on."

Tallis nodded. "One more thing. When we get to the Nabataeans' camp, can you help me locate something I'm supposed to return to Akilah? It's important."

The Edessan frowned. "Sentimentality can get you killed. Practicality keeps you alive. I'm practical. That's all I can promise." He stared into the fire until the air grew pregnant with silence. "Do you trust me?"

"As much as I trust anyone right now."

"Your arm still hurts from the branding, yes?"

"It's never stopped."

"I can remedy that. But I'll have to put fire to it again to heal it."

Again?

Tallis's hands closed around the Edessan's throat. "*You branded me?*"

Chapter 51

Reckoning

The Edessan pried Tallis's fingers from his throat. "That's the second time you've tried to strangle me."

He locked eyes with Tallis. "Yes, I branded you. On orders. Part of this job. You'll thank me later. Save your strength for what matters most. Get some sleep." He motioned to the Thracian. "He and I will take turns standing watch."

Tallis was in no position to argue.

The cheery morning sun belied the seriousness of this day of reckoning. It unsettled Tallis that the Edessan knew the exact location of the Nabataeans' camp—near Machaerus in a cavernous gorge cut by the Arnon River before it flowed into the Dead Sea.

The Thracian stopped the cart by a spot in the gorge still running with water.

With a firm grip on Tallis's arm, the Edessan led Tallis through the camp to its most ornate tent and threw open its flap. "Payment in full," he demanded. "Here's your captive, with news of Machaerus."

Tallis had seen the man in the tent only once before, but he couldn't forget him—or his armband festooned with gold loops, red and purple silks. He had ordered Tallis's capture. The man threw a jingling pouch at the Edessan. "Leave us."

He circled Tallis and eyed the bandages peeking out from the neck and shoulder of his tunic. "Hmm. Wounded in the line of duty. Speak quickly. You smell foul."

"First give me what belongs to my colleague. His astrolabe."

The leader laughed. "That heavy thing would slow you down as you try to escape."

"My concern, not yours."

"Huh." He pulled it from a chest and thrust it at Tallis. "Talk."

He took his time relaying all he had learned, starting with guard rotations, the bastions' signaling system, and what he knew of the prison's layout. Those small details would appeal to the Nabataeans' typical stealth tactics but not what he believed their larger objective was. He had to buy time—but for what, he didn't know. He had no escape plan. He would be disposed of as soon as he explained Antipas's plans for a new military base—or the Nabataeans would make sport of him by giving him a head start in trying to escape. He had no choice but to move on to the conversation he'd overhead in Machaerus's garden. He would draw out those details as long as possible.

A commotion rippled through the camp. A Nabataean scout burst into the tent, almost knocking Tallis over. "Fire!"

The Nabataean leader unsheathed his dagger and lunged for

Tallis. Swinging the astrolabe with all his might, he knocked the leader on the side of the head.

The scout collared Tallis. He spun and shoved the scout into the leader.

Hugging the astrolabe to his chest, Tallis dashed into the chaos. Flames leapt from one tent to another, surrounding the camp and his path to the wadi. It couldn't be. He had come so close to escaping.

Someone behind him threw a soaked blanket over him. "Time to walk through fire."

Chapter 52

Repairs

Cleaning took muscle, but repairs took skill. Despite his wisdom, Akilah lacked such expertise. He reluctantly approached the servants for help. All they had to work with were reeds and mud. "Who knows how to mend a roof?"

Three servants raised their hands. One offered instructions. "We need tight, flat lattices. I'll make one to show you how." Soon an assembly line formed. Some servants cut reeds. Others made lattices. Others scooped mud into buckets. Akilah watched from a distance with pride. Gone were the vestiges of two sets of servants simply working side by side. They were working together as a community. One might say almost like a family.

He retreated behind the barn. He knew so little about the servants other than their assigned duties. What did they like or dislike? What skills of theirs had he underused?

He strode toward the group. "I will help."

Soon, reed lattices alternating with layers of mud baked in

219

the sun on the roof. As more layers of both were applied, Akilah wondered if the repair would hold. Completely trusting the servants for this type of skilled labor was uncharted territory for him. If Rashidi had been here, Akilah would have consulted his engineering skills first. Hopefully when his colleague returned from Kher-Aha, he'd approve of the repairs.

Laden with a bucket of mud and a trowel, Akilah again climbed the ladder to the roof. An ache grew in his chest for all he wished for but couldn't have. If Tallis was alive, he was far away in Judaea. Rashidi was enjoying a respite away from this drudgery. Reaching Metariyeh was a triumph, but they were nowhere near home. If only Akilah could shed the burdens of leadership like he shed his outer cloak. He yearned to abandon this daily grind for survival and strike out on an adventure. Like search for Yeshua again.

The notion was ridiculous.

He'd have to cling to the hope that Adonai, the Lord of Lords, was in control of everyone's lives. And he had to choose to be faithful where he was, even when it wasn't where he wanted to be.

The next afternoon, Akilah had resumed his muddy task on the barn's roof when he saw Rashidi at a distance. He hailed his colleague and scrambled down the ladder.

"You're filthy," Rashidi exclaimed.

"We're patching the roof. Mud really does keep you cool. No wonder elephants and hippos roll in it." Akilah briskly rubbed his soil-caked hands together. "I have a surprise for you. But first, what news from Kher-Aha?"

Alighting from his camel, Rashidi produced his notes of fees and schedules, grumbling about the cost of fares and the taxes they must pay on top of that. Akilah scanned the total.

While Rashidi was in Kher-Aha, Akilah had moved the Magi's belongings and instruments into the small house where Joseph and Mary had stayed. Within the privacy of those walls, he had checked the money pouches hidden among their gear. Only one pouch still contained money, so he had locked it in their most secure trunk—the one that held their Magi robes.

He already knew they didn't have nearly enough funds to get the caravan to Alexandria. Despite all the energy he'd directed to that problem, he didn't have a firm plan for solving it.

Chapter 53

Thief

Akilah didn't want to tell Rashidi that news yet. "Come see what I've done with the groundskeeper's quarters." He smiled. "Go ahead while I wash my hands."

But as he headed toward the wash basin, Rashidi bellowed, "Thief! *Stop*."

Someone bolted from the house, with Rashidi in close pursuit. The thief outpaced him and sprinted down the dirt path.

Akilah raced after Rashidi.

Someone on horseback appeared at the far end of the path. An accomplice? Rashidi must not have considered that. He kept waving his hands and yelling for help.

Hooves thundered down the path. A rider flung himself onto the thief's back, knocking his bag from his shoulder. Something sharp pierced the bag from the inside.

"Contain him," Rashidi shouted. He needed to heed his own advice.

A second person kicked the bag out of reach while the other

rolled in the dirt with the flailing thief, who wasn't giving up without a fight. He landed a well-placed gut punch to the man wrestling him.

Rashidi grabbed the bag lying in the dirt and yanked the leather drawstring from it. Although their mystery rescuer had subdued the thief face-down in the dirt, Rashidi dove to bind the person's hands behind him.

Panting, Akilah caught up to the scene as the rescuer rolled the thief over and stepped back.

Tahrea.

"Explain yourself!" Akilah thundered.

The perennially unruly servant spat on the ground. "I'm sick of being dragged all over creation in your oh-so-noble search for knowledge. You say you can't pay us, but I know you can. I heard you talking about money and finding gold."

"You want to leave, then go. But you leave with only what you own and have earned." Akilah rummaged through Tahrea's bag. Beneath his clothes and blanket lay a small adze and a thin awl—plus a pouch with the money from the Magi's locked trunk.

Akilah flung the tools as far down the road toward the farm as he could. He counted a small sum of money from the pouch and threw it on the ground. "Your back wages." He motioned for Rashidi to take the money pouch while he untied Tahrea's hands. "You are free to leave."

Tahrea snatched the drawstring, glaring at Akilah with unbridled hatred.

"Take care. Money can slip through fingers as easily as it can slip through holes." Akilah's voice was as calm as a lake on a windless day. "Go. Don't come back here."

Tahrea grabbed the coins and raced down the dirt road.

Rashidi dusted himself off. "I'm glad he's gone. He was nothing but trouble."

"Perhaps. He could be so much more than he realizes."

Akilah turned to the two benefactor-strangers standing a respectful distance from the scene. "My new friends, thank you for your assistance." Akilah started toward them but froze. "*Tallis?*"

Chapter 54

Welcome Home?

Akilah remained rooted to the ground. "Tallis ... You're alive!"

"So it would seem."

Akilah found his feet. He ran and engulfed his friend in a muddy hug but pulled back at Tallis's wince. "Are you intact?" His eyes strayed to Tallis's heavily bandaged arm.

Tallis pulled an unwieldy bundle from a saddle bag. "I believe this is yours."

Akilah didn't need to unwrap it. "My astrolabe." He shook his head in amazement. When life became more settled, he would relish hearing the story behind its rescue.

Tallis motioned to the man next to him. "This is Ibn. You can thank him for subduing Tahrea."

Ibn waved the praise aside. "We don't have much time. I'm here to help you get home."

Persia? Akilah's heart stopped for a moment.

"You can trust Ibn," Tallis said. "I trust him with my life."

Ibn bobbed his head to Akilah. "I've secured *baris* that will leave from Kher-Aha for Alexandria in three days. That was the soonest I could rent enough of the largest barges to leave at the same time. One sank today."

Rashidi's face clouded. "Which one?" Distress suffused his overeager question.

"A ferrier named Mahen owned it. Two hippos rammed his barge near Merimda. Would have killed everyone on board except all were strong swimmers. One of the passengers was a diplomat's messenger. Did you know Mahen?"

Rashidi turned away. "We met. Once."

"What's wrong?" Alarm crept into Akilah's voice.

Rashidi wiped his brow. "I was supposed to be on that barge today."

Akilah took an unsteady step backward, his mouth agape in disbelief.

"When you sent me to Kher-Aha to inquire about rates and schedules to Alexandria, I sold my favorite turban pin for my own fare. To cover that up, I bought a scroll I intended to give you as a goodwill gesture of our studies together. But I was set on collecting my belongings and leaving for Alexandria today. By myself."

Rashidi's voice shook. "I couldn't fathom staying here after you went on about fixing roofs and farming when we …" He pointed northwest. "Kher-Aha is our gateway to Alexandria. Kher-Aha—a two-hour walk to a Nile ferry and our destination —a world away from this farm."

Rashidi paused. Akilah had no words for his friend, only a silent petition. *Please don't say anything about the gold wafer. This isn't the time.*

"All I could see before me was laboring for coin, season after season, hoping we could scrape together enough money to eventually return to Persia." Frustration and anger swirled through his words. "Whether we sold oil like Plato, grew crops, or milked goats … I hate goats almost as much as I hate sheep." He dropped his hands to his sides. "But Tahrea's attempted robbery and you two showing up at the right time saved me from a terrible fate today. I can't swim."

Silence blanketed the group.

Finally Ibn cleared his throat. "Then it is good we are all here, yes?"

"I was wrong to try to go my own way. Will you accept me back in the caravan?" Rashidi's eyes pleaded with Akilah.

Akilah laid a hand on his younger colleague's shoulder. "Of course."

"Well and good," Ibn said, "but we must hurry. You're under investigation."

Akilah swallowed hard. "How do you know? Wait. How did you find us?"

"Tallis can tell you later how we crossed paths. He knew you were trying to reach Heliopolis. Fast horses and the Via Maris got us that far," Ibn said. "The rest we learned in alleys."

Akilah raised an eyebrow to Tallis, who shrugged and nodded.

"Your landlord, Basa, was talking to the local magistrate about you," Ibn continued. "His voice is as big as he is. He's very curious about his newest tenants—men in worn-out clothes that are fluent in multiple languages, own jewels, and recognize rare metals."

Rashidi poked Akilah. "I warned you," he hissed.

"Basa claims you're hiding something." Ibn flapped his hand in the air. "He seems nosy enough for two people, even if the metalsmith isn't his informant. The magistrate told Basa he had ordered the land surveyor to assess your property—a legitimate ruse for gathering information to aid the formal investigation he's opened on you. The magistrate would gain a higher post and more prestige if he could prove you were running from some terrible crime. Their loose tongues are how we knew where to find you."

Akilah motioned to the group. "We're renting a small home. We should talk inside."

He opened the door to complete disarray. Suddenly the stolen adze and awl made sense. Tahrea had used both to break the locks on the Magi's trunks and slash the sleeping mats.

"Oh, that boy." Akilah groaned. He stepped around scattered papyri and damaged maps. The Magi robes, wadded in a corner, glinted faintly in the sunshine.

His eyes misted as he turned to the group. "We can still shut the door for privacy."

Ibn outlined in the briefest terms how unnamed "colleagues" had financed the caravan's fare to Alexandria—but the caravan would have to wait there for good weather to sail east on the Great Sea.

Akilah's forehead furrowed. "We can't afford the fare to cross the Great Sea."

"That's the easy part," Ibn said. "I'm a doctor. I treated a captain from Edessa and one of his passengers after his ship went down in a storm. The captain was happy to repay me by transporting your caravan from Alexandria to Edessa. You'll dock in his hometown, where you can exchange fresh camels for the rest of the trip home—all the way down the Royal Road. Persia still controls that route."

"I can't return to Persia without the camels. Most of them were loaned to us as part of a financing arrangement for our trip to Jerusalem." Akilah raked his fingers through his hair. "I'd have to make restitution if I didn't return them. I'm doubly bound to that. The help came from my cousin."

When Ibn learned the financier was Farzaneh, he laughed so hard tears squirted from his eyes. "I know a bit about your cousin. I don't know which will cause you more trouble—being absent from Magi society so long or reconciling your loans with her."

Akilah grimaced. That was only one layer of his complications with Farzaneh.

Chapter 55

River Revelation

Three days later, on the baris to Alexandria

When Hakeem confirmed the caravan's gear and people were accounted for and on board, Akilah relaxed a bit. The clear day and calm waters were surely a good omen. The sun's warmth and the Nile's rhythmic lapping against the baris lulled most of the servants to sleep. When all was quiet, Akilah motioned Tallis and Rashidi to a corner of the barge.

"Friends, we're on our way home," he whispered, gripping his colleagues' shoulders.

"This is like a dream," Tallis said. "I didn't think I'd survive Machaerus."

"I had stopped believing we'd get to Alexandria," Rashidi said. "When I bought that fare for myself, all I cared about was how I deserved to do what three generations of my family had been deprived of."

Akilah cleared his throat. "While we're admitting our imperfections, I have something to say too. Rashidi and I crossed paths with Joseph without realizing it when we first arrived in Heliopolis. That led us to the house and farm in Metariyeh. That same day, I overheard Mary, Joseph, and Yeshua in the marketplace but couldn't find them. Afterward, something happened to confirm we were renting the place where they'd stayed."

Rashidi's lips tightened to a thin line.

Akilah related all that happened with the gold wafer except where he hid it. Of that, he simply said it was safe from everyone, including the Magi. "It was the right decision, but I regret that it destroyed our unity." He locked eyes with Rashidi. "After that, the adventurous part of me wanted to leave the caravan to search for Yeshua's family. At the time, I didn't consider what danger I could put them in. All I wanted to do was fulfill my selfish desire. Our appetites can draw us in strange directions. We're only human, yes?

"In different ways, we let the hard things of life pull us apart. Maybe we needed to learn that our challenges were bigger than our ability to work them out on our own. We're stronger together. But we're not standing here because of our efforts. Adonai has protected and provided for us. He has rescued each of us from dangers we wouldn't have survived on our own. *He* has brought us this far. Praise be! I don't know His purposes for us, but no matter how dark the night gets, we must never forget to look up—and look to Him."

The three locked arms around each other in solidarity. Finally Akilah bent the circle to kneel. The gesture seemed inadequate, but appropriate, to acknowledge how great and good this all-powerful God was. Tallis and Rashidi joined him. If their action appeared odd to anyone on the barge, Akilah didn't care.

Day 2 on the baris to Alexandria

Tallis had always been the quietest of the Wise Men, but his brooding silence since returning from Machaerus was new to Akilah. He followed Tallis's gaze northwest toward Alexandria. "Are you well, my friend?"

"Mmm."

Tallis had shared little about his capture and only enough of his Machaerus experience for Akilah to know he'd suffered on both accounts. But his bandaged arm seemed to speak to something deeper.

"Is this healing?" Akilah nodded toward the swathing on Tallis's forearm.

Tallis slid two steps away.

"If you're concerned that Magi society won't let you serve in it anymore because your wound is an impurity, I'm fairly sure you'll be hailed as a hero and given leniency when you tell the Council what happened."

Tallis glanced up sharply.

Akilah stared at the water. "Rashidi will be absolved of any wrongdoing. But I ... As leader of this venture, I'm responsible for all decisions. The Council will put me on trial. The consequences will be severe. I'm ready to face that. But I'm unsure how I'll answer their questions."

"With truth, as you always do."

"How can I explain what we did? What we saw?" Akilah shook his head. "The Hebrew writings we found. The star. Yeshua. When I rehearse the facts in my mind, they sound like nonsense."

"I'll say again what I said at the oasis the day we fled Herod. Your head and heart need to reconcile what you know. Only then will you be sure of what you speak, no matter the consequences."

"You seemed to settle that faster than the rest of us."

Tallis turned to Akilah. "Remember the scroll from the Hebrew scribe we were going to ask the priests about in Jerusalem? I'd been doing genealogy work when that scroll was sent to me."

"You were tracing your ancestry."

"My family never spoke of relatives other than to say they were from Mesopotamia. That covers a lot of territory."

"Indeed."

"I traced my ancestors to the capital of Babylonia, but they weren't all Babylonian. Some were Jewish—from the era when King Nebuchadnezzar took Daniel and other Jews into captivity. When I tracked down that scribe, it was more than an academic exercise for me." Tallis studied his hands. "He's one of my distant relatives."

Akilah tipped his head. "When I was a child, my grandparents told me stories about a Danyal in Babylon. How he wrote about a Son of Man, a good king from God, that would rule forever. A kingdom that couldn't be destroyed. Some corner of my childhood heart felt the stories were more than adventure tales, but my family's beliefs smothered that curiosity for decades. Studying the star and reading Isaiah's words rekindled that spark." He clasped his hands, as if anticipating good tidings. "Your relative told you the Danyal stories?"

"They're more than stories. They're true. They're history. And prophecy."

Akilah swallowed a lump in his throat. "That changed how you viewed our study ... and finding Yeshua?"

"I met that relative. He told me about his faith and said he'd send me information to aid our study. As you saw, his message arrived heavily damaged. But what he'd already told me made more sense than any religion I'd studied or served. The Hebrews' God is concerned more about relationship than ritual. At least, that's how He intends it to be. Not everyone practices that."

Akilah shot Tallis an incredulous look. "The day after we found Yeshua, I wrestled with that same thing at the oasis. Remember? But you had reconciled the matter in your heart long before then. Why didn't you say something?"

"All your decisions about your study had to remain objective. As leader, you had to act on behalf of the entire caravan. I couldn't risk influencing your work. Moreover, what a person believes about Yeshua is their decision alone to make."

"You could have died ... I never would have known."

"I'm here, so don't walk down that path." Tallis trained his sights on the land passing by.

Akilah sighed. The conversation was over. Three years ago, Tallis had entrusted Akilah with knowledge of his past military career. Today he had shared his roots. But he still harbored secrets—including one wrapped in a bandage.

Chapter 56

The Great Library

When the caravan arrived at their lodgings in Alexandria, Akilah expected to pay for room and board, but the caravansary's owner said all expenses had been paid for a week. Another provision from Ibn or the people of influence he knew. Akilah was certain Ibn wasn't his real name. It wasn't even a proper full name—only the first part of a name. But he said nothing because Tallis maintained the man's intentions were honorable.

Rashidi could barely contain himself about visiting the Musaeum, which included the Great Library of Alexandria.

"We have a week here," Akilah said. "Make the most of it."

Tallis offered to stay at the caravansary to supervise the servants. That seemed odd. The library reportedly held the original Greek translations of all the Hebrew scriptures—the Septuagint. Tallis would be enthralled to dig into those writings. But standard practice was for one of the Wise Men to stay with the caravan at all times, and Tallis looked tired, so Akilah shelved his concern.

Rashidi reached for his Magi robes and exhaled audibly. "I was born for this moment."

Akilah stayed his colleague's hand. "Better if we wear the clothes Ibn gave us."

"You said we couldn't present our papers. It'll be hard to gain entry to the Musaeum or study there if we don't identify as Magi somehow."

"Precisely. We should remain anonymous. But we can look our best." Akilah smiled. "Let's go."

The moment they exited the caravansary, foreign languages engulfed them. Egyptian, Roman, Greek, Persian, and Hebrew culture surrounded them in grand edifices of sandstone, marble, and granite. "Find the Meson Pedion," Akilah said. "That street should take us to the library complex. It's in the Royal Quarter near the harbor."

The lighthouse on the island of Pharos towered in the distance, its mirrors shooting beams brighter than the noonday sun from the top tier of its 400-foot height. Akilah shielded his eyes as he peered in that direction.

The Musaeum complex was impossible to miss—a sprawling campus of Greek-style buildings and gardens linked by porticos and paved walks. Akilah spotted open lecture halls, a zoo, formal botanical garden, and buildings he presumed to be banquet halls and the medical school he'd heard of. Smaller buildings flanked the perimeter—likely housing for staff, groundskeepers, and visiting scholars. The grandest courtyard with the largest colonnades drew the visitor to the center of the campus. To the library.

Akilah stepped back to let Rashidi open the library's massive doors.

In unison, the two caught their breath. Light bathed a domed atrium, lifted on intricately chiseled pillars. Elegant marble statues of the world's greatest thinkers stood on exquisite mosaic floor tiles. But the seemingly endless walls of scrolls transfixed Akilah. Floor to ceiling, the only breaks in their expanse were vents, spaced at regular intervals, for circulating air around the volumes. Almost out of sight, more rooms stretched in every direction. He pictured connecting buildings housing more volumes. No library could compare to this.

Rashidi remained glued to the floor, his eyes closed, a rapturous smile on his face.

"You have to open your eyes before you can find something to read," Akilah whispered.

Chapter 57

Grandiosity

Three hours later, back at the caravansary

"Unbelievable." Rashidi tore off his turban. "I told you we should have worn our Magi robes. No papers, no one to vouch for us, no Magi robes, no entry. Now if we try to reenter wearing them, the head librarian will deem us imposters. What nerve to dismiss us and suggest we go to the annex—the public library. Who does he think he is? A god?"

He had words for his anger, but not the depths of his anguish. With a dismissive declaration, the head librarian had dashed Rashidi's hopes of Egypt embracing who he was, what he'd accomplished, and what he could have contributed to the Musaeum's holdings.

Akilah flapped his hands helplessly against his sides. "I know this is a disappointing setback—"

"Setback?" Rashidi shouted. "Is there any hallway in your head wide enough to comprehend how it feels to be the fourth generation of my family that's been denied access to Alexandria's Great Library? This entire city was designed to be

243

the world's greatest center for knowledge and learning. *Learning for everybody but me."*

"I—"

"Leave me alone." Rashidi seethed as he paced the floor of the Magi's shared sleeping room. He headed for the door.

"Where are you going?"

"Back to my roots," Rashidi snapped.

"We should always travel in pairs. I can go with you," Akilah offered.

"Where's Tallis?"

"Inventorying supplies with Hakeem."

"Do what you want."

Huffing, Rashidi strode down the street. Akilah, being a head taller than Rashidi, had no trouble catching up.

Rashidi stopped in the forecourt of an Egyptian temple his parents had frequented when he was a child. The exterior was more splendid than he remembered—probably because his adult-height gaze could take in the full height of the soaring columns topped with palm leaf capitals flanking the area. Reliefs of gods carved into stone gleamed golden in the early afternoon sun.

Life after Egypt had weaned him from such grandeur. The religion Rashidi upheld as part of Magi society was devoid of temples. But his teenage years in Harran were minus temples as well. His parents clung to their Egyptian roots and refused to conform to Harran's religion, even though the city was the center of worship for the "king of the gods," the moon god Sin. Although Rashidi never set foot in a Sin temple, he couldn't forget the metallic stench of blood from its sacrifices. Perhaps that had contributed to the city's booming perfume business.

He passed through the temple's forecourt into its vestibule. Again, its architecture commanded him to look up. Floor to ceiling, every column spoke through hieroglyphics. Carvings and paintings on every square foot of wall space shouted the necessity of worship and ritual. Kings making sacrifices. Gods pouring sacred water over kings. A king laying the temple cornerstone.

Donkey dung. Akilah had followed Rashidi into the Hall of Consecration. He pursed his lips, reminding himself to be civil to his superior regardless of his present anger toward him.

"That's odd," Rashidi said more to himself than anyone else. "Attendants should be here, waiting to pour holy water over each worshipper—for a fee."

"Many pardons for my ignorance, but what is the function of these vessels?" Akilah gestured to stations of urns with slots in the top.

Unwilling to admit he didn't know, Rashidi ignored Akilah. He confidently pulled a coin from his money pouch and dropped it in the slot. In response, water trickled from a spigot at the bottom of the urn. He lunged to catch some of it in his hands.

Akilah looked bemused. "These dispensers charge to give you holy water?" He shook his head. "It'll never catch on."

Flustered, Rashidi searched for an attendant.

He wandered from the Hall of Consecration to the temple library. Akilah followed at a respectful distance, but Rashidi waved him away. "You've already gone too far. You're not allowed in this part of the temple."

Rashidi paused at the library's entrance, flanked by a large sandstone relief of Seshat, the Egyptian goddess of writing and wisdom. "Can you help me?" he whispered.

Perhaps his voice carried farther than he realized because a female temple attendant in body-skimming, semi-transparent linen seemed to appear out of thin air.

Rashidi shook off his momentary astonishment. The

temple's laboratory, where the priests mixed incense and perfumes in preparation for rituals, was near the library.

She offered Rashidi a shallow bowl with a chunk of resinous material in it. "Come this way to burn your incense and make your petition." The attendant motioned toward an antechamber. "If the gods are pleased with your prayers, they will grant you an audience."

Chapter 58

The Prodigal

Akilah admired the wall murals as he worked his way back to the entrance of the Hall of Consecration. Secretly, he wanted learn more about those holy water dispensers. Rashidi's time spent in worship would provide ample time for Akilah to surreptitiously examine how they worked.

Arguing ahead of him curtailed his aspirations.

"The forecourt is for public worship. How did you get past the vestibule into the Hall of Consecration?" A male attendant's voice rose shrilly. "You're disturbing *ma'at* and inciting the gods' wrath."

"You're disturbing *me.*"

Akilah knew that voice. It belonged to his cousin's wayward servant, Tahrea.

"Your dispenser doesn't work. I put a coin in, but no holy water came out," Tahrea said heatedly.

Akilah meandered toward the attendant as a casual observer.

"You desecrated a sacrificial vessel. Where did you get the coin you used?" the attendant demanded.

"None of your business," Tahrea spat back. "My coin should be as good as the next person's."

Akilah approached the dispute. "Attendant, if I may … Perhaps this young man has another coin identical to the one he used. If so, that might help us solve the problem."

Glaring, Tahrea pulled a copper coin from his flat money pouch.

"That's not the right currency," the attendant grumbled. "Didn't you see the exchange booth near the courtyard pylons?"

Tahrea scowled but bit his lip.

"May I see the coin?" Akilah extended his hand and locked eyes momentarily with Tahrea.

He held up the coin and squinted. "This appears to have a bit of electrum on it, and the edge of the coin is irregular. Roughened, with a tiny ding in it." Akilah turned to the attendant. "The electrum suggests the coins may have been run over by an official's chariot. The weight of the wheel pressing on the coin, especially if rocks were underneath it, could have caused the blemish. If that happened to both coins, the defect might have caused the other coin to jam in the slot."

Akilah's deductive reasoning was lost on the attendant. His kohl-outlined eyes narrowed. "You stole the money." He grabbed Tahrea by the arm. "You didn't find those coins on the ground. You knocked someone to the ground and took them."

"My good sir." Akilah's voice resounded like a thunderclap. "We are in a temple, not a court. And you have absolutely no evidence for that accusation."

"He's filthy … he's been fighting … he's not fit to be here." The attendant's anger soared higher through the hall with each sentence. "Ma'at is ruined."

Tahrea's scowl deepened. "I don't know what ma'at is, but I didn't break it." He looked around wildly. Akilah grabbed Tahrea's other arm. Bolting would make matters much worse.

"Let's discuss this outside where we won't disturb anyone, yes?" Akilah said with a smile.

"I can't leave the temple until my time of service is finished."

"Quite right." Akilah shot Tahrea a "don't move" glare, then turned to the attendant. "I'll have a chat with this upstart regarding temple etiquette and protocol. We apologize if this has delayed you in providing service to others."

When the attendant finally let go of Tahrea's arm, Akilah hustled the glowering runaway through the Hall of Consecration.

"Why doesn't that attendant have eyebrows?" Tahrea whispered as Akilah whisked him out the front door. "And what is ma'at?"

"Harmony. Balance. Order. Very important to Egyptians."

Akilah kept a firm grip on Tahrea as he strode past the forecourt and pylons. At the street, he stopped and spun his fugitive servant around to face him. "How long have you been here?"

"Two days."

"Doing what?"

"Deciding whether to go in."

Akilah tightened his grip on Tahrea's arm. "I don't believe you. Speak truth."

"The temple is a good place to steal food. It has gardens to grow food for the gods. But that's not the only reason I'm here."

"Then what?"

"I … I have to try to get right."

"Get what right?"

"The gods are punishing me for leaving the caravan. I want to get right with the gods so they'll change things."

Akilah drew back a pace at this new side of Tahrea. Disturbingly, it gave him a better view of the deep bruises on his servant's arms and legs. Fighting would not have caused such welts.

"Start over. Where did you go when you left Metariyeh?"

"Kher-Aha. I got work as a dock hand. I had agreed to work for a foreman for two years. But he wasn't ... I couldn't ..." Tahrea's voice faltered.

"Did he hurt you?" Akilah's voice sharpened to a spear point.

Tahrea's wide eyes spoke more than his words. "I stowed away on the biggest baris headed north to Alexandria. I wanted to find you. But I couldn't face you.

"That's why I need help from the gods," Tahrea continued. "I didn't have money for holy water, so I couldn't ask for help. I looked around and found these coins in the street." His voice trailed off.

"I didn't steal them. You don't have any reason to believe that. But here." He thrust the coins at Akilah.

He gently pushed Tahrea's hand aside. "What were you going to ask the gods to do?"

"Get the foreman to stop hunting me. I owe him money for defaulting on my contract." Tahrea choked and looked down. "And I wanted the gods to make a way for me to get back with the caravan."

Akilah rubbed his beard. Given the time frame, Tahrea may have stowed away on one of the baris that had brought the caravan to Alexandria. If only he had known ...

Once again, the yoke of leadership weighted Akilah. Tahrea had acted out of desperation to escape the caravan's tribulations. Rashidi wanted to make his way to Alexandria alone for much the same reason. Both had lost hope. To change their lot, they were willing to risk everything—even the possibility of being hurtled into worse situations. *Adonai, I did the best I could. It wasn't good enough. I couldn't keep everyone together. I couldn't keep their hopes up. I couldn't keep them safe. I didn't have the strength. Show me how to restore what's been taken from us. Or restore what's been lost as only You can.*

Akilah cleared his throat. "If memory serves, I said, 'Don't return to this place'—'this place' being Metariyeh."

Tears filled Tahrea's eyes.

"Your actions in Metariyeh were damaging in many ways. You'll have to earn our trust again. That will take time. Some people in the caravan may never reach that point. You'll have to live with that. I will take you back and put you under my protection—on three conditions. One, you tell me the foreman's name. If he finds you before I find him, he settles his account with me—not you. Understood?"

Tahrea nodded.

"Two, he has a right to exact money from you if your contract states you must pay him for time you should have worked but didn't. You won't be released from his service until that happens. I'll pay what you owe." Akilah paused. That meant selling another cloak pin. He shook off the thought. It had to be done. He had to return or make restitution to Farzaneh for everything she had loaned him, including her servants. Selling another cloak pin might have happened anyway to pay for necessities if they were delayed in leaving Alexandria.

"Consider this a loan. You'll receive only a fourth of the wages you earned before—until your debt to me is paid. Agreed?"

Tahrea swallowed hard.

"And three, running from problems doesn't solve anything. *Stop running.*"

Akilah forced Tahrea to make eye contact with him. "Non-negotiable terms. Do you agree to them?"

"Yes." A breeze almost snatched his whisper.

"Good. Where are your belongings?"

"Hidden on the temple grounds."

"Let's get them."

"Wait." Tahrea froze in place. "I mean, I have to wait until

251

after nightfall when the attendants finish their work and go home."

"Hmm. The caravan's lodging is on the border of Alexandria's Greek and Egyptian quarters. A short walk from here. You can wash yourself first."

"May I ask you something?"

"Depends."

"Why do the temple attendants put jewelry and makeup on the gods' statues each day? And dress them for bed at night? Why serve the gods food no one sees them eat? If a god is powerful enough to change the weather or live in a statue, why does the statue need to be carried everywhere?"

Firing questions at Akilah fueled some of Tahrea's former bravado. "And *why* do the temple attendants not have any eyebrows or eyelashes or body hair?"

Akilah didn't know whether to laugh or cry. Tahrea's resourcefulness and observational skills were keener than ever. Based on what Farzaneh had said, they were already well developed when she found him in Assur's streets.

"The attendants shave all their hair to keep themselves pure and free from disease. It's part of their cleanliness rituals," he explained.

"What about dressing the statues, putting them to bed, and—"

"We'll need a longer street for that."

Chapter 59

Acceptable

Rashidi finished his ritualistic preparations and waited for the priest to appear. Gone was his childhood marveling of the temple. With open eyes, he saw how every inch of it was designed to elicit awe, wonder, or fear. Impressive as it was, his adult heart saw the temple's overbearing proportions. The outrageous human and financial price to build it.

The Parthian Empire's official religion didn't worship in edifices. But his Magi duties included serving other religions in opulent temples. Why had that never bothered him before now?

The female attendant announced the gods had accepted Rashidi's libation and sacrifice. He was granted the privilege of praying directly to the god.

An Egyptian priest appeared before double doors more than three times his height. With lavish praise to the gods, he intoned their favor. His incantations for one to appear rose to a fever pitch until the doors slowly swung outward.

"Behold!" the priest thundered. He dropped to his knees and pressed his face to the floor.

Rashidi did the same. Surprisingly, heat from the sandstone

slabs met his cheek. The altar fire couldn't transfer that much heat to the floor. Stone dissipated heat, providing cooling relief even during Egypt's hot summers. He dared glance up. A huge statue advanced toward him, seemingly moving on its own.

The priest stretched his right arm in Rashidi's direction and raised his left to the statue. "I am your oracle—the medium through which the gods will speak. Ask what you will. I will tell you their answer."

"I seek enlightenment."

Chapter 60

Steam Power

Rashidi had had enough of this day. First the crushing rejection in the Great Library and now his disturbing experience in the temple. He doubted very much that the oracle's utterances came from the gods. He could have concocted those words himself or recited them from a book of rituals. A wise god would have imparted specifics—including why Akilah had vanished and where he'd gone.

The Wise Men always had a plan for where to meet if they got separated. In anger, Rashidi spurned that thought and walked his own route instead.

He turned onto Canopus Way. *Great. Even on this street, I can't get away from people who act like they're gods.* In homage to Alexander the Great, the main east-west boulevard of Alexandria aligned with the star Sothis during the solstice that had marked the conqueror's birth. That omen, announcing Alexander as a god-king, had helped him become pharaoh of Egypt.

Lost in thought, Rashidi strode into the sixty-cubit-wide street, ignoring the babel approaching him. Child-sized hands and adult shoulders buffeted him as excited youngsters and watchful adults raced across the thoroughfare. A boy slammed into him and sped by without slowing. More chattering children and adults calling cautions streamed behind the boy.

The throng stopped at a nearby corner. Their prattle diminished to wondrous gasps at a strange sight—a spinning copper ball that quickly became a blur of motion, punctuated by steam shooting from two small right-angled nozzles.

"What is it?" Rashidi asked the nearest adult.

"An aeolipile," the person replied. "Have you been living in a cave? It's the latest high-priced curiosity for children."

Rashidi studied the toy. Its premise was ingenious. If a tiny boiler heating water in a copper ball with steam vents could make the ball rotate, what could a bigger version do?

His imagination spun faster than the aeolipile. If steam could be harnessed on a large enough scale, it could be used in building—to lift, move, and position heavy materials. The burden of hauling limestone would no longer rest on the backs of men. But if steam power eliminated people's jobs, what other work would they do? An empire's economy thrived on its ambitious building projects.

His speeding thoughts crashed to a halt. Panic clawed his chest.

Steam could open a fifteen-cubit temple door. And move a statue.

He stumbled into a run. "Was that a trick?" Rashidi yelled at the sky, his anger hot as the water inside the copper ball. "Is my heritage a sham? Are its priests deceivers? Is religion merely illusion?"

He ran faster. Dread chased him like death. All his work on comparative religions crumbled around him like sandstone in an earthquake. If Egypt worshipped gods that weren't real, did other cultures do the same? Were all religions just vain beliefs and useless practices?

He barely realized he'd reached the caravansary until he almost ran into Tallis talking with Ibn.

Chapter 61

Caged

Flora and fauna exhibits on the Musaeum's grounds

For Rashidi, the week inched along like a slow-flowing mudslide. Although he was free to read any volume in the Serapeum, Alexandria's public library, he resented doing so. Scouring its shelves was poor man's fare compared to the feast out of his reach in the Great Library at the center of the Musaeum's campus.

Akilah seemed content walking the grounds with the servants and giving them informal lessons in natural history. Rashidi grudgingly joined them and smirked. Despite Akilah's brilliance, he was a rather boring tutor. He couldn't capture the servants' attention in the botanical gardens.

The group moved on to the zoo and its vast collection of exotic animals. Akilah managed to dull the servants' fascination with the animals by droning on about how Ptolemy II created the zoo, how wealthy Egyptians kept exotic wild beasts, and how Rome had copied that practice. Pragmatism, not history, held the servants' interest. They interrupted Akilah frequently with questions like, "If someone had a pet cheetah and removed their teeth and claws so it wouldn't bite them, how could the animal eat?"

A roar drew the servants to a large enclosure. "What is it?" they said.

None of the servants had seen a bear before. The large brown beast seemed as curious about them as they were about it. As they neared the enclosure, the bear lumbered toward them and raised up on its hind legs, deep-throated rumbles pulsing from its gullet.

"Stay back," Akilah warned. His previous travels had introduced him to bears, and he knew their strength. But a servant reached his hand through the enclosure. A growl, then a roar erupted from the beast. Akilah snatched the servant away a second before the bear slammed against the barrier.

"That's enough for today." Akilah hurried the servants away from the area. "No need to anger the groundskeepers as well."

Rashidi doubted the bear could have seriously hurt anyone. One of its legs was chained.

"That bear is like us," one servant said. "Not free to go where it wants to."

"We'll be back in Persia soon," Akilah offered.

"That won't change anything except the scenery," the servant said.

Akilah looked at Rashidi for support, but he shrugged unsympathetically. Rashidi couldn't change the servants' lot. He was trapped in his own cage.

Chapter 62

Revelations at Sea

True to his vow, Ibn procured a ship for Akilah and the caravan. Large enough to be a grain ship, on this trip it carried only human and animal cargo. The sea journey was a milestone in conveying the caravan closer to home. Akilah finally allowed himself some measure of confidence in believing he could return most of Farzaneh's camels and all her servants to her.

He wanted to learn how Ibn and this mysterious captain were connected, but first he needed to show his colleagues something. Akilah motioned them to a far corner of the ship and unfolded a cloth, revealing an oversized cloak pin.

"It's stunning," Rashidi said. "A unique design. Where did you get it?"

"I had three of these made to commemorate our journey to find the child-king," Akilah said.

Tallis touched the upside-down triangle that formed the foot of the pin. Its glass and brass inlays shimmered in the sunlight. "Knowing you, each part of this design means something."

261

"It was meant to."

"And now?"

Akilah sighed. "It doesn't seem important because we can't share in it. I traded one cloak pin for our lodging in Ayla. When I found Tahrea, I used another to pay off his debt to the foreman who'd mistreated him. This is the only one of the three left."

Tallis touched Akilah's arm. "It's an extraordinary gesture. Tell us what the design means."

"The triangle is the three of us. The glass and brass in the triangle are reflections of the light and truth we set out to find. The arched segment connecting the triangle to the half-circle is our journey. The half-circle represents enlightenment at the end of the journey. The red spinels in the half-circle symbolize divine presence."

He folded the cloth around the cloak pin. "We will always carry the light of that star and the truth about Yeshua in us. But our journey hasn't ended, and I may need this last pin to finance another expense yet to come."

"You should keep it. Wouldn't you agree, Rashidi?"

"He paid for it, so it's always been his to do with as he saw fit. Nothing could have prepared us for all we needed on this trip."

Tallis nodded. "What we do have, we should cherish. Above all, life."

"This journey has taught me to hold onto possessions more lightly than I did in the past," Akilah said.

Rashidi turned away and stared at the sea. "Some things can never be held onto."

Tallis cleared his throat. "The captain says we're making good time. We should reach Edessa sooner than expected."

Akilah enlisted Ibn to introduce him to the captain. When he asked how they knew each other, the captain would say only that Ibn had treated him and a passenger after his ship sank in a storm near Crete.

Ibn nudged the captain. "You can speak freely. This person may know the man whose life you saved. Your passengers in the storm were Magi. Akilah is too."

Akilah didn't grasp the connection until the captain mentioned the reason for the trip—escorting a high-ranking Magus into exile in Macedonia.

"Did you learn their names?"

"The angry one got washed overboard in the storm. I can't remember his name, but it sounded like a snake's hiss."

Akilah's stomach heaved. Sassanak. "And the other?"

"I know him only as Gadiel."

Akilah turned aside for a moment to catch his breath. "Did he survive?"

"I was with him the first few weeks after we were rescued. Ibn treated both of us for injuries. Then Gadiel was taken somewhere else. I hope he still lives."

Akilah had left for Assur without knowing the outcome of the Chief's investigation. Sassanak must have been tried and convicted. Exile would have been a lenient sentence.

Akilah stared at Ibn and the captain. "Gadiel and I are … family. When I left Persia, we weren't on good terms. What else can you tell me? Please, I must know."

Ibn nodded to the captain then excused himself to check on someone in steerage who didn't feel well.

The captain rubbed his head as if friction would help his recall. "We were both bedridden from our injuries, so we had time to talk about many things." He laughed ruefully. "When you can't get out of bed, you're a captive audience for the person next to you—whether you want to hear what they have to say or not.

"During a particularly difficult week, Gadiel mentioned his son and someone named Fakhri. I gathered he was some sort of priest or prophet. Are you Gadiel's son?"

Akilah nodded.

"Shortly before Fakhri died, he predicted you were destined for greatness but no one would appreciate it for many years. Gadiel didn't know how to sort that, but he never stopped turning it over in his mind."

The captain shook his head. "People can say strange things after a head injury. Gadiel was in great pain too. Not always coherent."

When Akilah left for Jerusalem, Fakhri had prophesied about a coming dual reality. Akilah had dismissed it at the time. In hindsight, his mentor's words echoed what the Hebrew prophet Isaiah had described about the child-king being God and man at the same time. Maybe Fakhri had understood Akilah's quest all along. His final prediction certainly fit Akilah's current circumstances. Waves of loss crashed over him. He would never get the chance to tell his mentor that he was right.

"Gadiel was absolutely clear about one thing. He hoped you would succeed in finding what you were looking for."

"He did?"

The captain nodded. His gaze clouded. "I irritated him with my talk."

"In what way?"

"I told him why we never should have survived the storm. Nothing can control the sea. But the way the ship broke apart ... where the current carried us ... Only Adonai could have saved us. When I told Gadiel I was a God-fearer, that unsettled him.""

Adonai. Akilah's heart beat faster. "Do you believe Isaiah's prophecies about Immanuel who would come into the world as a child and be an eternal king?"

"Yes." The captain straightened, his eyes wide. "Did you—"

"My colleagues and I searched for the child-king." Tears

stung Akilah's eyes. "He's real. We found Him and worshipped Him. Adonai brought us through every trial we faced on our journey. I need to find my father and tell him that."

Akilah stopped, dumbfounded. That was the first time he'd uttered the word "father" in three decades. He prayed his father would live long enough to hear Akilah speak it.

Chapter 63

Proposal

Petra

A ntipas traveled to Petra without fanfare, accompanied by only two bodyguards, Varinius, and one other advisor. When they crossed his southern border of Perea into Nabataea, two of Aretas's men met Antipas's group to guide them to Petra's palace. He grudgingly admitted to himself it was good they had. The desert canyons they wound through were one tortuous maze after another.

A rivulet of sweat snaked from his neck down his back. Overhead, a sliver of azure sky broke through the heights of the burnt-orange cliffs hugging the twisting gorge they'd traveled in for the past half hour. Galilee had desert and mountains, but its climate was far milder than Petra's. Traveling all this way to meet the Nabataeans' king had better produce more results than goodwill and sweat.

Antipas shifted in his saddle and hoped he could bathe before seeing King Aretas IV. In this desert, a bath would probably be a basin of water. Surely nothing like the Roman baths he enjoyed in Galilee.

Antipas studied the buildings he passed on Petra's main thoroughfare. Lines more angular than Greek or Roman architecture, construction more primitive than Persian architecture, but designs possessing a stark beauty befitting of the environment. Not to his liking, but he appreciated the inhabitants' resolve in conquering their surroundings. If the Nabataeans' king had bred an equally resourceful, strong daughter, she might be worthy of being his wife. He would tolerate the desert heat to secure her.

Like other buildings, Petra's palace was carved into a sandstone cliff. Its surprisingly large interior offered cool relief from the sun's intensity.

A servant ushered Antipas and his group into private quarters, its stone walls swirling with mineral hues of blue, black, cream, and rose. To his surprise, the room had indoor plumbing and an ample supply of water for bathing. The servant instructed Antipas to bathe first, as only he would meet with the king. The others would wait where they were.

Herod would have derided the scale of the throne room deep within the palace, but Antipas strangely liked it. Minimal pomp, no superfluous people scraping and bowing. Other than a guard at the door, Antipas had an audience alone with the king. An environment conducive for transacting business.

Aretas IV made it clear he had no time for posturing, so Antipas ignored all the openers Varinius had suggested. Instead, he made his point directly. "You seek a faster trade route through Herod's former kingdom, particularly from Arabia to

Damascus. I control lands in the north and south and can provide you safe passage north to the Great Sea in return for a fair trade tariff."

"Your brother controls Damascus. Greeks control the Decapolis. You can't guarantee safety through either area." Aretas's knowledge of geography and recent power shifts was flawless.

"You need traverse only the northwest corner of the Ten Cities," Antipas countered. "My lands abut both sides of that sliver. The Decapolis functions independently under the Greeks as long as Rome allows it, and I have Rome's ear."

"Rome thinks well of Nabataea too … for the present."

"Yes, my king. But I can secure what you need and will deal with my indecisive brother who rules Damascus."

"That remains to be seen. What do you want in return?"

"To live in harmony along our shared border."

"By doing what?"

"Joining forces. I humbly ask that you pledge your daughter to me in marriage." Antipas knelt before the king and bowed his head.

Rustling of a date palm near Aretas's throne disturbed the crucial moment.

The king turned to his right. "Phasaelis? How did you get in here? Where is your nursemaid?"

A low-hanging palm branch bent. A girl, little more than a toddler, peeked from behind it.

Antipas turned his head aside to hide his amusement. Her antic reminded him of his childhood eavesdropping in the fountain room connecting Herod's banqueting halls. Clever girl.

"My daughter is spirited and inventive. Her mind never stops working." Aretas motioned for Antipas to rise. "Phasaelis, come here."

The little girl obligingly slid from behind the palm and approached her father. He scooped her into his lap. "Phasaelis, this is Antipas, ruler of Galilee and Perea, lands north of my kingdom. Would you like to know where those lands are?"

Aretas's title for Antipas wasn't lost on him. Calling him "ruler" instead of "tetrarch" had earned Aretas greater respect in Antipas's eyes.

Phasaelis nodded her response but kept her eyes trained on Antipas. Not with childish curiosity but complete fearlessness. Displaying such confidence for one so young moved him. He needed a strong, resourceful woman by his side who could handle the Herodian court. She could be that person.

A woman, flustered enough to be the nursemaid, raced into the throne room and prostrated herself before Aretas. "My king, it won't happen again."

"I doubt you can keep that promise." He deposited his daughter in front of the woman and waved them off but smiled as they left.

Returning his attention to Antipas, the Nabataean king leaned forward in his seat. "You offer something of interest to me, so I will consider your proposal. I will send my final word to you in a week. But know this. If I sign a trade agreement you do not keep, your land will suffer."

He rose and descended the throne's steps until his chin was level with Antipas's forehead. "My daughter means everything to me." Tipping his head down, he spoke with hot breaths into Antipas's ear. "If she becomes your wife and you mistreat her in the slightest way, I will not rest until you have paid ten thousand times over for your lapse of judgment. I will use every resource at my disposal to rain utter destruction upon you."

He returned to his throne and sat. "Enjoy whatever respite you need before returning to your kingdom."

The palace guest quarters in Petra

Varinius rose from a pile of cushions. "Well?"

"The deal is assured," Antipas said.

"Then consider our deal consummated as well. I will take your position to oversee the development of the Ornament of Galilee."

Chapter 64

Path to Sepphoris

Somewhere in Egypt

Mary fussed over the soup burbling over the cooking pit, but no amount of hovering could add more vegetables to the broth. She gently pulled her stirring spoon from Yeshua's grip and hitched him on her hip. As she turned away from the fire, she caught sight of Joseph in the distance. Hopefully he had news of work. Work might mean they could stay here a little longer. In a hut. But the tiny abode felt like a palace.

Ever since they'd left Bethlehem, "home" had been camping in a cave or a shelter—except for the groundskeeper's house they'd rented briefly at Metariyeh.

As much as she wanted to make this hut feel like a home, she trusted Joseph's divine sense of their need to keep moving.

When Adonai had told him to flee to Egypt, the reason was clear—Herod was intent on killing Yeshua. Mary's heart had split in two when she heard Herod had slaughtered life's youngest in and near Bethlehem. News from Judaea traveled in rapid waves to Egypt, and Joseph wanted to stay ahead of their crest.

Joseph said Adonai had promised to tell them when it was safe to leave Egypt. She longed for that day.

How can I honor this godly man who's already sacrificed so much for Yeshua and me? Adonai, please show me how.

"Herod has died," Joseph reported as he washed his feet outside the hut's door. "Now Archelaus rules Judaea. His cruelty to Jews is already wagging tongues. I'm sorry, Mary, but it's too dangerous to return to Judaea."

She squeezed Yeshua, wriggling in her arms. Joseph's news dashed all hopes of returning to their cozy little home between Bethlehem and Artus. That blessed place would always occupy a special spot in her heart, but only as memories—especially the memory of the glorious light that filled their cottage during the Wise Men's visit.

Joseph wadded the towel he'd used to dry his feet. "I can't give you the home you and Yeshua deserve. But in time, it will happen." He stroked her cheek. "Today I secured three weeks of work, so we can enjoy staying here for a while."

She leaned into his callused caress and tried to make light of the situation. "As long as you're back in time for Shabbat."

"I always am." Joseph smiled, but Mary didn't. As skilled as he was, moving so often kept him struggling to support their family.

Joseph tossed Yeshua in the air and caught him, prompting squeals of delight. Between boyish giggles, Joseph detailed the work he'd secured. Mary nodded but glanced past him, through a gap in the curtain that marked their sleeping area. Her eyes settled on a nondescript storage chest.

He followed her gaze. "No one can know we have those gifts," he whispered tenderly in her ear. "We use them only bit by bit, for others first. Frankincense and myrrh when healing is needed. The gold ..." His voice turned raspy. "The gold will buy scrolls of the holy writings for Yeshua when he starts Torah school."

Torah school where? They had talked about returning to Judaea to settle down. Now that wasn't an option. They might live in Nazareth in Galilee, but that posed its own challenges—including questions from relatives. Joseph favored that option, saying steady work was available nearby in Sepphoris.

Any dream of a real home seemed more distant than the east was from the west.

Joseph tipped Mary's chin upward until their eyes met. She looked deep into his sable eyes, full of quiet confidence no matter what the future held for them. He pressed Yeshua to his chest and wrapped his other arm around Mary.

In the safety of that holy circle, no one needed to speak their thoughts. They'd already had ample time to talk through them since trekking to Egypt. If Mary outlived her husband and son, the gold would provide for her.

Chapter 65

Advice

Farzaneh's regimen of tipping Gadiel on a plank helped, but didn't eliminate his lung congestion. Even so, he seemed strong enough for short daily walks in the back courtyard. Not that he made the task easy. He adamantly resisted walking with a servant. He insisted on walking only when the household wouldn't witness his unsteady, uncoordinated gait.

Farzaneh understood, but her land management responsibilities varied day to day, not to mention her new duties as envoy. When she told Gadiel she couldn't commit to walking with him at a set time, the news provoked an outburst of anger, an emotional display unlike him.

She tried to hide her worries about him. As Queen Helena had said, she couldn't let family matters interfere with her duties.

Still, Farzaneh's appointment as an envoy pleased Gadiel, and it seemed to calm his thoughts, so she walked with him every opportunity she could. Eager to tap the fount of

277

knowledge within him, she hoped that asking his advice on several pressing topics might focus him.

Other than mentioning a few Megistanes she could trust, he spoke in more general terms than she would have liked. Perhaps he still was bound by an oath to not divulge sensitive government matters. Maybe he was trying to protect her. She prayed his mind wasn't slipping. But one piece of his advice etched itself in her mind. "You will have to learn new ways to balance courage with compromise."

Courage, not compromise, had seen Farzaneh through every challenge life had thrown at her. Hard work, not trade-offs, had garnered her gains.

When she asked Gadiel how to strike that balance, he answered, "Exercise courage always. Exercise compromise only when necessary."

Neither seemed to work for her in her first trip to Ctesiphon as Adiabene's envoy.

The king's advisors in Ctesiphon had postured, digressed, and stalled. Some derisively said she should speak to a regional satrap instead.

Gadiel had been a Megistane for more than four decades. She couldn't imagine him acting like those advisors. Unless he was very different in and out of the royal court, she had always known him to be so straightforward and concise he often sounded curt.

She had faced Queen Helena with fear as she related the little she had to report. If all her trips to the royal capital would be as unproductive as this one, what hope did she have of achieving anything as Adiabene's envoy?

Farzaneh couldn't wait to retreat to the safety and comfort of Elyakim's home.

"How did you fare in Ctesiphon? Tell me about your first presentation as Adiabene's envoy." Elyakim clasped his hands in anticipation.

Farzaneh plopped onto the cushion Eliana offered her and summarized her lack of results. "Queen Helena was gracious and said, 'these things take time.' Time is our most limited commodity. Apparently a foreign concept to Parthia's officials. Why would anyone want to be in government?"

"Some are born into it." A half-smile played about Elyakim's lips.

Farzaneh was too busy fuming to appreciate his gentle joke. "I don't see how anything passes through Parthia's legal system. Whatever does must get tarnished along the way."

"We hope Parthia's advisors exercise a right sense of justice when they write Persian law—because not even the king can change it after it's enacted." Elyakim straightened, his eyes intense. "What Adonai writes in His book is penned in perfect justice. He can't change His Word because He can't change His character. But He takes another step to do what human law cannot. In His love, He blots out our transgressions. Isaiah said it this way, 'I have swept away your offenses like a cloud, your sins like the morning mist. Return to me, for I have redeemed you.'"[1]

Farzaneh rubbed the fresh scar on her forehead. Many of Isaiah's writings were too deep for her to comprehend. But what she did understand seemed to hold truth for every corner of her life.

Elyakim radiated the smile he reserved for talking about sacred Hebrew writings. A smile that rose from the depths of his being until it lit his entire face. "If this house was burning and I could save only one possession, it would be my scroll of Isaiah."

---

1. Isaiah 44:22 (NIV)

Farzaneh's hand paused on her forehead. Javad had saved her husband's scroll of Isaiah because it was his favorite. Apparently Adonai had a greater reason to protect that scroll, even before the orchard fire.

"Don't leave Isaiah's message on the doorstep of the legal system," Elyakim continued. "Adonai tells us to pardon—to forgive—those who wrong us."

As much as she enjoyed her talks with Elyakim, Farzaneh wanted to relax, not learn more about the Hebrews' ways. Besides, the notion didn't sound fair. "The person who caused the hurt should ask for forgiveness, not me."

"Whether that happens or not, when you pardon them, it releases your hurt to Adonai. He carries it away so it won't harm you any longer. You still bear the consequences of someone's wrongdoing, but it loses its power to darken your thoughts and actions."

She shook her head. "That isn't justice."

"Justice is right-proportioned judgment. Adonai is just, but He is also love. We can understand His ways only when we view His actions through His eyes."

"Isaiah also says Adonai forgives and forgets what we do against Him.[2] That's impossible for anyone to do. No one can forget past wrongs."

"True. He casts all our wrongdoings behind His back[3] and removes them as far as the east is from the west.[4] You may not forget, but you don't have to keep recalling it or letting it influence you. Adonai constantly uses broken things to create something new and good that serves His purposes."

"I don't understand." Bitterness crackled in her voice. Forgiveness sounded absurdly one-sided.

---

2. Isaiah 43:25 (BSB)
3. Isaiah 38:17 (ESV)
4. Psalm 103:12 (ESV)

"Let me show you." Elyakim unwound the scarf he always wore about his neck. The final fold parted to reveal raised red scars.

Farzaneh gasped. "Who did that to you?"

"Romans who don't like Jews."

"How ... When?"

"What matters is the injustice started me on a journey to help displaced and persecuted people. If I had been more concerned about staying angry than letting Adonai work His perfect will through the pain, I would have become bitter. I wouldn't be doing what I'm doing today. And I would not have met people like Ihsan and you." He rewound the scarf and raised his hands skyward. "You see, Adonai's plans always reach far beyond what we can imagine."[5]

"If I forgive someone and nothing changes, then what? They may not change, and I might not feel different. How would that help anything?"

"Adonai promises to bless the obedience of forgiveness. The blessing may not come when you expect it, and when it does, you may not recognize it right away. But He is always true to His word. He will fulfill all His promises someday."

Farzaneh's stomach churned. She'd harbored ill will against Akilah and Gadiel for almost three decades. Understanding the reasons for their actions had seeped into her slowly, like the ground receiving raindrops dripped from flower petals. Reconciling Akilah's and Gadiel's actions was another matter. Replacing her thoughts about them, even harder. *Forgiving them?* That would take time.

---

5. Isaiah 64:3-4 (BSB)

Chapter 66

Home at Last

I bn left Akilah and his group at Edessa but made sure the caravan was well supplied. Adamant to the end about not trading any animals entrusted to him, Akilah sold his last cloak pin to buy six fresh, rested camels, plus new sandals for the servants. It was the practical thing to do. The caravan faced a month-long trip overland from Edessa to Persia. The fresh camels would carry the heaviest loads, while the servants could take turns riding on camels without loads. When the servants had to walk, they'd do so in comfort. And the loads on the camels' backs wouldn't weigh so heavy on Akilah's heart.

Akilah couldn't ignore how much time Ibn spent talking with Tallis before departing. They clearly shared a bond, but not necessarily one of friendship. Although Akilah took care to remain out of earshot of their conversations, their tones sounded serious, much like a complex business transaction.

Ibn vowed the caravan would have an uneventful trip. Akilah didn't know how anyone could make such a promise, but he welcomed the thought.

The trip home offered Akilah time to mull over all that had transpired. He couldn't reconcile everything he wanted to. He still questioned some of his decisions. He'd never discerned the purpose of the gift Haruz had given him when they left Ayla. How or where to use the decorative Hebrew symbol, a letter of its alphabet, remained a mystery. Tallis was withholding something from him. Rashidi resented him. Hopefully time would ease all strains and reveal all secrets.

The camels' plodding but sure gait carried them across fertile lowlands and majestic mountains. Akilah had almost forgotten the beauty of both. The Wilderness of Paran had ground a survivalist mentality into him that strove to keep his eyes downcast and his mind on edge. He would have to remind himself, as often as needed, that he no longer needed to brace for the next endurance test.

Rashidi was quieter than usual most of the way but shared with Akilah and Tallis his proposal for his next study. In a departure from his previous studies comparing world religions, he announced his idea for an engineering study to harness the power of steam to perform heavy labor. Akilah couldn't envision all of Rashidi's intentions, but he didn't doubt the scope of his aspirations. Tallis remained silent about his plans as part of Magi society.

Before they could settle back into their former daily routines, they would face an inquiry. Akilah prayed it wouldn't hinder his colleagues' careers. But the only prayer he could muster for himself was "help."

Akilah made mental inventories for Farzaneh and the Magi's Lower Council. He'd pay Farzaneh first, although he could never repay her in full. Her loaned resources had enabled him to make the trek to Jerusalem and beyond. He couldn't put a price on finding Yeshua.

The Royal Road led the caravan straight to the turnoff for the Magi complex. They crested a rise, bringing their destination into view as banners of ruby, citrine, amber, and lapis streamed across the evening sky. Akilah couldn't remember a more beautiful sunset. He paused at the junction. "My friends, we're home."

The procession stared in silence at the sight they'd dreamed of seeing again for so long.

Home. A hollow space in Akilah's heart. Magi society had filled that void for three decades. Now his future in it was uncertain. Reconciling the stūrīh's provisions with Farzaneh would change his notion of home as well, but in what way? Married Magi weren't required to live in its complex, yet they always lived nearby. Assur was hours from the Magi facility.

"Ready?" Tallis motioned toward the complex.

Despite his eagerness to return to the familiar, Akilah forced himself to remain practical. "When we arrive, would you and Malachi oversee stabling the animals? Hakeem and I need to conduct a final inventory and account for all I must return to my cousin."

"Consider it done," Tallis said.

"Thank you. I'm a bit preoccupied with returning all I owe her ... and paying for what I can't return."

"If you mean your cousin's camels and servants, your vision of 'all' is too small."

Akilah couldn't handle more than camels and servants yet.

Akilah stepped gingerly through the door to his quarters. He had chosen to not send word ahead of their arrival, so no welcoming party greeted him. No matter, he would enjoy the solace of familiar surroundings.

Or not.

Although his quarters appeared intact, his gut said someone had searched them.

Fatigue dissuaded him from conducting an exhaustive search to confirm his fears. He scanned a shelf of scrolls. All seemed to be there, but some had been read, apparently in haste. Smaller scrolls with cords left untied. Larger scrolls with leather thongs secured differently than he would have. Once again he was grateful he'd taken the stūrīh with him—even though his cat statue was a casualty of the trip.

Akilah squeezed the bridge of his nose. He had no more capacity to parse variables over which he had no control.

He idled about his study, wondering if the scourers would be able to clean his cypress rug so it could grace the room's floor again. Hah. He couldn't control even that minute detail.

He checked on Rashidi, who also suspected his room had been searched. But he didn't seem concerned. "When we didn't send word or return as planned, the Council had a legitimate reason to search our rooms to try to determine our whereabouts. That's a comforting thought, yes?

"Nothing is missing," Rashidi added. "I'm going to unpack. I can't wait to sleep in my own bed."

"Rest well."

Rashidi could be right in part, but someone seemed to have searched Akilah's room for more than maps or an itinerary. Although his memorabilia from previous journeys were on their proper shelves as he'd left them, some items had been scooted aside or removed and replaced. The lack of dust in their original spots silently testified they'd been disturbed recently.

Akilah would warn Tallis when he saw him at the stables.

Chapter 67

Restitution and Restoration

Akilah and his head servant, Hakeem, led a bedraggled line of camels and servants through the back of Farzaneh's grounds to the stables. Akilah's palms moistened as he clutched the inventory he'd penned. He owed his cousin much, with no means to repay it. His retirement allotment, Magi ring, cloak pins, and self-assurance were things of the past.

He hailed a stable boy to fetch Javad. He and Hakeem could sort what needed to happen next with Farzaneh's camels and servants. Akilah was free to walk away from that responsibility now. He should have celebrated the freedom. Instead, loss panged him.

He wasn't ready to face his cousin yet, so he strolled into the back courtyard. Some time alone should compose him for his next step. But two people at its far end interrupted that thought.

One stopped and sat on a bench. The other approached.

"Farzaneh!"

"Akilah."

289

"You look well."

"You look … weathered."

"I've had a long journey."

"I heard."

Akilah nervously shifted his weight from one foot to the other. "I'm here to return your camels and servants." *That much is obvious. At the least, be adequate when you speak.*

What would his cousin think of him after he told her everything?

"Yes, well. Before you do …" She motioned to a tall, gaunt person on the bench. "Come with me."

He drew near. "Chief!"

"Akilah."

Farzaneh placed one hand on Akilah's shoulder and the other on Gadiel's. "Now that we've established we remember everyone, let's try this again. Cousin. Son. Uncle. Father."

The three sat on the bench together, almost like a family.

Before they could ease into a conversation, Gadiel blurted, "You should thank Farzaneh. She had a hand in finding you. She's also why I'm still alive. She devised a teetering device for me. I hate it, but it's helping my lungs. Her inventiveness is worthy of Magi status."

Incredulous, Akilah turned to his cousin. "He's staying with you?"

"For now."

"And you invented something?"

"A new use for something."

"You've been busy."

"You have no idea." Farzaneh shot a sideways glance at Gadiel. "There's more, but it can wait. Dine with us today."

A family dinner? Akilah had battled brilliant minds during Council debates and had faced the fury of a haboob. Either would be easier to weather than family dynamics. "I'd be honored, but—"

"You don't keep an envoy waiting." Gadiel's signature steely stare pierced Akilah.

"Envoy?"

"Yes."

Akilah's father under the same roof with Farzaneh? Farzaneh an envoy? What else had happened while he was gone?

With all the news they had to share, maybe Akilah could postpone talking with Farzaneh about the stūrīh's contractual obligations—at least until he'd finished his paperwork for the Lower Council. He'd also wait to talk with his father about losing his Nisean steed. For tonight, his greatest wish was to enjoy a substantial meal in a pleasant setting and share his news as well. He hoped his cousin and father would receive what he had to say about the child-king Yeshua.

When Gadiel excused himself to rest before dinner, Farzaneh signaled to Javad, who had been lingering at a discrete distance. She steered Akilah in the opposite direction before he could watch them exit.

Wait. She was headed toward the waterfall. The site of his last meeting with her—when she'd surprised him with the stūrīh. Sweat broke out on Akilah's neck.

She stopped at the hillside's first terraced step. "I want you to know that I can't forget what you did to me in the past. But now I understand why you did it. Oddly enough, the past makes the present possible."

She paused, as if waiting for his response.

"May the present be a bridge to a more pleasant future." Akilah stumbled over his words. The Magi's library of wisdom didn't include guidance on how to speak to women. Especially estranged ones.

Farzaneh digested the comment without blinking. "Your father doesn't want you to know how severe his injuries are. Guard his dignity at dinner. On another day, when he is less taxed, you can talk with him at length."

She stared at the waterfall as if she could see through it. "Aramaic isn't the world's common language. Grief is. It always arrives without permission, never leaves when bidden, and travels with a perpetual companion. Pain." She turned to Akilah. "I don't know what you suffered or lost in the wilderness, but it must have been painful. Whether you want to forget that pain or can't, I'd like to hear about it ... when you're willing."

She motioned toward the house. "There's much more for you to know. That can start tonight."

Gadiel appeared at dinner, his face drawn, but otherwise wearing the same determined look Akilah had known since childhood. He averted his eyes. He would need time to adjust to his father's physical transformation since the shipwreck.

Enough food for a large banquet appeared, luxurious choices often reserved for weddings or *Nowruz*—including Akilah's favorite, *fesenjān*. Nothing could have prepared him for the dinner's largesse—or the evening's bounty of disclosures. One night couldn't compensate for years of lost opportunities for conversations, but the evening was a worthy start.

He almost choked on his fesenjān when Farzaneh explained how her late husband's faith had led her to become a God-fearer and how it influenced her decision to fund Akilah's trip. What lightning-bolt revelations!

When Akilah left Assur for Jerusalem, Farzaneh wasn't present to see him on his way. That had puzzled and modestly offended him. He had assumed she wanted to avoid him, but she'd already left for Arbela. Now it made sense why she'd planted those sentences from Isaiah in the folds of the blankets Javad gave Akilah. What he'd considered an afterthought as the caravan departed was a deliberate act to ensure he received those words. They had provided comfort when he needed it most. He made a mental note to talk with Farzaneh privately about that. But not tonight. He wasn't ready to share the journey's rigors, its hopeless moments, or the encouragement she'd planted before he needed it.

Akilah raised his wine cup in his cousin's direction. "Health to your hands, Farzaneh. This is the most excellent meal anyone could ever enjoy."

She raised her cup in return. "I will share your blessing with the hands that prepared the food."

Without mentioning the stūrīh, Farzaneh related Ihsan's ties with Adiabene and how she'd met Elyakim when she fulfilled her husband's final wishes. She continued with Elyakim's connections to people who looked for Tallis—and then Akilah's caravan.

His nerves unwound as he listened with wonder.

Through a haze, Akilah absorbed what had happened to his father. With occasional prompts from Farzaneh, Gadiel related how the captain saved him during the storm, how they were washed to land instead of farther out to sea, how they were found, then treated by none other than Ibn. She supplied details when he stopped to cough or catch his breath. She took over in sharing particulars of his return to Ctesiphon and coaxed a laugh from Gadiel when she described how he left the place of the sick without a doctor's permission.

Gratitude clogged Akilah's throat until he was hard pressed to swallow. Despite decades of family strain, he had assumed his father would always be with him. He couldn't risk making that mistake again. Time was precious. Tomorrow wasn't guaranteed.

Talk of Ibn offered Akilah an opening to share how Ibn had found Tallis, then the caravan, and had overseen its safe return to Persia.

With every round of revelations, another course of food appeared, each as festive as the last. Akilah heartily approved. This truly was a night for celebrating life and its connections. Who could have imagined—or engineered—such improbable intersections?

Akilah gazed out the window at the stars. Oh, how he loved them. He'd traced the constellations' outlines many times. Their connecting points were easy to miss unless one knew where to look or had a guide to direct one's gaze. More important, only the One who placed the stars in the sky could create the connections Akilah, his caravan, and his family had experienced.

The story unfolding was bigger than the sum of its parts. *Adonai, You are truly God Almighty as your Books of Moses say. You are the Master Planner.*

Servants brought each guest *zereshk polo*, a layered dish of sweet-tart barberries and saffron rice. The dish, often part of a Persian wedding feast, turned Akilah's thoughts to Yeshua's family. They had sacrificed the certainties of a normal wedded life to risk fulfilling an extraordinary purpose. Akilah understood that better now. His wilderness experience had taught him everything worthwhile came with a cost—sometimes a painfully high personal cost. But Adonai had guided him through his wilderness. He surely could steer Akilah's way through the risks and discomfort of forging family relations.

He couldn't let this evening pass without putting his faith

into words, but how? He prayed for guidance on what to share of his incomparable experience in finding Yeshua.

He dwelt on the discovery while minimizing the journey. "This God your captain talked about is real," he said to Gadiel. "I've seen Him manifested in a child, a light brighter than all the stars, and an Almighty Presence that guided and protected us to bring us safely home. He is what the Hebrew writings say He is. He is truly worthy of worship."

As if in affirmation, a panorama of Adonai's provision unfolded before Akilah's eyes. From Haruz's hidden food to Tallis's return and a ship to convey the caravan from Alexandria, the Almighty's intervention was evident. Without discounting human effort, the rapidly scrolling scenes shined a light on how Adonai was greater. Overwhelmed with gratitude, Akilah stood and lifted his hands in spontaneous praise. "Praise be to You, Lord God Almighty, maker and giver of all things!" Farzaneh joined in the chorus. Gadiel seemed uncomfortable with, but not disapproving of, their demonstration.

Only the sublime experience of finding Yeshua near Bethlehem surpassed this moment.

Chapter 68

Summons

Akilah, Rashidi, and Tallis waited in the Hall of Audiences for Azazel to finish his business. He had summoned them to his office, likely to discuss Akilah's report and outline preliminaries for the formal inquiry.

Akilah had recounted events as objectively as he could, leaning into the science and scholarship of his endeavor. Despite the carefully worded logic in his report, he was acutely aware he'd likely need to answer for more than its contents.

When the three filed into Azazel's office, Akilah barely recognized Sassanak's old quarters. Gone was his former boss's penchant for opulence. Although Azazel had kept some of Sassanak's furniture, starker décor, devoid of Zoroastrian symbolism, dominated the room. None of the motifs in the rugs, tapestries, or tablecloth reflected Magi tenets. The *Faravahar* entrusted to the Head Magus's care was not in sight, possibly hidden or stored for safekeeping. Notably absent was a copy of *The Spirit of Wisdom's Commandments for the Body and Soul*, displayed with reverence in virtually every Magi official's office.

297

Glaringly present were two cataphracts waiting inside the doorway.

"I read your report." Azazel cocked his head toward Akilah. "You have been very busy."

"We returned as soon as we could—"

"What part of 'I read your report' did you not understand?"

"Many pardons, Head Magus."

"Your circumstances are most unusual. Rashidi, as the Magus with the least seniority of the group, you acted under Akilah's guidance. In writing, you have recommitted to all the ways of Magi society, so you are exonerated from all charges that might pertain to other members of this party. We will meet soon to discuss your future plans. You may go."

A cataphract whisked Rashidi away before Akilah could say anything to him.

"Tallis, your circumstances warrant further study. Until you hear from me again, you are restricted to this complex." He handed Tallis a small scroll. "You will limit your activities to these events and locations until further notice. You may go."

The remaining cataphract escorted Tallis out of the office in a hurry.

"Akilah, your actions present a particular challenge ... one without precedent, actually." Azazel leaned back in his chair and rubbed his hands the length of its armrests. "This requires delicate handling." He handed Akilah a triple-sealed scroll. "I will see you in Ctesiphon. You may go."

Akilah composed himself long enough to exit Azazel's office then rushed out of the Audience Hall. He had never seen a scroll bear both the Lower and Upper Councils' seals, as well as Parthia's royal seal. How could the Head Magus gain consensus so quickly from all three entities—and why was the empire's king involved? Quick cooperation was a rarity between the two Council divisions. A snail could move faster than deliberations in the royal palace.

Intuition told him to not read the scroll alone. He needed the wisdom of someone familiar with Parthia's government to guide his actions. Mounting his fastest Arabian, he tore down the road to Assur.

"Where is Gadiel?" Akilah thundered the question to a cowering stable boy.

"I-I don't know," he stammered.

Akilah wasn't sure if he could walk into Farzaneh's house unannounced, even though they were contractually married. They'd barely had time for casual conversation. Serious matters such as the stūrīh were for future discussion. At the risk of some great breach in protocol, he strode through the back door.

Javad intercepted him.

"I need to speak with Gadiel immediately."

"He's in the middle of his morning treatment and can't be disturbed."

"This can't wait. Take me to his room."

Javad didn't move.

"Then I'll find his quarters myself."

Akilah pushed past Javad and headed to the guest wing. Barging in to Gadiel's quarters, he tripped over an odd plank sitting on a fulcrum. Gadiel was in bed, deep in conversation with Farzaneh by his side. She rose with a frown at Akilah's commotion.

"Many pardons, but I have something in my hand that may change all our lives. I do not feel it wise to read it alone."

He handed the scroll to Gadiel and pointed to the three seals. "Would you read this ... and advise me?" Akilah exhaled forcibly at the monumental admission of needing help from his father.

Gadiel's face hardened as he read the scroll. "You are being summoned to the royal palace complex in Ctesiphon to stand trial for crimes against the Magi Council and the Parthian Empire." He glanced at Akilah.

"I'm sure the charges are listed. Read them."

Gadiel hesitated, anguish etching his face.

"You are charged as follows. Pursuit of a study you were advised to abandon. Inappropriate use of Magi funds to continue that study. Failure to report results within the study's time frame. Failure to notify the Council of your location or request assistance. Reckless endangerment to everyone in your caravan. Loss of possessions, including Magi property, due to negligence. Attempting to undermine the empire's religion. Breaking Magi code that upholds the empire's religion. Espousing beliefs contradictory to its religion. Starting a cult and practicing magic. Jeopardizing national security and international relations through the sum of your actions.

"The trial will take place in the southern building." Gadiel's stare impaled Akilah. "It holds more people than any place in the royal complex."

He crushed the summons. "They're going to make an example of you. Then silence those who believe like you."

(To be continued ...)

Can you trace the Wise Men's round trip, staring from Persia?

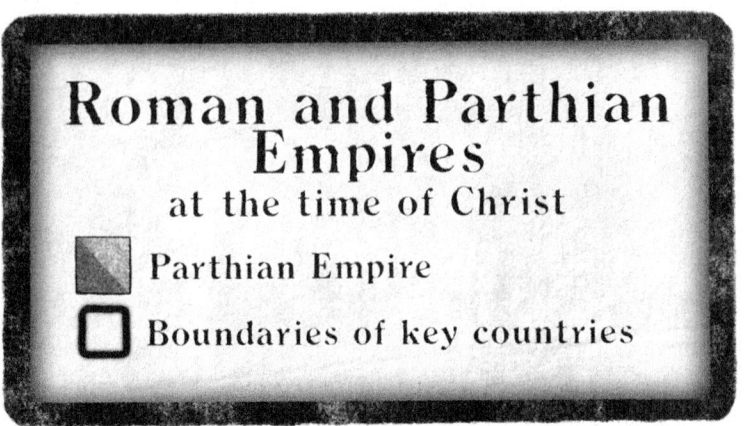

Roman and Parthian Empires
at the time of Christ

Parthian Empire

Boundaries of key countries

ASIA

Roman Empire

Macedononia

ANATOLIA

ARMENIA

ADIABENE

Nineveh

THE GREAT SEA

Assur

Alexandria

JUDEA

Jerusalem

Ayla   Petra

NABATAE

EGYPT

RED
SEA

Thanks for Sharing in this Journey

Thank you for continuing the Wise Men's story with me. If this is your first time reading about them, I invite you to also read *New Star*, the first book in this series.

You have many choices of books to read. I'm humbled and thrilled you chose to read mine. Thank you from the bottom of my heart! Word of mouth carries great weight with people's reading choices. Would you please take a few minutes to review *Survival Skills*, recommend it, and tell others about it on social media? I'd be very grateful if you did.

To get book updates, sneak peeks, and other bookish news, sign up for my free newsletter. I send it (ad-free) every other month. It also unlocks free supplemental resources on my website (lanachristian.com).

Want to email me with your comments? Please do so on my website's contact page. I answer every legitimate email.

For clean, good reads by other Scrivenings Press authors, browse Scrivenings' website.

May God richly bless you and all who read the Wise Men's story.

There's More to this Book than the Book!

Check out the Resources section of my website (https://www. lanachristian.com/resources) for these free downloadable goodies to go with *Survival Secrets*:

A book club kit

- Discussion questions and tips for making your book club meeting an immersive experience. Includes recipes for food mentioned in *Survival Secrets* so you can nosh authentically while chatting about the book.
- Want to have me join your book club? Live and virtual options are in the kit.

Bible study questions

- Want to dig deeper? Download a personal or group study based on the themes in this book.

Family Extras

- Age-appropriate information on different topics mentioned in the book

Enjoy these topics just for fun or use them as the basis for homeschooling or a school project. Whatever you do, let me know all the creative ways you use this material!

Acknowledgments

After the initial excitement of writing and publishing one book wears off, the most burning question for many authors is, "Can I do it again?" I raise my hand as part of that crowd.

The many moving parts in *Survival Secrets* posed unique challenges for me to write. I asked myself repeatedly whether I was equal to the task. I couldn't have done it without support from my author communities, especially ACFW WI(SE), the ERASERS (Edit, Rewrite, And Save. Edit. Repeat. Save.), Biblical Fiction Aficionados (BFA), and my Scrivenings Press "family." Many thanks also to my high school Facebook group and other friends who encouraged me and bolstered my confidence when I needed it the most.

Special credit goes to my beta readers: Barbara Britton, Mary Van Peursem, Karl Bunch, and Tony Perona. Thank you for identifying the manuscript's lingering weak spots. Kudos also go to my amazing content editor, Suzie Waltner. *Survival Secrets* is stronger because of your wisdom and diligence, your unique perspective and thoughtful suggestions.

A big shout-out goes to Bree Cook, who designed the gorgeous maps in this book. I hope you like them as much as I do.

Most of all, I praise God for allowing me to co-create with Him. He never fails to supply me with inspiration, ideas, strength, fortitude, and perseverance for this awesome task of writing. To God be the glory!

About the Author

Lana Christian started her writing career in business and healthcare, where she garnered numerous APEX awards, a patent, published books, and many millions of dollars in grants for clients. Her faith-based writing sprang from years of writing devotionals and marketing materials for Christian organizations. She stepped into writing faith-based novels in 2017.

Lana is passionate about crafting stories that make the Bible come to life and is relentless in her research to make each scene authentic. Her tag line says it all: "Immersive stories from history."

Since 2019, she has won a dozen faith-based awards: eight for her biblical fiction novels, three for her short stories, and one for an online devotional.

Her author website features her award-winning "Encouragement from Living History" devotional blogs that connect the dots between the Bible, history, archaeology, and practical application for today. Connect with Lana at www. lanachristian.com/contact and sign up for her bimonthly newsletter. That also gives you early access to her devotionals, other free resources, and an occasional giveaway.

Also by Lana Christian

New Star: **Book One of** *The Magi's Encounters*

How far would you go to protect what you believe in?

Akilah, a highly respected priest-scholar in Magi society, considers all his astronomy discoveries well-deserved stepping-stones to a more fulfilling life. But the appearance of a new star challenges his priorities. As Persia totters on the brink of an undesirable king coming to power, Akilah declines a position that could turn that tide. Instead, he studies a star that doesn't appear in any almanac or religious writings. Except Jewish.

When he and his colleagues uncover a few Jewish prophecies linking the star to an eternal king, Akilah becomes the target of Persia's religious and governmental conflicts. Jailed for crimes he didn't commit, Akilah must rely on questionable resources to free himself and reach Jerusalem.

Persia's purists aren't the only ones bent on keeping their country free of Jewish influences. As dangers at home and abroad plunge Akilah and his colleagues into three countries' religious conflicts and circumstances beyond their imagining, Akilah realizes his knowledge of Yeshua could potentially destroy Magi society and its power over Persia's official religion and government. Untrusting of his Council, a thousand miles from aid, and bound in a potentially career-ending contract, Akilah must decide how far he will go to protect what he knows of Yeshua—and whether the cost of his belief is worth the risk.

Get your copy here:

https://scrivenings.link/newstar

More Biblical Fiction from Scrivenings Press

A Certain Man by Linda Dindzans

A Certain Future—Book One

Mara is a young Samaritan beginning to discover her love for Samuel—and his for her. Soon she will be deemed mature enough to marry. Her hopes are dashed when her greedy father brokers a match with the cruel son of the wealthy High Priest of Shechem. When her loathsome betrothed is killed, her beloved Samuel must run for his life. Mara and Samuel struggle to survive and reunite during the treacherous and scandalous times of the Bible under the merciless rule of Rome.

Along the way, they are entangled within the snares of such notable figures as King Herod, Herodias, Pontius Pilate, Caiaphas, and Salome.

The heartrending tales of Mara and Samuel are interwoven with their desperate love story. Before either meets Yeshua the Nazarene face to face. Before He sets the political, religious, and spiritual landscape on fire. And before either Mara or Samuel are immortalized in the gospels.

Get your copy here:

https://scrivenings.link/acertainman

Stay up-to-date on your favorite books and authors with our free e-newsletters.

ScriveningsPress.com

Printed in Dunstable, United Kingdom

72123060R00191